Father Tierney ✝ Stumbles

John Shekleton

iUniverse, Inc.
Bloomington

Father Tierney Stumbles

iUniverse books may be ordered through booksellers or by contacting:

iUniverse
1663 Liberty Drive
Bloomington, IN 47403
www.iuniverse.com
1-800-Authors (1-800-288-4677)

ISBN: 978-1-4620-0922-0 (sc)
ISBN: 978-1-4620-0926-8 (hc)
ISBN: 978-1-4620-0925-1 (ebk)

Library of Congress Control Number: 2011905536

Printed in the United States of America

iUniverse rev. date: 08/27/2011

Chapter 1

F ather Joe Tierney felt trapped. He needed to get away—far away.

He shoved open the heavy metal door of the STD clinic and then skipped once to gain momentum before plunging into the Monday morning springtime mist. He ran the length of the red-brick warehouse. He ran until his side hurt and he was gasping for air.

Joe's mind raced. The clinic was in a neighboring county, and he'd dressed down. He'd worn jeans, dirty tennis shoes, and the torn denim jacket he used for work in the parish garden. He'd even glued on a fake mustache, the one that he had bought for last year's Halloween party when he'd gone as Pancho Villa.

Joe knew he looked like another illegal from Oaxaca, a foreign wanderer in the oldest part of the *gringo* city. For once, he thanked God his mom's *indigena* genes had made him short and dark-skinned.

Joe knew the invisibility of a Mexican in an *Anglo* city. No one noticed you unless you talked too loudly or acted crazy. He had ambled toward the clinic's door and stared up as if he were a recently arrived Mexican peasant amazed by all the tall buildings and the somberness of the brick.

Now he was booking it down a busy avenue like a thief after a heist. He'd run seven blocks and had just turned right toward the river and his Honda Civic. He'd have to slow down. He had to be careful. He tugged off the fake moustache and then threw it in the gutter.

Joe hadn't wanted to park near the clinic, so he'd parked near the hospital. It was part of his plan. If any parishioners saw him, they'd think he was visiting the sick or tending to an emergency.

God, Joe wished that were true. The truth was he was now one of the sick.

Father Joe Tierney was HIV positive.

* * *

Joe parked his car in the parish's back lot. He didn't move. Something awful was happening inside him. Could a man's heart break in an hour? He could barely turn his head to stare at the old stone building that housed the parish. Mater Dei. He loved it—and not just the weathered limestone that shimmered on a sunny day. Joe loved the people who came there, who prayed for their newborn or their dead. He loved being their priest, part of their cycle of life. That role rooted him, deep and firm. It had nourished his soul.

Joe turned away from the building and shook his head. He nearly cried. His heart ached. He'd let them all down. This diagnosis made it all so clear.

Joe still clutched the steering wheel with both hands. He needed to sit there a few more minutes. He flashed back to her words, to Nurse Helen's words at the clinic. He knew she'd talked of therapy and drugs and support groups, but through it all, he'd mainly concentrated on suppressing the urge to get up and run. Now he had to force himself to get out of the car and go inside his parish. Joe had to step back into his normal life. But he wondered how anyone could do that after hearing what he'd just heard.

Joe released the steering wheel, cracked open the Civic's door, and smelled the spring air. He remembered Nurse Helen's last piece of advice: "You have to tell someone." He felt the words grip him. It was the same advice he would have given some isolated, fearful soul who'd come to him with a festering secret. Joe sighed and stared, unfocused, into the gray sky, fixing his mind on this new piece of self-knowledge. Joe Tierney could become that soul. In some ways, he already was.

Joe finally climbed out of the Civic. He bumped the door shut behind him and stared at the rectory. No matter what happened, this was still his life. And this rectory was his home. He walked across the lot, entered the tiny mudroom, stepped down the short hall, and stopped outside the kitchen's old oak door. Man alive, he was nervous. He could feel the sweat steaming up his armpits. At least he could avoid talking to any of the staff.

Joe knew where the other two priests of Mater Dei would be. Father Velker was on a nursing home visit. Father Fitzgerald would be in a front parlor counseling a parishioner. He knew their schedules. He was rector of an important downtown parish and a careful steward. Father Joe Tierney liked directing staff. He liked knowing that the Holy Roman Catholic Church, which he had served for ten years as a priest, was a busy maze of praying, learning, laughing, weeping, scrubbing, and dusting. Many an hour, the busyness of it had made him happy, swept his own soul of any downtime gloom that might settle in—had swept it clean most years.

Joe opened the kitchen door and called out, "Anybody here?" as he stepped onto the shellacked kitchen floor. No one answered. The kitchen was empty, but Joe's heart raced. He looked at his watch. He'd be alone a while longer. Gloria, cook and mother figure, wouldn't arrive till 11:00 a.m.

He took a deep breath. Okay, this was feeling better. He could pace the kitchen's thirty feet, past the heavy steel blenders, the ovens, and the polished aluminum refrigerator—all needed for the frequent socials concocted in the kitchen's industrial-sized space. These had been some of his best pastoral tools, he thought as he walked up and down the kitchen's length. He had slaved to keep the downtown parish busy and in the black. He used the kitchen as a major asset. Serve food, and they will come.

Besides, Joe liked the uncluttered surfaces and scrubbed-clean smell of the kitchen. He moved his right hand over one of the speckled laminate counters. This kitchen was a refuge, a sacred space. He came there often, morning, afternoon, and night, especially after a rough council meeting when everyone's wisdom had been as puffed out as a peacock's proud span. "Father, I'm a businessman. I know."

Joe leaned back against the counter and scanned the space. Yeah, he found this kitchen peaceful. Some of his best childhood memories were set in a kitchen.

A smile raced across his face. His *abuelita*. She had been a savior in his life. After she'd moved in with them, she took over the family kitchen and made it her haven. He remembered sitting at the red Formica-topped table, an observant *niño* listening as *la abuelita* chattered on about her life in Oaxaca, watching as she patted the dough into tortillas, noting her quickness in dicing the vegetables for a salsa, hearing her pray to the statue of the *Virgen* at the far end of the counter whenever an impossible need crossed her mind.

Joe began to frown. Not everything had been happy in that childhood kitchen. He remembered that over the years, *la abuelita* had acquired many impossible needs. Chief among them was the reformation of Joe Tierney's *gringo padre*, owner of a corner market whose financial trials kept him at an even keel of lower-middle-class anger and frustration—anger at their impoverished neighborhood, the greedy superstores, the lousy police protection, and a son who was pious like his mom.

His dad. Joe pushed away from the counter. He paced across the kitchen. He felt sick. He stood over the deep metal sink and shook his head. His dad could never find out.

Joe had always played the macho for his dad, sweating across the wrestling mat, playing goalie on his soccer team, even getting his girlfriend Maria as near pregnant as she could get—with one late period. For a semester in high school, Joe had thought fathering a child was the only way to prove his worth—to show that even a boy who knelt before the Virgin with pleading eyes could be a macho who knew how to take a woman.

Joe began to hyperventilate. Even a quick memory of that childhood folly brought back the adolescent fear. He opened the cabinet and took out a green plastic glass. Joe needed a drink of water. His throat felt dry.

As a kid, Joe had believed his dad would blast out of his chair in fury at hearing the news of an out-of-wedlock pregnancy only to settle back into its reclining comfort with an inner glow of pride.

God, that was a foolish child's dream. Joe gulped down the water. He refilled the glass and then went over to the refrigerator to get some ice. He felt his body heat up.

Joe stood quietly in front of the broad surface of the stainless-steel refrigerator and studied his reflection. He worried he was becoming more like his dad every day—not in body, but in spirit. Joe's dad was one of those stoic men who had kept his triumphs, his moments of joy, hidden—so no one could steal them. Joe remembered his mom explaining this to him and his sister, offering what even then seemed a fragile excuse for their dad's alternating aloofness and rages.

Joe sighed. He knew he was becoming aloof like his father. He knew he had become a hider of thoughts and feelings. Even on the day of his ordination, ten years ago, Joe knew there were things that could never come out.

If only. Joe gulped down the now-cool water. He put the glass in the sink. Today, everything had changed.

Joe knew it would happen sometime. There was a reason he'd gone to the clinic. You couldn't keep a living force wrapped up forever. It always broke out, often in a destructive burst. He'd spent too many hours in the confessional to be naive, for Christ's sake!

Joe leaned over the counter and then closed his eyes. He'd been so stupid!

Maybe his life hadn't had to come to this. Joe straightened up and clenched his hands into fists. Maybe if his dad had been different, a man of studied thoughts; maybe if his dad had been someone who sought the meaning behind his gut feelings and his angry outbursts; maybe if Joe's dad had been like a seminary professor, a man of words who would gift his son with principles and insights, gifts of subtle logic rather than angry tirades, maybe a different outcome ...

Maybe Joe could have coped better.

Joe took his balled fists and then beat his chest hard. He started to cry again but immediately forced himself to stop, clamping his eyelids shut. Even at this hour, someone could walk in. He drew in a deep breath, held it, and listened. Joe ripped off a paper towel to wipe his face dry and then walked over to the hallway door. He put his ear to the wood, muttering as he stood there, "I hope no one's there. I need to be alone for a while." He looked at his watch, whispering, "I should have the kitchen to myself for another half hour."

Joe heard nothing. He walked over to the small table at the far wall and then pulled out one of the two chairs, commenting, "What's happening to me? I've become such a mutterer lately."

Joe settled in to the old wooden chair. Slowly, he folded his hands. He was remembering the monologue he'd delivered after his first night with Kenny O'Connor. That was when the muttering had started.

Joe wasn't clear on the exact words he'd used to berate himself on the drive home, but he was sure he'd concluded he was a total fool for acting out that lunatic desire. Joe had never done anything like that before, and he swore on the drive back to the rectory that he would never do it again.

It hadn't seemed like lunacy at the time. Kenny was his type. He had that long, flaxen hair that made him look rebellious and nerdy despite his rugby-player build. In their chat session, Kenny had said he'd been out for a night with a *papi*.

At the kitchen table, Joe pressed his palms together, as if he were struggling to compress his tension into a ball so he could toss it away. That night, he had learned how agony and ecstasy combined. And the combination had a name: Kenny. It was such an *Anglo* name. Just the man Joe had always wanted. Golden. Tough. Bright smile. Endless in his desires.

For the last year, Joe had sneaked online before going to bed. But nothing had happened until Kenny had logged on late one summer night nine months earlier and messaged him. Joe shuddered just remembering his reaction to Kenny's first contact. It was elation. And this cute guy was looking for someone like him, a *papi*. Joe had seen the word in online ads, although he never thought of himself as one. But Kenny obviously did.

Joe felt himself relax a bit. This part of the story wasn't all bad. Up until his exchange with Kenny, Joe's presence online had been purely voyeuristic—distant, maybe dicey, but empty of involvement. He ignored messages from users who wanted to chat. Only in response to Kenny's message did Joe type a reply and then press the send key.

Joe shot out of his chair, almost flipping it over. The AIDS fear was back, forcing him to jump with the balled-up energy of a teenager in a horror flick who's been tapped from behind. Joe shoved his hands through his thick curls. This morning had been a boot camp in Fate with a capital *F*. It was like one of those Greek myths he'd read as a kid in high school, like one of those unbelievable moments when the feathered god swoops down and disrupts a human's life forever.

Only Joe's mythic god had moved away. Kenny had moved to San Diego. "Come with me, *Papi*," Kenny had said, as they sat at the kitchen table in his small studio studying a cheap travel guide. Joe remembered Kenny's eyes looking up from a picture of the ocean. His eyes were steady and focused. Joe knew the words were more than casual banter, more than a passing desire to be with his *papi* and continue their athletic lovemaking.

Kenny could be quick with his words, even irreverent. "*Papi*, you spice my life." Joe would always smile at that phrase, maybe because he, too, could say anything he wanted with Kenny.

"Am I just an *ancho* to mix into your dull white-bread day?" Then they'd wrestle about for a while, almost like brothers.

Joe looked over at the rectory kitchen's clock. He had some more time. He relaxed into the memory of one night when the wrestling had turned into lovemaking, and Kenny ended up with his head on Joe's stomach. Kenny had told him again of his dream to go west. "You should come with me, Joe," he'd said, lifting his head up to stare into Joe's eyes. Kenny was always serious when he used a first name.

The professional priest-counselor in Joe had wanted to tell Kenny that he was young and that Joe was older and had made commitments. His words would be a simple, clinical summary. Then he should leave.

Instead, Joe had scooted up in the bed, tucked the pillow behind his head, and told Kenny about his ordination, about lying flat on the cathedral's marble floor asking for the prayers of the people of God, of the entire people of God, way back to the dusty-footed apostles and martyrs. Joe even recalled some of the words he'd used explaining it all to Kenny. "That ceremony really did change me.

It's still changing me, Kenny. Your invitation is very welcome, but I'm not ready to move away from my priesthood. It's me, you know. It's who I am."

Saying those words that night had made Joe sad, the way he felt now in the rectory's kitchen. It was a murky, brown sad, the sad someone feels when he realizes all his tromping around has loosened the topsoil and the hillside will come crashing down in the next rain, wrecking the structures of life. He had lost Kenny. He felt he was losing his priesthood. And now, he was sick.

But Kenny was still a light in Joe's life. How could that be? That night, Kenny hadn't just rolled over and then walked away from Joe. Kenny had gotten out of bed to stand up, as if it might be all over, but then he'd bent down and looked into Joe's eyes and said, "I want you to keep being that special guy. I really do. You care for people. It's very sexy."

Joe remembered smiling back at Kenny, realizing at that moment that his old, gilded dream was fighting with this new, sinewy dream. And for the younger dream to win, it had to kill the other. That's when Joe had gotten up and left.

Joe hadn't seen Kenny since then. He still thought a lot about him. Kenny was now wrapped up in Joe's vocation story. And he was mostly a positive force, adding strength and energy. That was Kenny, Joe nodded in memory.

Kenny had professed his love so strongly, with worn hands that produced the softest caresses. He showed he could pursue a dream, studying hard at Tech, getting his electrician's license, joining the union, pleasing his vast blond family, pleasing his *papi*.

Joe took a deep breath and leaned down to touch his toes. He had felt the tension knotting in his back. Now some of it had sifted out. Then he stood back up. Joe looked at the clock. He was about ready to head out. He wondered one more time if he could have worked out a life with Kenny. Surely such a life wouldn't be as bad as this life he had started to live. Joe had begun to live the nightmare of the priestly vocation—a modern dark night of the soul with an increased distance between friends, the rapid and rote performance of once-nourishing rituals, the crowding of meetings and blessings and funerals, and the death of inner silence. He had enumerated these laments to his confessor, Father Dan Boyer. But so far, nothing had improved.

Joe walked over to the south window that looked out onto the kitchen garden, preparing himself to get on with the rest of the day. He had to keep going. Joe paused just a second to gaze at the green heads of the new carrots. The garden had always made him feel hopeful.

Then one final thought, *Did Kenny know? Did he know when they were together?* Joe took a step back. His heart froze. It had to be Kenny. There wasn't anyone else.

Maybe Kenny didn't know. Either way, he'd have to contact Kenny to tell him.

* * *

Joe left the kitchen and then stopped a moment in the hallway. He needed to focus on his immediate needs. What was his plan? He'd cancel his meetings for the day, leave a note for Father Velker to take evening Mass, hole up in his room, and figure out what to do next.

Then Joe heard footsteps and saw that the rest of the day was walking toward him with a sassy smile. Lucy Walker. She was his best receptionist ever, a young, African-American single mother with two children, who had declared in her interview that she was ready to drag herself out of the "drama-drenched swampland of daytime talk shows, even though I do love my Oprah!"

Joe saw Lucy hesitate. He wondered if he looked ill.

"You're not well?" Lucy asked, knitting her eyebrows.

"Right," Joe answered, looking out from the hallway window into the busy street. "I'm going to crash in my room."

"You're supposed to meet with the Darlings," Lucy said.

"Please ask them to reschedule. Same time next week, maybe," Joe said. He knew the Darlings well, a mega-rich couple who lived in a ranch house, drove a rusted car, and helped out at the St. Martha's soup line. Joe was sure a change in plans wouldn't cause them any concern. They were as mellow as any beach-loving Californian. Joe had never figured out if their detachment to things and schedules was due to a vegan lifestyle of good works and meditation or to the transformative impact of never experiencing a financial want.

"You got it, Father T," Lucy said as she continued on to the kitchen. "You go and take care of yourself. Let me know if you need anything."

Joe entered the office reception room with its handful of chairs and Lucy's desk, its wooden expanse rimmed by pictures of her children. He wrote a note asking Father Velker to take the evening Mass and then left it in his mailbox. That was the easy part of his plan.

Next, Joe walked into his office. He shut the door and stood a moment, looking at the office clock. He had most of the day to pull himself together. He needed at least a week.

He was starting to feel punchy. Joe felt like laughing hysterically. What had he gotten himself into? His best friend from seminary, Pascal LaVigne, would be surprised to see him like this. Pascal would never have messed up like this.

Pascal was the queer that everyone had admired—well, not the outstate guys. They were well weeded by their zealous bishops who discarded any vocation with even one discolored leaf of unorthodoxy. Everybody at the seminary had known Pascal's story, either learning it directly from him or plucking it easily off the seminary grapevine.

He was the short, dirty blond who could have disappeared in any crowd but chose not to hide. He wore bright colors and covered his shrunken chest with antiwar, antipoverty, and antihate pins.

Pascal, he had taken such a different road. The thought made Joe feel worse; he saw himself trapped in a slow-motion tunnel of misfortune. His heart rate slowed for a moment. But he had to keep moving.

Joe looked around the office. There wasn't much he needed. He walked over to his desk to pick up a fresh notepad. Maybe he could think through the next steps by making some lists. Joe stood a moment at his desk. He had always thought that the big mahogany landmark was the desk of someone who mattered. It was the kind of idea his father would have had.

Joe felt a trickle of tears push out at his eyes. He gripped the notepad and then crossed back to the office door. He'd better hurry over to the rector's suite. No one ever came there unless he invited them. He'd be alone. Joe was feeling his energy ebb. He was drained. He needed to barricade himself away for a while—to plan … to pray.

CHAPTER 2

P ascal LaVigne was in shock. He stood at the front window of his upstairs room at Casa Romero, the Catholic Worker house and gazed out with the lifeless stare of a zombie. His second-floor bedroom in the aging Victorian looked onto the busy street where a large oak filtered the traffic noises. Pascal usually stood in the same spot every evening to pray with his palms open to heaven asking that he might share the oak's strength and virtue. Tonight, he stared outward, focusing on nothing, his arms limp at his side.

Pascal finally pulled himself away from his view of the darkening form of the oak. He went back to his small desk to pick up the newspaper article: "AIDS in the Catholic Priesthood."

Pascal decided to sit a moment before going down to the community kitchen. It was his night to make dinner, but his usual enthusiasm for cooking was gone. His stomach was rumbling—not from hunger, from some emotion. That rarely happened to him anymore. Pascal was the soul of healthy living, striving for spiritual and physical peace. He'd come out and created his own niche in service to others. He had made a good life.

Tonight, Pascal sat quietly on his single bed. He placed the article flat on the white cotton bedspread and leaned over to start reading. He'd read just the first paragraph, to make sure he had the context.

> It's been two decades since AIDS devastated the gay community. We have discovered that the disease didn't spare the Catholic priesthood. Some priests are dead, and their death notices never mention the real cause. We think it's time to examine this little-discussed aspect of the AIDS crisis and to ask: what does it mean?

Maybe it was that final question that bothered Pascal. It sounded snarky to him, the sort of broad, poking question Ron Saville-Jones, his most recent ex-boyfriend, would have written. It was a good question, but too big to be answered.

Pascal folded the paper and then rose to put it back on the desk. He needed to head downstairs and get the meal together. The beans were already boiling. He couldn't turn them to mush again.

Pascal smiled, thinking of Ron. Ron hated beans. Ron liked good, interesting questions, but he hated healthy food.

Of course, Pascal liked Ron precisely because of his interest in the bigger questions. And he had supported Ron in his effort to break into the world of reporting by doing lifestyle articles for the *GLRegister* when he wasn't swamped with his real work architecting Internet security strategies.

Pascal was excited for a moment, thinking how he might enjoy an evening with Ron, a friends-with-benefits type of evening. But not tonight. Pascal felt lonely tonight—lonely in a way that only being alone could reduce the melancholy. Pascal chuckled. He was weird that way. Maybe that was why Ron had broken it off. Pascal winced. The barbs in that memory stung.

Pascal plodded down the house's main stairs, holding on to the decades-old railing. He was actually feeling weak. Then the house phone rang, and Pascal hurried down the stairs and into the kitchen to pick it up.

"Did you see the 'AIDS in the Catholic Priesthood' article?" Ron asked.

Pascal was happy to hear his voice. "Father George faxed me a copy yesterday at St. Martha's. I think he's constantly scouring the religious newswires for gay-related stuff. Then I bought a copy last night at Barnard's."

"So you've read it?"

"Five times yesterday." Pascal hurried over to take the beans off the flame. "The lunch line at St. Martha's opened half an hour late. The regulars weren't happy, but I couldn't put the article down. An exposé on Catholic priests with AIDS! This priesthood-sex link just keeps on growing. Did you notice that all the priests in the article were gay? And I knew two of those guys who were quoted. Eerie."

Pascal was adept at nestling the cordless phone between shoulder and ear. He picked up the lid of the beans to test them for consistency.

"How did you know them?"

The beans felt good, which was a relief, but this question surprised Pascal. "Are you about to take notes?" Pascal carefully reached up for the large skillet hanging over the stove. He was going to sauté carrots, onions, and mushrooms to add them to the beans. "Are you going to do a follow-up? Am I to be a source? You once said you loved me."

Pascal felt like teasing. His earlier gloom was lifting. He was always playful with Ron. And he missed that. He was really only playful with Ron and with Joe.

"I did love you." Ron's voice sounded defensive to Pascal. Or canny. "And I respected you. And now I need you. I told you I've wanted to write something about the Catholic sex scandal. Now I've got the idea. I'll write a story similar to the 'AIDS in the Catholic Priesthood' article, but with a local angle. A story about the consequences of breaking those archaic vows. A really big consequence."

Ron's words had rushed out, hurried and breathy. This pattern perplexed Pascal. Ron's speech was usually more studied. When they were first dating, Pascal had dinged Ron about his slow, studied delivery, saying he sounded like an economist discussing demand slopes.

"I can keep any guy's identity hidden," Ron said. "I'm good at secrets. Surely you remember that. I never told anyone about that little thing you like to do." Ron paused a second.

Pascal knew he had to end this conversation, at least for the moment. He needed both hands to complete the dinner, and he certainly wouldn't put this dialogue on speakerphone.

"I just need to find the right priest. He's got to be in town," Ron said, persisting.

Pascal felt his eyes narrow, the way they did when someone spouted easy assertions. He knew that reaction came from his seminary days. He was irked. But this was no naive seminarian on the phone; this was Ron. "So, you call the certain somebody who you think has all the dirt ... or who knows the alley where the trash cans are kept," Pascal said as he began to rummage through the cupboards for oil. "I'm not comfortable with being your mole, Ron."

Pascal had hoped for a companion, someone who could share his feelings about the article. Pascal wasn't even sure how to describe those feelings, but they felt strong, even deep. He needed to talk to someone. Now Ron was playing the butthead.

Pascal found the can of olive oil and put it on the counter. Or was there something in his feelings that was sinister, wanting to hide its name? Pascal noticed his defensiveness rise, in his quick replies, his jittery movements. He realized he was having one of those "protective" moments. Something had to be protected. Was he, Pascal LaVigne, the most liberal of liberal Catholics, feeling the need to protect the church? The thought stunned him.

"What's to make you uncomfortable, Pascal? I'm not a witch hunter."

"Yeah, sure, Buffy." Pascal stood still in the kitchen, desperately wanting *not* to have this conversation—at least *not* now and *not* in his present mood.

"Pascal, you've told me many a time that the RC Church needs a good housecleaning."

"Housecleaning, yes. Person-dangling, no. An article ... an article on this topic needs to be written with grace and kindness." *That's it,* Pascal thought. *I'm tired of all the screechy accusations. I'm tired of the hysteria.*

"Yes, yes. I can handle this with grace and kindness." A pause, and then Ron's sigh of exasperation washed across the line. Pascal waited. He knew Ron had tried many times to find the "right" story to get him noticed. But his story on local gay entrepreneurs stayed local. His story on chat rooms lacked sizzle, as dull as most online conversations. His man-about-town series competed with the writings of a dozen others. Ron needed an angle.

"You really want to do this, don't you?" Pascal asked, gaining himself time.

"I think there's a story here that will grip our community, a story that matters, to people and organizations. Powerful organizations, many people. It could be a landmark story. Yes, I want to write it."

Pascal looked over at the kitchen clock. Now was not the time for snap decisions. At least his seminary training had taught him to avoid the "snap trap."

"Okay. Let me think about it. I don't know of anyone offhand, anyone here. But I'll get back to you."

* * *

Angela Roth stopped at the foot of the chancery's grand stairway, studying the many carved flowers. The day felt special. It was another Monday morning, and she stood for a moment to reflect on her luck in working in a place steeped in reverence and power. The thought made her happy. And this staircase, such a wonder of molded mahogany! It still delighted her. The building, like that of many chanceries of the American Catholic Church, had once been the mansion of a poor European immigrant from a pious country who had made a fortune in grain and railroads. It was exactly the sort of image that appealed to Angela. The Horatio Alger myth come alive. In many ways, she thought, self-acceptance in the thought, she was a simple American.

And in many ways, she was a fierce American feminist. So Angela moved on from the splendid view in the reception hallway down the main corridor toward her own small quarters, two renovated workrooms behind the old pantry. There Angela headed the diocese's communications and public relations department. As she walked down the corridor, she reminded herself that even though her office wasn't a wood-paneled sanctuary, it was on the first floor. Only Bishop Healy's office, the chancellor's office, and the office of worship were on the first floor, in the old parlors and dining room. Angela resided on the floor of power.

Angela stopped outside her office door and remembered her first day walking down the slightly drab hallway; its width had been narrowed when the offices were created. She was wondering if she had made a mistake, taken a step down. But then she heard Bishop Healy's voice as he welcomed an early guest out front. She knew then that she was where she needed to be.

When Angela had worked at the local newspaper, her office sat four doors from the publisher's. Proximity made a difference. These days, every CEO knew that an institution's reputation was a pearl of unparalleled value. She smiled before opening her office door, recalling how Bishop Healy had told her in their first interview that her value wasn't in performing daily tasks. Her value to him was in spinning gold out of hay. "Blessed is the subtle and cunning tongue," he had said, as he began to lay out his fears and needs.

Angela closed her door quietly, concentrating on making the closure one smooth action. She had arrived early, as was her wont, because now was her time to meditate. But Angela's mind was busy today. It would take a while to center herself. Maybe it was the smell of spring coming from the damp earth. She was feeling full of life.

Angela took off her light raincoat and hung it in the small closet. She walked back to her desk and saw that her message light was already blinking. She knew others would be annoyed by the constant demands for time and opinion. Not Angela. She recalled explaining it to her therapist.

"After a decade in public relations, I know that an executive buffeted by crisis winds will look to me for steady navigation."

Her therapist, Frau Schmidt, as Angela called her, had said, "You feel like an Amazon, don't you?"

"Not an Amazon," Angela had said. "A guide, calm and stable."

"Yes, yes," Frau Schmidt had answered, huffing her reply. She had shifted in her chair. "Let's nail down the correct image. I'd say you like to be near the center, but not in the center." The old therapist had raised one hand up, turning it back and forth. "Guiding, but from a distance. Like a night star. Or a goddess."

Angela had laughed out loud at the comparison, but the image stayed with her. Frau Schmidt had, indeed, nailed it.

She looked again at the flashing light. Maybe she'd listen to the messages before meditating. It was going to be a hard day to settle down.

There was only one message. Bishop Healy wanted to see her as soon as possible.

* * *

Angela knocked twice and then waited for Bishop Healy to invite her in. He had sounded disturbed. It had to be that article. The thought of it made her want to groan, but she put on a discreet smile as she entered the bishop's office. This topic was toxic.

"I assume you've seen this headline?" Bishop Healy asked as he turned the paper around on his broad desk. Angela watched him thump the offending words with the tip of his black Mont Blanc pen. "Sunday's paper," Bishop Healy said. "Bishop McGee couriered it to me last night."

Angela stifled a desire to tell Bishop Healy how exasperating she found these gay-priest discussions. One of her first lessons in working in the church was how to deal with the whole priest/sexuality topic. An individual's opinion on the validity of ordaining gay clergy or married clergy was sure to signal who was a dissenter, working his or her own beliefs in the confessional and classroom, and who was an orthodox defender of the faith with the sword of St. Michael ready at the side to gut any spiritual laggards. Thankfully, Bishop Healy wasn't one of those neocons who'd been saying that the sex abuse scandal was all a "gay" issue.

Angela stood silently for a second before Bishop Healy's desk, trying to clear her mind, reminding herself that her job was to help this good man. Bishop Healy would've been a cardinal, Angela was sure, except for a minor leftward bent on certain social issues and a fondness for phrases like "personal conscience."

"AIDS in the Catholic Priesthood," Bishop Healy said with a raspy, tired voice, interrupting Angela's meditation. "You know from this headline alone that it's going to be another bumpy ride for us, even though the article's from a city that just barred cattle drives and public lynchings a few years ago."

Angela smiled without looking up at Bishop Healy's eyes. She knew he'd see her pleasure in his mockery. He'd admitted to being a student of eye movement and head position, a skill he tried to teach his priests. "You have to read the whole person," he'd say. In response, Angela tried to control the obvious body signals whenever in his presence, unwilling to be read too easily even by Bishop Healy's benign eminence.

A second later, Angela shifted her feet and exhaled a deep sigh, reluctantly giving away her inner feelings. "I heard about the article on CNN but haven't seen the paper yet."

Angela looked up from the newspaper headline laid out on the desk and searched Bishop Healy's eyes. She could see this issue was hard for the old man. Angela suddenly felt the need to put away her own thoughts, her fear that this was about to become another gigantic distraction that would once again expose the real flaws in church policies and politics. Instead, she needed to help Bishop Healy think and speak. That was her job. She was neither theologian nor ordained with a teaching authority.

Bishop Healy looked back at her. "I hear McGee's got a stack of copies in his office. He's airmailing ten to Rome. This is a piece of Americana the Vatican won't quickly file in the archives." He was again pointing at the headline with his pen. Angela saw a scowl ripple out over Bishop Healy's recently shaved cheeks.

Angela leaned over to pick up the paper. "May I?" she asked. She might as well get acquainted with the facts. She gave the paper a quick glance. Clearly, the article bled onto another page.

"It's yours." Bishop Healy sat back in his chair. He folded his arms over his chest. "McGee called me late last night. He said I had to get involved, make a stink, that it was my responsibility as a member of the bishops' committee assigned to draw up the new guidelines on clergy sex abuse, even though no abuse is alleged in the article. Then McGee patted himself on the back explaining how he had refused to cooperate with the reporter working on this article. 'Devil's work,' he had called it. I think he wanted me to take the same tack."

Angela tilted her head. "Bishop McGee can be a bit dramatic," she said, playing into Bishop Healy's long-standing difficulties with the other prelate. At least she and Bishop Healy could commiserate. Angela could see him relax a bit; his arms unfolded. He liked to let off steam with her.

"Dramatic is an understatement. He's got the worst personality for this sort of thing." Bishop Healy was shaking his head. "He told me that the reporter had started asking questions months before the Boston sex abuse scandal broke. And after that ecclesiastical catastrophe, my words, not his, Bishop McGee promptly told her this topic was a witch hunt—an attempt to besmirch the Catholic Church brought on by a liberal, anti-Catholic press. I'm sure he shut his door to her as if he were defending Rome from the Vandal horde."

Angela gave Bishop Healy a wry smile. Best not to offer too many words, yet.

"Read the article, Angela," Bishop Healy said, pointing to the paper she had neatly folded under her arm. "Can you come back in an hour and tell me what you think we should do?"

Angela raised her eyebrows. This was definitely fast action for the Roman Church. "I'll read it and consider our options. But tell me, what's Bishop McGee's office saying?"

Angela didn't look forward to getting caught in a war of words between the two bishops. That would end poorly for both. She had learned that collegiality, even if strained, was a prime virtue of the hierarchy.

"McGee's office is saying, 'No comment,'" Bishop Healy answered. He stopped to chuckle. "What would you expect? Of course he wants to talk to the papal nuncio first, to get a Vatican spin."

Angela heard a tremolo of disgust in that last comment. It was one of the things she liked about Bishop Healy. He was no one's lackey. And he had a tolerable intellect, although it was mainly filled with well-memorized Thomistic conclusions. But add in a kind smile, a quick wit, and a cathedral-sized belief that prayer solves everything, and you got a great man of God.

"McGee is such a wimp!" Bishop Healy sat upright in his chair. "I told him to get on the phone with the USCCB, with Father John Fasopov, that I'd call Cardinal Hughes, that we didn't need Rome to get involved with this."

Bishop Healy paused to take off his glasses. He rubbed his eyes. Angela knew he'd been up for four hours already, one of them spent on his knees praying for his diocese, praying to be a good servant. That was one of the reasons Angela had taken this job. This man was for real.

"You know what McGee and his coterie are going to do with this, don't you?" Bishop Healy asked, leaning his elbows on the desk.

"I can imagine," Angela answered, keeping her voice calm. *They can be a pack of weasels.*

"I'm sure we'll come up with a considered response," Angela added. She felt her PR-personality already starting to kick into overdrive.

Angela left Bishop Healy's office and headed immediately to her own. By now, a few more of the chancery staff were arriving. Soon, the gossip would begin. She didn't need to get drawn into that sinkhole.

In her office, Angela sat for a second at her desk chair with her hands folded in her lap. The article was open before her. She took a deep breath and then started to read.

Angela's mood turned dark after reading the story for the third time. She stifled an urge to scream, to bang on the walls. Once again, a story about the male clerical culture—nothing about nuns with AIDS or Catholic Workers with AIDS or Opus Dei financial backers with AIDS. Priests with AIDS.

Why did this wrinkle on the face of the church fascinate so? Because it's on the face. She saw it clearly. And the face of the church was male—and supposedly celibate. Some days, this new vocation of hers didn't make sense at all.

After subduing her scream response, Angela's second urge was to call Father Tierney. They'd met at Mater Dei five years earlier, and he'd since become her interpreter of the more abstruse rites of the clerical caste, even the machinations of the United States Conference of Catholic Bishops. Indeed, she wouldn't be in this job if it weren't for Father Tierney. He'd helped her decide to follow a calling into church work. It had been a bad time for her. One more failed relationship. Too many lonely Sunday afternoons. She had gone to seek his counsel, to absorb some of the peace he radiated from the altar. After a few minutes listening to her story of self-doubt and despair, Father Tierney had shifted to the end game: "You need to be alone with your thoughts, Angela. But try to quiet your soul. Dial back your fears. Remember, you're not really alone. Not totally. None of us is. We live in a web of spirits." Father Tierney had seemed to glow with a steady energy when speaking those words, moving his brown hands as if he were manipulating a hidden cat's cradle.

That night, Angela had struggled to make sense of a life stalled in midstream. She'd curled up in front of a fire in her second-story den, alone. There had been this new feeling building inside her. It had felt like a "pulling." She'd laughed at herself because the word would have fit well in the mouth of some long-dead druid priestess speaking of moon power and goddess worship.

When she later told Father Tierney, he hadn't laughed. He'd looked thoughtful. He'd said that he'd felt the same way and that he'd often thought that the feeling was more of a "calling." Then he'd prodded her with brochures from schools of divinity.

Angela still had those tattered pamphlets. Back then, she had studied them as if they were holy artifacts, even stuffing them in her briefcase so she could take them out at work.

Angela stood up from her desk. She needed to move around. She went over to get her coat. She'd go for a stroll in the chancery garden.

Angela paused a moment. She could feel the melancholy slip in. Going to the garden did that, opened up the pores of her mind to let the memories shift in. The garden reminded her of St. Edmunds where she'd spent two years studying for a masters in theology. Her days there had been revelatory. She read theology for hours. The texts never bored her. She had liked everything about St. Edmunds. It was an urban Catholic theology school with a small courtyard where students would gather on the good days for laughter and argument amid the well-tended flowers. And there were few young men in collars.

Sadly, Angela often thought these days—especially this day of troubling headlines—her years in the land of liberal Catholicism had not prepared her for work in the mundane, political, and flatly human institution of an ordinary diocese where a reference to Hildegard of Bingen brought polite stares and secretive gossip about women's theology.

But at least Angela was now sure she was not alone. She had met others like her at St. Edmunds. So she walked briskly out the door of her office and headed to the land of memories. Maybe one of those memories would provide the key she needed today: how to respond so neither she nor Bishop Healy would regret their words?

Chapter 3

J oe was tense as he took his seat at the window table, yet he was glad he would finally fulfill Nurse Helen's request. It had been over twenty-four hours since she'd made the request. He was going to tell someone. He was going to tell Pascal.

Only Joe didn't like the location, the Nightly Bean, a loud coffee shop near the university. Pascal had suggested it. Pascal, the neo-ascetic, loved being out in the crowd. Usually Joe did, too, but not tonight. It didn't seem right to tell Pascal here, surrounded by undergrads and chatter. Joe felt exposed. Some kid from the parish could show up, overhear.

Joe thought he should be having this conversation in a rectory— or someplace quiet and removed.

He watched briefly as a young man moved about setting up his music on the small coffeehouse stage. *He's the Salvadoran refugee, Felipe,* Joe recalled, shaking his head. He suddenly realized why Pascal had insisted on this place. Pascal had always had a weakness for dark-skinned types.

Then Joe looked back outside and saw Pascal hurrying across the street heading toward the Nightly Bean. And with equal speed, Joe felt an iron vice clamp around his heart. He started to sweat even before Pascal had entered the coffee shop. Joe's tenseness was turning into something more menacing.

"I'm late, I'm late," Pascal said as he neared the table, first waving briefly at Felipe. His voice sounded bright.

Joe faked looking at his watch. He smiled awkwardly. This was going to be hard. Felipe was going to be a distraction. Maybe he shouldn't say anything tonight.

Pascal took off his thin polyester jacket and settled into a chair next to Joe, positioning himself to look inward toward the small coffee-shop stage. From all appearances, Pascal hadn't picked up on Joe's discomfort.

After a second, Pascal took his eyes off Felipe, who was settling onto a stool, and turned to Joe. Pascal leaned into the table. "The other night I was thinking, I can hear the moon, but I can't hear the sun."

"What? Pascal, what are you saying?" Joe knew his voice was too loud and harsh. He felt so on edge. It was usually so easy bantering with Pascal. Now he was just bleating.

"I was speaking poetically," Pascal replied, still bright and positive. "It's a poetic explanation of my attraction to the night and to night things ... compline, candlelit chapels, and sex in a pitch-black room."

Joe quickly looked around, scanning the nearby tables, and then whispered, "Please, Pascal. That's confused thinking." Joe had hoped to sound less distraught but knew that that last comment had come off sharp and accusatory.

"You always hated imagery," Pascal said. Joe saw his friend stiffen a bit. This evening wasn't going well. "You even wanted religion to be nothing but social work. Well, it's not. Not for me, anyway."

"Unfairly accused am I!" Joe said, with his lips clamped tight for two seconds before he burst into his usual, big-lipped smile. Finally, a relaxation. Joe had picked up that silly phrase from Pascal their first month in seminary. Pascal had been a grade-school teacher for two years and often constructed sentences that sounded like Dr. Seuss prattle—until Pascal had started to read Matthew Fox and found a hip new jargon.

"Falsely accused you're not! You wanted every religious statement to be parsible. Simple declarations. Computer code." Pascal accompanied each terse phrase with a finger wag.

Joe's shoulders drooped. "Let's not argue."

Pascal was looking at him with an open mouth and concerned eyes. He was reading him now, and Pascal was good at that. He had relished Bishop Healy's exhortation to trust the body's language, a phrase often used at the seminary before concerned minds reported it to the Vatican.

"But I like arguing with you." Pascal smiled, paused again, and continued to peer at Joe over his dark-rimmed glasses. "At least I used to like arguing with you."

"Do it while you can."

"What's that?" Pascal asked. Joe heard the concern, something beyond curiosity. He must be giving off a vibe.

Joe felt a grim silence settle between them while his eyes examined the dark surface of his Guatemalan brew. He still didn't want to say the words. But it had been twenty-four hours, twenty-four hours lying in the coffin—or so it seemed. Then there was that article, the priests with AIDS article that he kept on reading and reading, a story in which each man had died, each death explained away by other illnesses in order to save the "people" from scandal.

Pascal leaned over the worn table, his eyes clearly on Joe even though Felipe was now strumming his guitar.

At least Joe had Pascal's attention. Still, he remained silent.

"So, tell me," Pascal said, the words slow and kind, a cadence Joe knew well from seminary halls.

Joe inhaled deeply and then looked away—out onto the busy

avenue. He hated being so obvious, with his emotions on display. He bit his lower lip. He didn't want to cry, not yet, not again, but his brown eyes already shimmered, the way his mother's had often when they pooled with the moistness of fresh pain. He closed his eyes and clamped his hands tightly together, as if he were mashing something between them, a mannerism of his that Pascal had often seen. But when he started crying, he released the clamp and pressed his hands over his eyes. He tried to stop the flow. This was too much! Joe shot out of his chair and ran outside into the mild evening air. He'd rarely been so dramatic in public. He hated making a scene. He'd always been the rock, visible and unmovable and etched with a divine covenant.

Joe stopped when he reached the intersection. He was facing the street, sobbing on the corner. Joe heard footsteps come running up behind him. He looked down and back, seeing Pascal's worn tennis shoes.

Then Pascal's hands were around him, Pascal's head over his shoulder, Pascal's mouth in his ear.

"Joe," Pascal said, his voice now sharp with concern. "Joe, poor baby. What's wrong?"

*　*　*

Joe shut his office door and then leaned against it. His legs felt like rubber. He locked his knees and let his head drop back against the door. He shut his eyes a moment. When he opened his eyes, he glanced around the dim confines of his office. A pink slip rested on the edge of his desk. Joe walked over to pick it up.

Lucy's handwriting, her script all precise slants and full tails, informed him that Angela had called.

Joe headed off to the rector's quarters, the note in his right hand. He'd pour himself a Scotch, light a few candles, put on some Peruvian flutes, sit for a while, and think about what had just happened, recalling the few facts he remembered—that he'd told Pascal, out on an evening street with people walking by; that he'd made his announcement in a whisper into his friend's ear, "I'm HIV positive"; that Pascal had gasped and his eyes had widened; that Pascal hadn't said a thing. Not at first.

"How?" Pascal finally had asked.

"I can't say," Joe had replied. "I can't say any more." He was so afraid to tell it all.

Joe shook his head recalling the scene. Maybe it was a step in the right direction, but it was a very small one, a shuffle, really—a fearful man's shuffle.

∗   ∗   ∗

Two feet into his suite, Joe saw the answering machine blinking and wondered who it could be.

He kept his personal landline number private, almost as private as his cell phone. Only a dozen people had it. Even then, most of those people contacted him through the church office. He took a deep breath and then walked quickly past the phone, as if it might suck him in. Joe couldn't risk listening to the message. He suddenly felt near the cliff's edge—too near. He couldn't listen to someone else's needs, even a close friend's. His inner light was burning low, flickering out.

Joe went into his bedroom and switched on the overhead, closing his eyes to its brightness. He undressed down to his boxers, turned on the reading light, and then shut off the overhead. He sat on the bed a moment, rubbing his legs. His body was aching. It couldn't be the disease, he thought. Or could it? Joe knew so little about AIDS. His experience was limited, but he'd seen what it did to people. He wasn't that cut off from the epidemic. It was just never his passion.

Joe lay back on the bedcovers. He needed to concentrate on his job. There were things he had to do.

Joe looked over at the clock. It was only 9:30. He was meeting with the newlyweds' group tomorrow night. The afternoon was preparation time. He had Mass in the morning and a four o'clock meeting at the chancery to discuss the housing crisis. Would he be ready for tomorrow? Maybe if he slept. Joe remembered the bottle of Nyquil he had from last month's cold and the medication's promise of quiet rest. He chuckled, thinking he might as well get used to drugging himself, because from what he'd read, he was about to become a pharmacist's retirement plan.

The thought made Joe sit up straight, made his heart beat fast. That was the other thing Nurse Helen had said. He'd have to see a doctor. And who would that be? He couldn't see Dr. Courtland. He played golf with her husband.

This diagnosis was not just a spiritual crisis. He was really sick now. He was HIV positive. Everything was going to change, and for the worse. Joe was going to be like one of those guys in the article. He was going to become a pariah. Would people even share the Communion cup with him?

Chapter 4

Angela preferred the peace and quiet of a morning at the office. Although she usually meditated her first half hour at work, this day, Angela decided she had to get right to task. She sat at her desk and began to review the editorials that busy opinion leaders had already churned out on the "AIDS in the Catholic Priesthood" article. Bishop Healy had asked her to stay on top of reactions to the article and write a summary every week. After ten minutes and several hundred serious, moaning sentences, Angela gave up. She shoved the papers away from her. She couldn't start the day this way.

Angela rose from her chair and went over to the closet to get her prayer rug. She unfolded it and then placed it next to the wall. After bending to touch her toes several times and stretching out her thirty-six-year-old muscles, she sat down in lotus position. It was only 8:00 a.m., and this was supposed to be her meditation time.

Angela and Joe had taken yoga class together last fall after he had complained about losing his concentration. It had brought them even closer. She had confided in him that she had received other offers—not church offers. She needed to be clear about her future. Joe didn't say anything right away. Then he smiled his wide, handsome smile and said, "So forty years in the wilderness might be too many?" Angela recalled punching his arm, joking with him that he shouldn't make fun of her. He'd turned serious. "I'm not," Joe said. "If it's a vocation, the summoning doesn't end."

That phrase hung in Angela's brain as she shifted to get more comfortable on the rug. She decided to concentrate on that one word: *summoning*. For a moment, it was working. She was focused on a rich thought.

Then the phone rang. Angela sprang up and dashed to grab the receiver. Only Bishop Healy would call at this hour. Before picking up, she checked the caller ID. It wasn't Bishop Healy. Angela squinted at the number as she tried to tamp down her annoyance. She looked at the travel alarm next to the phone. It was 8:00 a.m. Who needed to reach her first thing?

Angela decided to answer. Maybe it was a call from the local press. She had been expecting them. But the number on the caller ID wasn't from a news organization.

"Hello?" she said, tentatively. It could just be a wrong number.

"Hello, I'm Ron Saville-Jones, a reporter with the *GLRegister*, and I'm calling to speak with Angela Roth."

Angela suppressed a growl. *What a rotten morning*, she thought as she considered her response, feeling a sadness deepen inside. Something in this article made her bones weep.

So far, Angela had been lucky. The local mainstream media had been quiet. The television stations had only used the story to entice a few more eyes before an evening bar melee, which ended in death and riot, had pushed all other stories aside. The TV stations had solicited a local quote to go along with their oft-used graphic of a Roman collar. Angela supplied them with the brief statement she and Bishop Healy had concocted. "We offer prayers for any person caught up in this disease." The comment was nonjudgmental, slightly vague yet compassionate, and empty of political or theological fodder. That is, it was a dead end. The metro daily hadn't contacted her at all. *No surprise,* Angela thought. She had a tepid relationship with the religion lady, Lois, a middle-aged Lutheran with little taste for popery, even of the less dressy post-Vatican II kind.

Angela moved around to her chair. She sat down. "I'm Angela Roth. How can I help you?"

This Ron Saville-Jones immediately launched into what he assured her was a brief introduction of his journalistic interest. Soon Angela dropped her head onto the desk. Brief would be one sentence. *This guy is a rookie.*

"Are you aware of the 'AIDS in the Catholic Priesthood' article?" Ron asked. "What's been the reaction? How many priests in the dioceses are HIV positive? Are there any restrictions on them?"

Angela raised her head up from the desk. *Well, he's got quite a list of questions,* she thought, twirling her sapphire-blue Waterman pen in her right hand. And he'd offered no explanation of what the *GLRegister* was. So he assumed she was up on the local gay press.

"Yes, I've read the article and some of the editorials." Angela began to rummage through her brain in the "alternative newspapers" file. *GLRegister. GLBT. Small-circulation. Twenty thousand? Metro distribution, obviously. Maybe outstate in some of the university towns. Tab format. Weren't there two gay papers in town? Was this the one that attempted to cover hard news, or was it the bar rag that stitched together ten pages of dating ads and realtor pictures with a few wire stories?*

"In-depth article," she mouthed to the side of the room and its framed picture of Mother Theresa's wrinkled smile, which hung next to Dorothy Day's aged elegance. "Lots of different perspectives," she whispered, quietly echoing another fragment of Ron's pitch. *He's not just looking for a good ten-word quote,* she thought. *Is he after a Pulitzer?* GLRegister *must not be the bar rag.*

"An article with real names and events," Ron said. "An article that shows how AIDS has touched this important part of our society, the clergy."

"You remember Father Stephens," Angela said, already playing her trump card. It had been twenty-four hours, and she had to admit she wasn't comfortably prepared for this call. She was having trouble getting on top of this story and couldn't understand why. "Father Stephens died ten years ago. His story was well covered."

Angela was looking over the list she'd been able to pull together yesterday. The vicar for administration had come up with Father Stephens's name. "His story is well known and gives most reporters all they want," Sister Cecilia, the ever-vigilant vicar, had said. Did this surname-enhanced reporter really think that anyone kept a registry of clergy with AIDS? She stopped to look at her fingernails, deciding they needed a new color. Angela could feel her tongue start to sharpen. She wanted to tell Ron that if anybody in the church were keeping a list, it was written in Syriac and filed away in the tomb of an out-of-favor pope. The church had millennia of practice in dissimulation and disguise.

Since her tête-à-tête with Bishop Healy, she'd been calling around nonstop and had finally cajoled a wealthy gay Catholic donor, a man who dined with every significant Catholic in the diocese where he regularly uncorked the best distillations of clergy gossip, to produce a list of three local priests with AIDS. Of that infected triad, only one was alive: Father Peterson. He'd spent many years in and out of drug rehabilitation and was notorious for that failing. He was known as funny and kind. Father Peterson was currently chaplain at the children's hospital where he usually walked the halls in a Holstein cow costume. Folks called him the Holy Cow Clown. He was doing well on the meds and didn't want to come out as HIV positive. "He has enough baggage to lug around—and none of it on wheels," her wealthy informant had said, chuckling happily.

"Yes, Father Stephens's story was compelling." Ron huffed his answer over the line as if the whole world knew that. "But the landscape of AIDS has changed."

"It does seem that AIDS is a different disease now, more a chronic disease than a virulent and fatal one." Angela became aware of a glint of sharpness flashing in her tone. "I'm not sure it's that big of a story locally."

This Ron Saville-Jones should just say: "I'm interested in queer priests." *That's your story, right? Queer priests, oppression, bad choices, and bad luck. Your readers will love it. Who wouldn't?*

A long pause. "I want to write more than a simple news piece," Ron said. "Not an exposé. Not a documentary. More like a reflection. A story of a soul."

"Story of a soul." Good Catholic phrase, Angela thought. *He's definitely one of us. And not a bad idea. St. Thérèse had been tubercular.*

Chapter 5

J oe's afternoon chancery meeting went smoothly. He wanted to set up a women's shelter for undocumenteds and had petitioned the diocese for aid. His plan was good, even the details about secrecy and potential legal problems. Joe was pleased to see the serious heads at the table nod as he went through the what-ifs. He sat at the middle of the table, and all those eyes studied him. These people still thought of him as a leader—as a man guided by principle and a desire to care for others. He stopped a second at that realization, during an exchange between two participants, and welcomed the freshness of the realization, even daring to hope its presence might signal a sea change in the emotional currents coursing inside him, might signal the advance of cleansing waves that would break up the shame-infused oil slick left by his HIV diagnosis.

After the meeting, Joe headed over to his parents' house for an evening dinner. His mom would cook—probably something *la abuelita* used to make. They'd relive old times, and Joe would be able to assess the tension level in the household. But as soon as they sat down to dinner at the kitchen table, his mind was back on the diagnosis and its ramifications. Joe could barely make conversation. He spent a lot of time chewing and listening to his mom talk about spices. He only offered an occasional smile. He saw his mom stop several times in her cooking commentary to look at him with her wry, Olmec big-lipped look, the one that said: "I see, but will wait for you to tell me why."

As was his routine, Joe stayed in the kitchen to help his mom clean up. His dad went into the living room and turned on the TV, catching the tag end of a national talk show.

"They're still talking about that AIDS article," Joe's dad yelled out. "They're asking how many Catholic priests have AIDS."

Joe looked over at his mom, who was scrubbing a frying pan. She looked back at him with a gaze that said, "Your father has no sense."

"I warned you about that church business," Joe's dad scoffed. "It's getting worse every year."

"What's that?" his mom called out.

Joe gestured for her to be quiet. He didn't want to deal with a fight tonight. All the fight he felt before his afternoon meeting had evaporated. Now he was feeling arid and alone, as shriveled up as an unwatered cactus plant in an old woman's windowsill.

"The priesthood! All them queers!" Joe's dad yelled.

His mom had finished with the pan and was drying her hands. "Frank, watch your language!" she shouted back.

Joe suspected his mom knew her son was one of those queers. Her supportive comments about Dignity, the Catholic gay support group, were a clue. "It's good they still worship the Lord." But his father surely didn't suspect. After all, there was the pregnancy scare when he was in high school. And he'd been no saint.

Joe walked into the living room. He sat down in the armchair next to his father's recliner. His father kept staring at the TV. It was now a sports show.

Joe remembered his teenage preoccupation with being shorter than the other boys. He remembered the need that had burned inside him to act tough, to give off a scent of danger. Once he had let that greasy fire come close to destroying everything in its path.

It had been a warm night, and the kids his age and younger were hanging near the roller rink. It was time for the younger kids to go home, so Joe told them to head off. Just as he was prodding his sheep along to their shed, the "three kings" showed up. They were baby hoodlums from deep in the *barrio*. One of them, a wide fat kid, stopped in front of Joe and told him to stop his braying. Pointing to the young ones, the wide boy said, "They can do whatever they want, *chulo*."

Maybe it was the heat, maybe it was the bully word "*chulo*," maybe it was the wide brick wall's sneer, but Joe drew out his pocketknife. He opened the blade, and it clicked loud in the evening air. There was a sudden silence. Joe's crowd backed away. Most of them had seen him throw before. Everyone knew he was as accurate as old Robin Hood with his arrows. Joe felt their fear. And he felt it himself. This was not mumbly pegs, but he was comfortable with a blade.

The brick wall stood quiet for a second and then lunged for Joe's knife arm. Joe's wrestler instinct guided his dive at the brick wall's legs. He wouldn't need the knife. The fool was standing close to the curb, and it didn't take much thrust to get him to stumble. But when the brick wall came back at him, it was as a bull blinded with rage. That's when Joe slashed his opponent's right cheek, making sure the blade didn't go deep.

Blood was everywhere. People were screaming. Adults came running out of the building; the police arrived with their sirens and lights and soon escorted Joe into a squad car to drive down to the station. In the back of that squad car, Joe remembered later, as he confessed his sin, he hadn't been frozen by fear. He was in his groove.

But that knife-wielder was not the persona young Joe envisioned for himself. The blade guy was a sideshow freak, a distraction. Still, Joe knew that the street-brawling boy was real—a bantam weight inside him—and keen to punch out. So Joe worked hard to build up that other persona, running it through scenes of charity and kindness that would entice its soft heart to come out.

Joe volunteered at the parish soup kitchen with its adjacent twelve-bunk shelter. He would beg his mom to let him stay overnight, despite her fears for his youth and the rough crowd she imagined came there.

Joe remembered the hard time he had convincing his mom that he felt at home in the shelter. How could a kid explain that rush of feeling that comes when you know you're in your element? "I'll be okay, *Mamá. Mi ángel* will watch over me."

Joe took to being in charge. He liked to stay up late and show the men to their bunks, checking the bed number off as soon as it was claimed. Joe would explain the rules to the newcomers. He knew his voice was still a boy's, a little high and sweet, but the men listened. Only later in life, after he had gained a man's perspective, would he wonder why they were docile and kind to him.

Joe remembered the man called Eagle. He was from a tribe two states over but had tried to make a living as a short-order cook in the city. Eagle was older than the others. He moved slower than most and never swore. Joe remembered their first meeting at the check-in desk.

"Hello, young man," Eagle had said, his voice smooth and dusky, sounding like a gentleman, or how Joe had imagined a gentleman sounded. It was unusual for anyone at the shelter to speak first to him, maybe because he was so young or they were so weary, so Joe was surprised by this man's open directness.

"Hello, sir," Joe had replied, a little stiffly, as he opened the evening logbook. "I need to get your name for our registry. Some of our funding is from the state. You know how it is." Joe was poised to write, pen in hand and face down. He assumed from the man's accent that he was no illegal. Joe might even get a real name.

"Just put down Eagle," the man said.

Instead of writing, Joe looked up at the old man and into his wrinkled face. The man was smiling kindly, and there was a flash of cleverness in his eyes. Joe smiled back. This man was different. Usually the shelter's residents had one or two believable aliases ready at hand. Joe could hear the falseness when they spoke them.

"Eagle. That's a good name," Joe said, as he leaned forward to write it in his book.

"It's kind of a family name," the man said. "Maybe I'll explain it to you someday."

When he had finished writing the name, Joe put his pen down and looked up, saying, "I'd like that." Then Joe stood up. It was just before midnight. Soon, he and the older staff person—that night it was Howie—would lock the doors and turn off the lights. The shelter enforced quiet and sleep, or at least bed rest, after midnight.

"I'll show you to your bunk, Eagle," Joe said. "May I call you Eagle?"

The old man reached over and placed his hand on Joe's head, ruffling his hair. *He speaks without words,* Joe thought to himself.

Joe reached over to pick up Eagle's stained backpack, saying, "Let me carry it." Eagle stood back and let him.

Joe remembered that it was often like that at the shelter—so much meaning in gestures. And he remembered the way time passed. The time spent at the shelter was a lazy companion, as unrushed as the flow of a muddy summer river.

Joe now wondered if that evening shelter pace might be part of what made him become more aware—more aware, or more expectant. Maybe it had started with Eagle. But Joe began to pay special attention to the eyes of the men who came late to their shelter. He was looking for Jesus' stare of approval, hoping for a nod from the disguised man-God who might say, "You're okay, little guy."

The image of Eagle faded. Joe's parents' clean but shabby living room snapped into focus. His dad had changed the channel back to the commentator who was signing off with a snarl and swagger.

He shifted in his recliner. Joe looked at his dad's bitter face. That night, Joe felt no anger. His dad was right. Joe's life was now a mockery. He had debased everything he'd ever stood for. The housing projects, the cooperative of immigrant painters and carpenters, Casa Magdalena for battered women—all of it would be tainted with the stain of his sin.

Joe felt short of breath. "I've got to go. An early session tomorrow." He stood up.

His father didn't get up. His mom hugged him.

Joe drove home gripped by silence. He could say nothing about his diagnosis to his parents. He shuddered. He was becoming a tiny little bird with darting eyes.

Chapter 6

As soon as Joe entered the rector's suite after dinner with his parents, the phone began to ring. He hurried across the room to get the call. It was Pascal.

With the cordless phone to his ear, Joe walked over to the loveseat on the wall opposite his small writing table and then dropped into its padded comfort.

"How are things today?" was all Pascal asked, as if Joe's "things" could possibly be anything but wreckage and skid marks.

Joe shucked off his shoes and curled his legs up on the loveseat. "I'm okay. I just got back from my folks'. What's up with you?" He had to admit it. It was a pleasure to hear Pascal's voice. He was a good friend.

"Well, I've got news. So I'll just come right out with it."

There was a brief pause. Joe tensed up.

"I think Ron is going to do a story on HIV-positive priests."

Joe closed his eyes and let his phone hand drop into his lap. He felt limp—a sudden deflation. Now a reporter was sniffing around near him. Could things get worse? Joe had just been diagnosed. It was all too much—too much, too soon.

"Joe! Joe!" Pascal called out after a few seconds. "Are you still there?"

43

Joe opened his eyes and tried to refocus them. He had trouble seeing the wall clock across the room. It had been a long day and now this. Joe heard Pascal still calling his name. Had Pascal ratted on him?

Joe raised the phone back up. "I'm here." He felt defeated.

"I didn't mean to upset you any more. Really, Joe. I thought you'd want to know. And there's more. Ron's been talking to your friend Angela Roth."

That news made Joe uncurl his legs and sit up straight. "She'd never get involved in a witch hunt!" Joe felt a surge of anger. "The church isn't looking to stoke the fires of scandal right now. Why would she cooperate?"

Ron didn't know what he was getting into. Secrecy within the Catholic Church was ancient, bred in the bone.

"You're probably right." Pascal sounded hesitant. "And I don't mean to upset you. Really. But the conservatives have already started to use this article as more proof that gay men are unsuitable for the priesthood."

Now Joe heard Pascal getting heated. This topic was close to Pascal's heart, ever since he was forced out of the seminary. "They want to get rid of gay priests. Send them off to Devil's Island, or direct to hell if they could manage the logistics. I got an e-mail from my Jesuit contact just this morning. The article he forwarded was vicious!"

Joe stood up and then walked over to his picture of the Virgin of Guadalupe. He stared at the stars in her cloak, into their cosmic sparkle where he had once found peace as a confused kid. "You know, Pascal, I can't have this conversation right now." He and *la Virgen* didn't need another invader coming into their land, tramping down the crops.

"I ... I'm sorry. I just thought I'd warn you."

"Warn me?" Joe was exasperated. This conversation was not helping.

"Let you know."

Neither spoke. Joe was feeling the coldness of fear again, the permafrost coldness. He waited for Pascal to get the hint.

"Have you made an appointment yet?" Pascal asked, moving on to that other topic.

Joe turned away from the picture. His arm almost flung the phone across the room, an involuntary response, as if a madman were inside him and taking control. Joe knew Pascal was talking about seeing a doctor. Pascal wasn't the type to let up on that topic.

"Not yet." Joe clipped the two words.

"Like I said, Dr. Trongard is safe. He's gay. He's savvy. He understands privacy."

Joe started to wedge out his Roman collar. He needed to get to bed. But Pascal was a friend. He meant well. Joe could be reasonable for a second more. He dug a little deeper, looked back at *la Virgen*.

"But ninety percent of his clientele is gay and probably half of them positive. People would find out. And I already see a physician. She sees a lot of priests." As soon as he said it, Joe shivered at the thought. That was why he was afraid to contact Dr. Courtland. She was part of the fraternity.

"So make an appointment with her."

Joe didn't want to say anything more. He undid his belt and let his trousers drop. He stepped out of them and then walked to the door to flip off the lights.

"You have to see *someone*." Pascal's voice had taken on the slightly humid sound of a pleading mother.

Joe just wanted to get into bed. He'd had enough tension today.

"I know ... I will. And good night now, *Pascualito*."

With a press of his thumb, Joe hung up. He could feel his heart beat, its rhythm panicky. He got light-headed. Joe dropped down to his knees, bent over with his head touching the floor, and began to sob.

* * *

The weariness of his restless night strained Joe's smile as he greeted Lucy the next morning.

"You're still not okay?" she asked.

"I'm okay, but I had trouble sleeping last night. Excitement about that project." Joe didn't want Lucy to get involved in Casa Magdalena because what they were planning was skirting the law, so he called it "that project." Luckily, she just let it pass.

Joe settled into his desk and picked up his calendar, making sure it matched what he had tried to recall as he was getting dressed that morning. It had been a rough night, lots of tossing and turning, his sheets winding around him.

It was now 9:00 a.m., and like clockwork, his phone rang. Joe picked it up and heard Lucy asking if he'd take a call from Angela Roth at the chancery.

Joe hesitated a second. He'd already ignored a couple of her calls. He knew she wanted to talk about the article, maybe about Ron's inquiries. Joe shook his head, wishing there was some way to shield himself from this issue of priests with AIDS, especially from the personal, pointed, sitting-in-your-own-bedroomness of it.

Finally, Joe decided he had to take the call. He offered a silent prayer for wisdom. He'd need to gulp down a pitcherful of that long-brewed virtue to move forward.

"Joe, you've been avoiding me," Angela said, starting off with a jab, even if she sounded cheery.

"I've been swamped. Really swamped." *You have no idea how swamped,* Joe thought, wanting to keep it that way. *Like stuck deep in the muck.*

"I know how it is. I've heard that you're getting close to setting up Casa Magdalena. I think it's a great undertaking. And so does Bishop Healy."

"It's supposed to be a secret." It annoyed Joe that the project might be discussed openly at the chancery.

"It *is* a secret, but you know I'm privy to what the bishop is doing and thinking." She spoke with the tone of an assuring mother.

Joe heard Angela's secretary asking a question, which Angela must have answered with a head nod.

"I'm calling about something Bishop Healy has asked me to research."

Joe felt his jaw tighten. Here it came.

"He wants me to come up with a more robust response to the 'AIDS in the Catholic Priesthood' article. And I'm having difficulty getting a good take on it. I was hoping you could help me out. So I'm calling to invite you over for dinner." Angela paused a moment. "Besides, we could catch up. We always laugh together."

"Yeah, you laughing at me!" Joe said, proud that he was still able to disguise his despair. But Angela was a good friend. He picked up his calendar to check his free evenings.

"So? Make me happy, Joe. Dinner tonight? I'll cook. Refried beans. Beef and rice. You know I can cook as well as your mother."

"But your tortillas are store-bought!" Joe moved his finger down the day's schedule. His dinnertime was free.

"I'll serve corn bread. Even a *gringa* can cook that!"

"I don't know …"

Joe wanted to make an excuse. He feared this meeting. Angela was dear to him. She shared her life with him. He respected that. He encouraged the sharing. But he wasn't ready to share this new—this personal—development.

He still didn't believe it. HIV positive. He still had moments when he wanted to pack up and run. He looked up through his open door at Lucy, wondering how he could ever tell her, how she'd react.

Joe knew, in the jargon of self-help, he was slightly beyond stage one. He had accepted the facts. Now he was absorbing the meaning of his diagnosis, like monitoring a dial, something you'd do with a Geiger counter. And he knew there would soon be practical consequences—public shame being consequence *número uno*. The details of that shaming were becoming clearer. If he saw a doctor, the bills would need to be paid. The diocesan health-care system would surely spit him out as a data point of interest. Someone would wonder. It would only take time.

Joe stood up from his chair and then turned to look out his window onto the busy downtown street. People were passing by, some still heading to work, some already on coffee break. *Normal life.*

Joe sighed. He needed to get a plan in place. He needed to take care of himself. But every time he thought of a possible action, his heart started to race, his gut churned, and he started to sweat like an overdressed marathoner at mile twenty.

And he still needed to contact Kenny, a simple action he had put off, but not out of fear of the words he'd say, the warning, the advice he'd offer. They hadn't spoken since Kenny had left. What did a contact imply, any contact, even this worthy and righteous contact? Joe had vowed to turn away from the path Kenny had showed him, despite the young man's naked presence in his bedtime thoughts. He wanted to get back to his priesthood, the way it once was.

"I need your advice, Joe," Angela said, breaking into his thoughts. "I've been contacted by a local gay reporter. I'm thinking of cooperating with this guy, and I'm not really sure why."

Joe's heart nearly stopped. Even the street life seemed to stand still. He shook his head and then forced an answer, "Okay. I'll come over for dinner. But I don't know what to say."

"Just listen. I'd like a priest to listen."

"Not fair. You'd like everyone to listen!" Joe smiled. At least with Angela he didn't have to be politic.

* * *

Joe found a parking spot right in front of Angela's Lennox Hill condo. He shut off the car engine and then turned his head to study the old brownstone. Angela had been lucky to buy it when she did, preconversion. Now the neighborhood was getting swanky. A cellist for the chamber orchestra lived in the unit above her.

Joe got out of the car. After locking the door, he stood a second to observe the street. Lennox Hill had become the sort of neighborhood that made Joe feel out of place. He looked over at the French bakery that had taken over an old corner grocery. He thought of his dad's business. Joe smiled a moment. His dad probably would've found something to complain about, even in a neighborhood like this. His dad would have aimed his tirades at the type of woman Joe was watching come down the street, a slender, fiftyish woman in a pleated jacket carrying a baguette in one hand.

Joe shook his head to clear his mind. He had more pressing issues to address. He looked up the steps to the condo building's front door. He felt a sudden evening chill. Beyond that door could be traps—unintentional traps, but traps just the same. He'd have to be careful. And he'd probably be lying as boldly as Peter at the high priest's gate.

Joe walked up the steps, drew a deep gulp of evening air, and then rang Angela's buzzer.

"Smells good," Joe said as he hugged Angela at her unit's door.

"Me or the *arroz con carne?*"

"Sadly, my nose I got from my mom, and it's Mexican peasant—mostly attuned to the subtleties of earthy spices. Are you wearing anything particularly *picante?*" Joe was determined to make this evening as breezy as possible. He might dip into his childhood bag of tricks, one of which was to pretend he was on a broad beach rather than sitting in his father's cramped store. But he didn't need to go to the beach quite yet. He liked to banter with Angela.

"I'm giving off my natural, womanly smell," Angela said, leaning against the doorframe.

"Then sorry." Joe winked at Angela, and she smiled back, working her lips to disguise her wince, that little mouth tug that meant she still wasn't 100 percent over her attraction to Joe. They had never talked about it, but Joe knew it was there. She wasn't the first woman to find him attractive.

"Come on in and pop open a Dos Equis. I'll put the food on the table." Angela headed down the hallway to the kitchen and gestured for Joe to follow.

"No little chitchat and *tapas* in the living room tonight?"

"It's a working dinner," Angela answered, flipping her hair. "I left early from the chancery to cook, so now I'm back at work."

"Story of my life. All my entertainment turns into work."

"*Pobrecito, no llores,*" Angela said. Joe smiled back. Angela liked to test her Spanish with him.

It only took a few minutes to finish the cooking. They exchanged a couple of words about the rich smells and moved to the kitchen's eat-in nook with two heaping plates. Joe was feeling relaxed, thinking of the pleasure of a good friend and good food. The meal talk was all silly prattle and catching up with diocesan gossip, with a brief yet heated discussion of possible parish closings.

Soon, they had put the dishes in the sink, and Angela told Joe to head to the living room. "I'll just rinse them. You go make yourself comfortable."

Joe didn't say a word. Obediently, he walked back down the hallway to the living room. He had always liked this space. It had the feel of old-time elegance, with a marble mantle over the fireplace and large oils on the walls. Joe reminded himself that Angela had once pulled down an impressive salary.

He settled into one of the armchairs near the fireplace and coddled his beer bottle in both hands. He was almost relaxed, except for that feeling of foreboding that had driven over with him. Joe was still annoyed that Pascal had called last night with his warning. It had been wearing away at him all day.

Joe was studying the details of Angela's Persian carpet when she suddenly appeared before him offering coffee. He had been lost in his thoughts.

"*Café?*" Angela asked as she brought in two cups.

"Sure." Joe put the beer on the side table. *Now it comes,* he was thinking. Angela had so studiously avoided the article. She wanted him to be comfortable. That was her style. But she also wanted to address the facts. He should be ready.

Angela settled into the other armchair. Then came the question. "So, did you read the article?"

"No," Joe said, flatly lying; it was the way he had planned to keep himself far from the topic. "I only heard summaries. Statistics. That some orders tried to cover up the truth."

Angela shifted in her chair and took a sip of coffee. *She knows I'm lying,* Joe thought. *Maybe she'll stay away from it.*

"Well, it's been a constant topic at the chancery. But luckily the story has had very short legs here, which is a great relief to Bishop Healy. In his early seventies, the last thing he wants is another sex scandal to disturb his sleep." Angela was staring over her cup.

Joe finished the coffee and then set it next to his beer. He crossed his ankles, pushing himself back into the red damask. He could feel it coming.

"Do you think it should have legs?" Angela asked.

Joe paused to consider his answer. He was ready to be evasive. "What would be the point?"

Angela settled her cup in her lap and looked down at it as if studying the dregs. "This sex abuse scandal has all been about evil acts: adults abusing children, bishops and chanceries covering up—and not even understanding the impact of this kind of abuse," she said, sounding meditative.

"Yes. I think you're right on that."

"But isn't a pivotal issue getting clouded?"

"A pivotal issue being?"

Now Angela looked straight at him. Joe could sense her discomfort.

"How do I say it? This 'sex' abuse scandal is about problems with a closed-loop, all-male, secret society. The sex part, which is clearly disordered, plays a crucial but supporting role in the scandal."

Joe hadn't expected that angle. He was just enough of an outsider to understand what she was saying. But he was amazed how well he fit into the club, the all-male society, except that it was mostly white. "I'll buy that," Joe said.

"Today's stories are about sick men and the intransigent, out-of-touch geriatrics who govern them."

Joe laughed. "They're not all geriatric."

Why did he try to make a joke? Maybe because she wasn't coming after him.

Angela smirked but kept on.

"Most of the conservative bishops are saying the solution is a return to discipline. Praying the rosary. Adoration. And getting rid of the homos."

"I've heard all that crap," Joe said. "Neither you nor I can do much about it."

"But we can talk about it. And think. Especially about this current article. And this is what I wonder: what's at the heart?"

"I'm sorry?" Joe asked. Angela's question pulled him in. He had always been one to look for meaning in events. He uncrossed his ankles and leaned toward her.

"Isn't a part of this AIDS story, the broad-picture story, about sexual connections—about a longing for love and intimacy? And you only get to the bottom of a story like this when you get into somebody's heart."

Angela leaned back in her chair, as if she'd made her final point.

But it was a fresh cut for Joe, a question that went in deep and fast, with the brutality of a surgical mishap that requires emergency tactics.

Joe had an image of himself stumbling about these last days, having lost his course, wishing things were different. Now Angela had suggested that there was an impulse behind what was happening, something to do with love maybe, or whatever goes on inside the heart. Joe trembled at the idea. Was he being moved by fate in a different direction?

In a second, Joe shot up from the armchair and turned his face to the outside window. He balled his fists and clamped down a sob.

Angela was suddenly up from her chair. Joe turned to look at her and saw the astonishment in her face.

"I'm sorry, Angela; I just can't discuss this now. I'm really tired. Stressed. I need sleep." Then Joe said his good-byes and hurried out.

Chapter 7

P ascal listened to the rain tap on the tall glass panes of Ron's bedroom windows. He had glowed inside when Ron had invited him over for dinner. He could get some good food, a little corporal intimacy, and maybe a clue as to where Ron was going with his article. But he hadn't wanted an evening of gay clergy sex talk. Luckily, they dined on poached cod and couscous with no chatter about gay priests, AIDS, or the state of society. Ron had promised a healthy meal with no serious talk, and he had delivered.

Pascal remembered how, while in the kitchen cleaning up and giggling over their shared infatuation for Harry Potter and all things wizardly, they had started to bump into each other—at the sink, near the wastebasket, by the pantry door. Ron had been the first to make unambiguous contact, placing a full-on, let's-do-it kiss on Pascal's lips after Pascal had set the wineglasses back in the cupboard. That memory of Ron's desire pleased Pascal as the rain turned heavier and lightning lit up the sky. Pascal liked that sense of being wanted sexually; it was something he rarely experienced at the Casa Romero dinner table or at St. Martha's soup line. His life choices had taken him so far from the gay mainstream. This evening with Ron was like getting giddy with champagne and grapes at midnight on Christmas Eve.

Ron began to stir. The thunder was getting louder and the lightning brighter.

Pascal stretched his arms back and grabbed a bar of the metal headboard, flexing his biceps. "Our sex is so much better now."

Ron turned slightly and raised an arm to tweak Pascal's blond soul patch. "The truth is you finally learned how to top—letting me relax more."

"That was relaxing? It was more like *pilates!*"

"It's either have sex or go to the gym," Ron said, sitting up halfway and yawning.

"Or both at the same time, I hear." Pascal nudged Ron with his knee.

"Not for me. I go to the Y, work out, and towel off."

"Yeah, Ron, but what's on your towel after that post-exercise exercise?"

Ron slapped Pascal's stomach. "You know I'm not that type!"

Pascal rubbed his hands over Ron's buzz cut, thinking how odd he would seem to most religious folks. He lived in the confines of Dorothy Day religiosity, enjoyed spoofing the antics of modern gay society, and kept a rosary next to the condom in his front right pocket. But his life seemed of a whole to him, a seamless weave.

"Any update on the article?" Pascal's mind was coming back to serious thoughts.

"I thought we weren't to discuss religion." Ron pressed his hand to Pascal's stomach. "Wasn't that the agreement?"

But now Pascal was curious. "And you've fulfilled all the obligations of a true gentleman. So I am releasing you from that vow and permitting you to discuss what you've wanted to talk about all night."

Ron laughed and then pulled himself up in the bed, leaning on one elbow.

"I did want to talk about the article. You know I spoke with Ms. Roth at the chancery. She's still considering the possibility of helping me. She asked for an outline of my approach. Isn't that great?"

"I can't believe it!" Pascal said, a low-grade panic vibrating in his voice. "But why would anyone at the chancery want to help you with this article? They'd rather stamp your passport to Hades."

"Calm down, honey." Ron bent forward to rub the nearly invisible hair on Pascal's legs. "I'm not really sure myself why she might want to help. But she's thinking about something. That exposé has her thinking."

Pascal didn't respond. He thought of Joe. He thought that he had to shield Joe. This could get tricky.

"Aren't you happy for me?" Ron asked. "Mr. Hot Top."

Pascal hefted himself up to lean against the headboard. He felt stern—an emotion that rarely entered his life. "This is what I have to say." Pascal stopped to clear his throat. "If you're going to write this article, you've got to do some preparation."

"Like what? Pray a novena?"

"Something less ethereal. We'll start with reading. Some Merton, surely. And maybe Hammarskjold."

"Not theology books!"

"No, not for your computer-game-loving brain. We'll add some Graham Greene and Morris West. These are personal stories and novels. You need to understand more about religious men: why some men are religious, what it means to us. You can't write this story without understanding that."

CHAPTER 8

After his meeting with Angela, Joe felt an urgent need to speak with Pascal. He didn't want to discuss Angela's love thesis. He wanted to discuss what it might mean if Ron learned about his sero-status. Joe's fear had spiked again, and there was only one person he could speak with openly. So the next Friday evening, Joe picked Pascal up and drove him out into suburbia to sip coffee and chat in a chain store.

"Why did you drag me out here?" Pascal asked as he got out of the car, moving hesitantly.

Joe was already at Pascal's door. He pointed to the store, saying, "This place is big and empty. People drive up, park, get their coffee, and drive away. That means we can talk freely—if you don't get too emotional." Joe ended with a grin. He wanted Pascal to help him.

Pascal didn't seem to get the point. He turned around and appeared to stare at each of the empty parking spaces and their white delimiters. "But I feel I'm supporting the paving over of America." Pascal finally turned to face Joe.

Joe gave Pascal one of the *anathema sit* stares he had perfected in the seminary. They came in handy at the tensest moments with his sweet but eccentric friend. Joe shut Pascal's door and gave him a little shove toward the coffee shop.

Once inside, they ordered two decaf lattes. Joe led Pascal to a back corner of the fake-rustic coffeehouse where they sat silently for a minute and sipped the milk-rich brew.

Joe was formulating his approach to this conversation; how could he get Pascal to keep Ron off his track?

Pascal was the first to break their silence.

"You're looking okay." Pascal sounded relieved. "I'm glad. On the phone, you sounded harried, as if you were losing it."

"Thanks. I feel like shit."

Pascal sat forward, almost spilling his latte. "Like there's something wrong?"

"No, no. Not like something physically wrong."

"Oh," Pascal said, settling back. "I was just concerned ..."

Joe set his coffee mug down on the polyurethaned oak table and leaned forward. "I'm having trouble thinking this through. I don't know what to do ... what to do next. And now with Ron snooping about ..." Joe's voice trailed off into an unwelcome silence. Every time he started to talk about his new situation, he lost it.

Pascal reached under the table to touch Joe's knee. Joe jerked away and then looked around to see if anyone was watching.

"Sorry," Pascal said.

"No," Joe answered, shaking his head, "I'm sorry." He sat back, took a deep breath, and then leaned forward. "I deal with tragic situations all the time, but when I'm the one ... the one with the tragedy ... I'm just incompetent."

"That's okay," Pascal said as he started to reach a hand across the table and then abruptly took it back. "I've got a number, if you want it."

"For?"

"A group."

"I can't go to some AIDS support group." Joe whispered the word *AIDS*. "That type of organization is too public."

"This is a secret organization."

"Secret, huh. So, how did you find out about it? Is there an AIDS underground?"

Joe kept his gaze on Pascal and started drumming his fingers on the table. Pascal was taking this conversation down a path he hadn't planned to travel. It made him edgy. For a moment, Joe turned to look at the ponytailed barista who had started a new latte. Then he turned back to Pascal.

"I got the number from a friend," Pascal said. "And it is like an underground. It's made up of cells. Like Mattachine when it started out … or the Communist Party."

Joe said nothing. Pascal knew how closeted Joe's life was. How could he suggest such a group?

"Let's say it's a group like the early Christians during the persecution of Diocletian," Pascal added, "with secret sayings and decorations of ambiguous meaning. Would that make it sound okay?"

Joe nodded and smiled. That was Pascal, with his church history references. "Maybe, tell me more."

At least this conversation was about the main issue in his life. At least he had told Pascal. Nurse Helen had been right. It was a relief having told someone. And Joe knew more things in his life would have to change. But every time that awareness stormed in, he ducked for cover.

Joe was going to need help, help beyond keeping Ron at bay.

Pascal was smiling at him with an impish grin. "This friend, who will remain unnamed as of the moment, is at the center of the local cell." Pascal leaned over the table and whispered, turning serious, "He runs a group for clergy with HIV."

*   *   *

Pascal's unnamed friend turned out to be Dan Beecher. Joe knew Dan Beecher, but not well. He was an Episcopal priest with AIDS. His story had been told many times. The local media often sought him out as a source of commentary on all things AIDS-related.

Joe had not done a lot of AIDS work. His parish had a group that walked in the annual fundraiser, but he never walked at the head of the contingent, afraid how he might interact with the gay men in his parish; he might let a smile seem too warm, or a laugh too knowing. How ironic!

Joe had only ministered to three men with AIDS. All had been single immigrants. Two had been drug injectors. One had raped a positive prostitute multiple times during a hot summer night. Joe had known those men in the early nineties and had buried all three. That was Joe's experience of HIV: loneliness, tortured death, and interment.

Still, it wouldn't seem abnormal to meet with Dan Beecher. They were both clergy in prominent downtown churches. No one would assume that Joe's health situation was the topic of their discussion. Joe made the call on Monday morning.

*   *   *

Joe's appointment with Dan was at the Episcopal Office for Social Justice on Wednesday morning. Joe had been to the stately granite building many times but never feeling the way he did today. Once again, a moist warm front had pushed in under his arms. As he walked up the slate walkway, despite a growing surety that this was the right move, Joe realized he hated having this meeting, hated being the supplicant, hated being HIV positive, hated what he saw as a future crammed with apologies and public scorn. Telling Pascal had been easy. Pascal loved him.

The receptionist pointed Joe down a long hall, stating that Father Beecher's office was the last on the right and that Joe was expected.

Joe found the office easily. The door was shut. He checked his watch, noting he was right on time, and then knocked.

A booming voice called out, "Come in." Joe felt skittish, as if he were a young seminarian at his first meeting with the rector. The man with all the power was on the other side of the door.

Joe had a rough image of Dan in his mind. The Episcopal priest was easily six foot four with a barrel chest and thick thighs. When he first met him, Joe had thought of Dan as a man bred to herd cattle, with the power to pick up a good-sized calf or two. Sexually, he was not Joe's type.

Joe opened the door and stood a moment. Dan rose from his desk, hefting himself with his palms flat on the desktop, and then came around to greet Joe. He was smiling broadly, one meaty hand extended in greeting. Joe was sure Dan had no idea of his motives.

"It's a beautiful day," Dan said as he ushered Joe into the office.

Joe felt small next to him. He had to look up into the tall priest's eyes.

"It is," Joe said and quickly looked away, afraid he would stare too long at the furrowed landscape of Dan's HIV-sculpted face, wishing he could look in a mirror to see if he had already started to change. *Lipodystrophy.* Joe was already learning the disease lexicon by clicking through website after website. Yes, Dan had the look of a man with a sickness, despite his girth. But his eyes had seemed clear and strong, exuding kindness and a promise of wit.

"Thanks for seeing me." Joe looked briefly back at Dan and then crossed over to the office's latticed windows, not ready to settle in yet. A view of one of the city's busiest boulevards filtered through a row of old ash trees at the base of the sloping grounds.

"It is a very beautiful day," Joe said and turned, looking again at his host.

"Well, Joe, I'm surprised you're free for a 10:00 a.m. appointment." Dan's answer came wrapped in a sweet, flirty tone that belied his bull-wrestler's size. "You're known as one of those clergy with a schedule as busy as a bishop's—or any other mitered hierarch's." Dan, still at the office entrance, closed the door. He headed back behind his desk and gestured for Joe to sit in one of the chairs on the other side.

Dan must think this is a business meeting.

Joe smiled a moment at Dan's compliment as he looked back out the open window. Yes, he was a busy man. Then he stared down at his hands, which he had been wringing. His smile vanished. Joe wasn't himself, not the confident man who made things happen. He didn't feel any fire inside him. The kindling was gone. There was nothing to light.

Joe moved back from the window and sat quietly in one of the guest chairs, using his hands to straighten the pleats in his black pants. Already, he could feel the muscles of his face start to droop. He wasn't going to cry, he knew. Today, Joe was too miserable to cry. It actually felt good to sit and look back at the massive and gentle man on the other side of the oak desk, the way he used to feel sitting in the adoration chapel at Mater Dei, before this virus had consumed the gene for peaceful prayer, the gene which had saved his vocation many a time. Joe was waiting for a message. Maybe Dan Beecher was his angel.

Joe waited.

But Dan Beecher said nothing. Instead, he leaned back in his old wooden swivel chair and folded his hands over his ample abdomen, smiling yet clearly signaling that the meeting was Joe's.

For a minute or two, Joe sat without speaking, his eyes flitting from his now folded hands to a point on the plaster wall just beyond

Dan's head. He listened to the traffic outside. He overheard a couple of snippets of conversation from passersby, something about coffee later.

Joe took a deep breath. By now, Dan may have realized what this visit was about.

Joe looked at Dan. He couldn't quite bring himself to make eye contact, so he looked at Dan's collar. "I don't want to waste your time." Great. A canned apology that sounded common and empty. Was that the type of first impression he wanted to make?

Dan blinked a couple of times and nodded back.

Okay, the ball was still in Joe's court. So he'd pick it up, dribble, and try a jump shot. He looked directly into Dan's eyes. "I've experienced a recent reversal. Of a medical sort."

Dan didn't move. Now Joe's eyes were poring over Dan's face. The man seemed a Buddha, stone-faced yet tranquil. Then Dan's mouth opened. "I see," he said. He shifted up from his reclining position and planted both elbows on the desk, resting his head on his hands. Dan was totally focused on Joe now, his eyes squinting a bit, as if he was trying to figure out what was going on.

"Maybe you can guess what it is." Joe almost groaned. More stupidity! Out with it!

Dan was smiling. Joe wouldn't call it a grin, but an expression that said something like, "Go ahead. Leap. I'm waiting."

"That was a stupid question, sorry." Joe had to say it now. Use the words. Dan would be the second person. He'd use the clinical words from the websites.

"I recently sero-converted."

Despite the electricity of the words, Joe felt his whole body relax, as if he'd just been injected with a relaxant. He'd said it. And no one had screamed. "I'm HIV positive," he added, to be clear.

Dan leaned back again in his chair. The hinges groaned. His face looked more serious. "I'm sorry to hear that, Joe. That's tough news to get."

More silence. Joe slumped back, but it was a satisfied slump. He felt a swell of relief. Maybe this was getting easier. He took a deep breath. Then he sat up a bit.

"I've heard through a friend that you run a group for clergy with HIV."

"I do," Dan said, smiling again, nodding his head.

"Good." Joe exhaled a moist sigh. "I think I'd like to join ... to try it out ... the group."

Chapter 9

Angela was in her office at the chancery. It had been a week since that strange dinner with Joe that had ended with him stampeding out her door. She was in and out of her chair, walking around the office, fidgety and in a mood. But today she couldn't lay it to the fine spring weather. Angela was annoyed with Joe, more annoyed than concerned. He was supposed to help her sort out her approach to the AIDS in the Catholic priesthood issue. He was supposed to help her figure out what to do about this gay writer. Instead, he had fled into the night.

So she had to move forward on her own. And at the top of her day's task list was the gay reporter.

Angela finally sat herself firmly in her chair. She'd decided to make the call. She could deny it no longer. She was curious where this might lead. Her gut was telling her to make contact, but even paying attention to that abdominal push was in itself unnerving. That wasn't the way she made decisions. Still, she was fairly certain everything would work out with Mr. Saville-Jones; all she wanted to do was give the reporter a nudge in a different direction.

Angela took a deep breath, glanced quickly at the number, and then picked up her phone.

"Can we talk on this line?" Angela asked after a few brief pleasantries.

"It'd be easier if I called you back. Five minutes, okay?"

"Sure." Angela thrummed her fingers on her desk. She got up to pace some more.

Angela's meeting with Father Tierney had reinforced her intuition that there was, indeed, a story about sex and the priesthood, about the perception of a priest's holiness, about individual struggles for connection, about a public person's right to privacy, and about how HIV made the issues more prominent. But today's church scandal was a sex *abuse* scandal and a cover-up scandal. The abuse angle colored every aspect of the story and tainted any story that was in any way related.

She was certain that this wasn't the right time to delve into the sexual lives of Catholic priests. How many people could keep the two separate: priestly sex lives and priestly sex abuse? Not many in the faith community, as her theology professors had taught her to call the modern church, and certainly fewer in the ratings-addicted media. That was the problem: the main story line would be sex—the "sex" that made grandparents cringe, bishops thump their staffs, and TV producers speed-dial their writers.

Then the phone rang, and Angela jumped. She hurried back to her desk, sat a moment, and then answered.

"This is Ron Saville-Jones calling back." He sounded eager. That pleased her.

Angela had decided to be blunt. She hoped she didn't scare him off right away. "Mr. Saville-Jones, I've had some time to think about your request on a local follow-up to the recent exposé. I'm sorry to tell you that we won't be able to cooperate."

A pause. Ron must be wondering why she had called at all.

"That's disappointing," Ron finally said. He sounded annoyed. "Was there any particular reason? Do you think the issue isn't relevant in this diocese?"

Angela looked over to make sure her door was closed. "Can I speak off the record?"

Another pause. He must be getting confused.

"Yes. Off the record."

She had to get him to see why this was not the right time for an exposé about her church. She hoped he'd stay with her and not hang up.

"I personally think your proposal is a topic of interest. But in today's climate, in the Catholic Church, it would add another unfortunate bit of background noise to the current sex-abuse scandal. It would highlight the presence of gay men in the priesthood, an already sensitive discussion. And it would link gay priests with sex, with being noncelibate, with being active homosexuals." She paused a second. She could hear his breathing. He was still with her. "And, sadly, pedophilia and homosexuality are joined in many people's minds. The way I see it, an exposé would cause pain and confusion, needlessly."

Angela stopped. She'd played her first hand. She held her breath.

"But the issue of priests with AIDS has already been broached!" Ron countered. His voice had gotten louder and defiant. Angela moved the phone back from her ear and smiled. "A large metropolitan daily newspaper just published a three-day series. It was picked up on the national news!" Now Ron paused a second. She could imagine his face getting red. "And the gay community knows that pedophilia isn't part of being gay. Believe me!"

Ron was still with her. Angela was pleased. Now for the delicate part.

"It's a story that's going nowhere," Angela said, maybe too tersely. "You're the only print reporter who's contacted me."

She didn't have to wait long for his response. "In my community, it's still a topic of interest." Ron sounded riled up.

"These are gay priests we're talking about. Men who are serving their church."

Now to plant her seed. "If you want to do a story on men with HIV serving in a church, there are plenty of other denominations. And most of them don't allow their gay clergy to have sex either."

Chapter 10

J oe parked his car on the tree-lined street. He checked his watch
and saw he was still early. He was supposed to arrive late for the
first meeting so Dan would have a chance to explain to the group
that a new guy was joining and so he could deal with the edginess
that particular announcement always evoked.

He had a few minutes to waste, so he turned off the engine and
sat. He rolled down two windows to let in a cross breeze and then
looked up the street to watch the sparrows swarm through the dusk
air.

Joe thought how glad he was that the group met in a Protestant
church. He didn't need any suspicious, ultraorthodox Catholic
asking too many questions. And this church, deep in a humble
south-side neighborhood, looked more like a gym or a community
center. There was only a small red cross sticking out over the sign
in the front lawn. Joe smiled. No one would take special note of a
group of professional guys meeting here.

He looked at his watch again. He still had time. He went back
over the questions he'd asked Dan Beecher in that first meeting.
"What if somebody sees us—someone who knows that so-and-so
is gay or HIV?"

Dan's response had been quick, a practiced answer. "Everyone has that concern. I'm the only one known to be infected. Only one other man is somewhat out about his HIV status, and he's only spoken to his bishop and his brother. Oh, and another, who's not a local, has told his provincial superiors. The other men are closeted, like yourself, several about being gay and being HIV. A couple of the men are or were married."

Joe recalled the ruse that Dan had set up, how he had explained the meeting to anyone who asked. Dan told people it was an ecumenical discussion group. But Joe had pointed out that the group was all men. That would seem strange in today's religious landscape, even to a Catholic.

Dan had been philosophical. "There are some risks—as in all of life."

The risks didn't deter Joe. He decided to make at least one appearance. Now he was getting excited, maybe more excited than fearful. He checked his watch again. It was time to move. He rolled up the windows.

Joe got out of the car and then locked the door, testing it twice. He turned to face the church and breathed in the night-fresh air. He made his way down the side walkway to a door with a church office sign.

Joe opened the door and stepped into a small, spartanly decorated office where a gray-haired gentleman volunteer, sporting a crimson sweater vest, waited to greet people. The old man, Dennis, told Joe there were two meetings that evening and then asked which one Joe was attending.

"The ecumenical meeting led by Father Beecher."

Dennis didn't seem to care which meeting Joe was joining. He pointed down a long hall. At the end of the hall, Joe would find a stairway. He was to go up the stairs and then down a short hall to the church library where his group always met.

So far so good. No questions or quizzical looks.

Dennis cast a quick glance at the wall clock. "You're a little late."

Joe smiled back. He surmised the men of the group were punctual.

It only took a minute to get to the library. Joe hesitated at the room's door. He rubbed his hands, which were sweaty. He stopped to look at his watch. It was 7:15—the appointed time. He felt his heart pump. But he'd made his decision. He'd go one time. He just needed to see other faces, faces of other clergy with HIV.

He took a deep, cleansing breath. Then he knocked. "Come in," boomed Dan Beecher from inside the library.

Joe opened the door and stood quietly, checking out the scene, his eyes as busy as a design major's in a museum period room, identifying and cataloging. Six men sat in the room, five of them on wooden folding chairs. Dan Beecher was the only one in a leather wing chair. There was one empty chair and a small table within the circle of chairs. The walls of the room were lined with bookshelves and some homespun banners with the name "Christ" always in gold stitching.

The first scan was quick, but Joe saw no threat—no one he knew. Dan rose and crossed the room, extending his hand. "Come on in. I've just explained to the group that I've invited a new member."

Dan sounded overly welcoming, cheerful. *He must be compensating,* Joe thought. He could feel the tension in the air—not just his own, but that of the other men as well. He was still at the door and did another review of the group. Something like an electrical current shifted among them. It bounced off their eyes and tensed up their bodies. Joe felt it, too.

Now Joe was taking in more details. They all looked about his age. Maybe they ranged in age from thirty to fifty. Most were in civvies except for one man in a sport coat with leather elbows. He wore crimson clerics and had thick gray hair. He was tall and thin, with long legs which he'd scrunched up when Joe had entered.

"We've got a seat for you," Dan said, breaking Joe's reverie and retreating to his leather chair. "Please, come in and shut the door."

Carefully, Joe closed the door, listening for that final click, and then crossed over to the folding chair. He had expected an uncomfortable hardness. Instead, he found that he fit well into the wooden form. He tried to smile. It used to be instinctual for him. What did his face look like? Like that of a guilty man being hauled into judgment?

Joe wondered if he should say something, start the conversation. That was usually his job. Instead, he continued to check out the men, not wanting to make any strong connection or display his growing curiosity.

"We use a first name in this group," Dan said, breaking the still buzzing tension of the group. Joe turned to look at him. "It's up to you to decide whether to use your real name or not."

Then he heard another voice, older and silky, from the man next to him.

"We all eventually get to our real name," the gray-haired man in the sport coat said, shifting his long legs and looking kindly over at Joe. "This is a safe space." His voice was fatherly and kind. Joe had met many men like this one.

Joe nodded back at the older man and tried again to smile. He still felt off his game.

Dan started speaking again. "You also don't have to go through your story. We all know what we have in common." A pause. "In fact, you aren't required to share anything. Just listen for a while, if you want. Relax. This is a safe place."

"Okaaaay," Joe said. He leaned back as much as he could in the straight-backed chair.

Joe began again to look around the group, stopping again at

each face, this time experiencing more welcome than apprehension. He wanted to say something, to let out a little bit of what was inside him. "I appreciate your permitting me to attend."

With the words out, Joe felt a sudden wave of tears forming and quickly clenched his teeth. He balled his hands into fists and looked down at the floor. He didn't want to start bawling, not in front of these strangers.

"We're glad you made the choice to come," said a pudgy bald man in yellow shorts and a green Hawaiian shirt. His voice had the ring of unwarranted cheerfulness to it, as if he didn't want Joe to cry either, so he would distract him with a burst of happiness.

Joe looked up at the man. He wanted to say something in response but couldn't think of anything. He noticed the other men were nodding their heads. Were those head nods a silent relief that Joe hadn't broken down or a signal that he could cry if he needed to?

Joe took a deep breath. He nodded back at the group. His emotions were on a roller coaster about to turn a corner, but he would hang on.

"Of course, we have rules," Dan said. Everyone turned to look at him. "Jim, would you like to review them?"

Jim was the curly-haired man seated almost across from Joe. He appeared to be in his early thirties. He had a goatee and a day's worth of dark stubble on his cheeks. When he leaned forward to speak, he clasped his hands as if in supplication. Joe was thinking, *He looks so sincere. Definitely like someone who would become a disciple, a true believer.*

"I'm one of the newest members," Jim started, "so I may not get all the rules correct." He smiled. His teeth shone bright against his well-tanned skin. Joe wondered if his mother, too, were *Latina.* "Rule number one: nothing said in this room goes outside this room, unless you're discussing murder, suicide, or the abuse of a minor."

Jim stopped a second. Joe assumed he wanted to make sure the rule had sunk in.

"Dan will handle that issue, if it comes up," Jim said. Then he turned to look directly into Joe's eyes. "You understand the law, I'm sure."

Joe nodded back, suddenly wondering if Jim knew he was a Catholic priest and so was suspicious.

Jim turned back to focus into the group. He raised two fingers. "Rule number two: no one has to answer any question he's not ready to answer. Rule number three: say whatever is in your heart. We're not here to report you to your bishop or congregation or whatever." Finished, Jim straightened up and did a neck flex right and left.

He's got an athlete's body, Joe thought.

"Sounds fair," Joe said, looking straight at Jim and aiming to sound macho and in command. He found Jim's masculinity enticing.

The group was still silent, which puzzled Joe. So often, he'd been in meetings where people fought to get a word in. This group had a different vibe. He told himself to go with it, see how the conversation developed.

"Let's just go around and say our names," Dan said, looking at the circle. "Each man can share whatever he wants with our new member. First," Dan said now looking straight at Joe, "what name do you want to use?"

Joe paused. "Salvador," he said. It was his Mexican grandfather's first name. "Or Sal," he added, remembering it was a group of *Anglos.*

"Sal it is," Dan said and then turned to look at the plump man to his left. Joe thought he saw Dan suppress a smile at the man's luau attire. Joe, himself, was never comfortable with too much showiness.

The little round man shifted in his seat. A seriousness came over him; it contrasted with the bright colors of his print shirt. "My name is Paul." He had a mild lisp. "I've been positive for eight years. My numbers are okay. I thank God every day for that." Paul raised his hands in what seemed a praise gesture. "I thank God every day I'm doing so well. This disease ..." Paul stopped to clear his throat. "This disease has brought me closer to Jesus." He stopped again and looked down at the oak-plank floor. Then looking up, his face having lost all its praise-glow, he said, "That's all for now."

Next to Paul sat Jim, the curly-haired beauty. Jim sat forward before speaking. "I'm a UCC pastor. I was ordained as a gay man. I'm definitely not in the closet about my sexuality." Joe noticed how steady Jim's tone was, thinking he had never sounded that way talking about his own sexuality. "The UCC ordains gay men. That means men who have sex with other men. Of course, gay means more than male-on-male sex, as I guess we all know," Jim added, lifting and opening his hands, a gesture that revealed his strong forearms. Joe enjoyed watching him.

Then a dark sadness showed up around Jim's eyes. "I sero-converted two years ago. I'm sure how it happened, which is, I guess, a good thing. My ex and I had been dating a short while. It was a surprise to both of us."

Jim started to ramble on, telling a story with lots of details, describing a trip on a cruise, beaches, dancing, and drugs.

"No one—no one at my congregation—knows I'm HIV positive." Jim abruptly ended his story and also looked down at the floor, just as Paul had.

These men are ashamed, Joe thought in a flash of awareness. *Just like me.*

"I guess that's enough for now," Jim added, sitting back and tipping his chair with his muscled legs.

Next to Jim sat a plain-looking man with thin blond hair, a slight paunch, and pale white skin. "My name is Søren," he said with one of those Scandinavian accents that came after years in America, nearly perfect but still bowing the vowels. "I'm married, but no children. And Lutheran. ELCA. I've been positive for five years."

Søren neither smiled nor frowned, delivering everything at a deliberate pace, which made Joe wonder if Søren's preaching style were as stark. Or maybe he preached in his own tongue and was more expressive in it.

Next came the gray-haired man who had been the first to speak. Joe turned to smile at him. This one seemed really normal, even dignified.

"My name is Edward. I've been divorced for six years … before I got infected. I have two children, a boy and a girl, Saul and Leah. They're twenty and eighteen now." Edward had held up one hand for each child. Joe thought he'd be good with rituals. "I, too, have been positive for five years, a year after my divorce. But we hadn't had sex for a decade prior."

Joe hoped Edward didn't notice that he was glued to his sapphire-blue eyes, a color he had only seen as a child after he had started to explore the landscape outside his mostly immigrant neighborhood. Eye color had fascinated Joe since childhood—Edward's color in particular.

"And I am an Episcopal priest," Edward continued. "A priest at St. George's on the Lake. I'm not sure if people know I'm gay or not. No one asks. Perhaps my congregants would deem such an inquiry impolite." He ended with a grin and folded his hands in his lap.

The final man, who sat next to Joe, was the only one who looked familiar. He appeared to be in his early thirties. His head was shaved, but there was no balding. The stubbly hair was an orange red, and his skin was a luminescent white. He had a look of intelligence, although his eyes were a little close together, making his gaze seem strained, or too intense. It was obvious that he spent plenty of time at the gym. He wore a tight top and his biceps stretched the fabric.

"My name is Rocco. I'm a Catholic priest, a Salutarian. I'm here getting a doctorate at the university in American studies. I've been here a year. And ..."

Rocco began to sob, one of those sobs that came on suddenly, as if a tidal wave had crashed in. Joe was shocked. The tears seemed so out of place for the muscleman. Others were reacting. Edward reached behind him to touch Rocco's shoulder. Dan reached out to squeeze his leg. "And ... and I found out I was positive ... my first month here," Rocco added, looking over at Joe with his eyes swimming in tears.

After a short while, the force of his crying started to diminish, and Rocco started to breathe more evenly. The group seemed to settle back.

"I'm sorry," Rocco said. "I'm still in shock. This thing is ruining my life. I think I'm going to have to withdraw from my program at the university. It's so hard to concentrate."

"I bet," Joe said. "I bet." Rocco's were the emotions he had been expecting: devastation and overwhelming despair. Wasn't everyone in the group just a second away from this kind of breakdown? Why were the others so stoic? Could a person, a priest, really live a normal life with this diagnosis?

Then Dan spoke up. "Well, Sal, that's our group. We meet every other week for an hour and a half. Our agenda is to talk about whatever anyone brings up. And there's always something," he added, smiling.

With the introductions done, the other guys all looked at Joe. He felt their hungry curiosity. And their hunger was drumming under his skin. Or maybe the drumming came from within his now-anxious body. It was his turn—even though he knew he didn't have to say anything. He took a deep breath and exhaled with a long sigh. But he was feeling better, more relaxed, more relaxed than he had been in days. Maybe it was Rocco's meltdown. Maybe that outpouring had begun to loosen up something inside him.

"My name isn't really Sal," he began. This group seemed trustworthy. "My name is Joe." He looked over at Rocco. "I, too, am a Catholic priest. I've been a priest for ten years." He took another deep breath. Even in this group, the next words were hard. He could feel his eyes dim, his heart sink into the cold, wet darkness. "I was diagnosed a couple of weeks ago." He raised his right hand to wipe away the trickle of tears that had shown up.

"We're all sorry to hear this," Edward said, handing him a tissue from the Kleenex box on the table in the middle of the circle. "It's a tough diagnosis to get."

Joe dabbed his eyes and blew his nose. He didn't want to dissolve in front of this group, not now, not like Rocco. He took yet another deep breath. He wanted to keep talking. He'd been thinking about this for days.

"I guess I see myself as bruised, kind of like a corpse, a badly beaten corpse—a corpse like you'd find in a crime lab. The bruises, they're deep. And they reach down into my organs." Joe's voice was choking. "But the problem is: no one else sees the bruises. No one else knows how deep they go. I'm not even sure how deep they go."

CHAPTER 11

The city's evening lights shone brightly as Joe pulled into the parish parking lot. He shut off the car's engine and reflected, for the first time that he could recall, that this neon and halogen glow didn't seem harsh. It seemed kind, even protective—perhaps enticing.

Joe got out of the car, stretched his head back, and looked up beyond the parking lot lights at the distant, pale moon. He smiled. He was definitely feeling lighter inside.

After a few minutes gazing up, Joe locked the car and headed for the rectory. He was tired but not foot-dragging tired, maybe a good tired. As if he'd worked hard but had accomplished something of value.

Joe decided to stop in the rectory living room to see if his assistants were there. He didn't usually hang out with the other two. He was either busy or needing privacy. But tonight, he felt an urge to show himself, maybe to test the waters, to see if those two observant souls would notice anything different. They had both mentioned how exhausted he'd seemed the last weeks.

As he walked down the rectory's main hallway, Joe remembered how he had complained when Bishop Healy assigned newly ordained

Father Fitzgerald to his progressive parish. And how just yesterday, when Joe had told Father Fitzgerald about the ecumenical discussion group, the young priest's face had paled. Joe had read disdain in his face. Clearly, Father Fitzgerald, a full-bore traditionalist, didn't think there was any need to spend time huddling with the separated brethren. As he continued down the long hall, Joe hoped he hadn't told the young man too much. Father Fitzgerald might want to know the names of the other clerics in the group, facts Joe had just sworn to keep secret.

Joe stopped a second, a couple of feet from the rectory living room door. Maybe he should go straight to his room. Even though he was good at dodging personal questions, this new secret life presented a different challenge. The stakes felt higher. He started to turn around but changed his mind. He needed to be normal in public. It was a new skill he had to hone. He'd just pop in and pop out.

Joe could see that the lights were on in the rectory living room. Maybe a radio was playing. Father Velker was probably stretched out on the couch and listening to the game. The old priest was always good for some banter, although many of his memories had been lost in the alcoholic haze that had hovered over him for the last twenty years. At least now he was sober. Joe started down the hall again.

"Good evening, men," Joe said as he entered the long rectangle.

Father Velker lifted his head from the tattered green sofa and said, "Evening, Pastor. Enjoy your meeting?"

Joe stuck his hands in his pockets and rocked on his feet. He wanted to seem cool and normal, his athletic self. "It was an interesting meeting. I'm still digesting all the comments."

Joe glanced to his left and saw Father Fitzgerald at the card table at the far end of the room. The young man had lifted his head up from a game of solitaire. Joe noticed a strain in his face. Probably not from a bad hand.

"Any luck?" Joe asked, preempting an open attack.

Father Fitzgerald put the cards down. Joe knew Father Fitzgerald had been writing letters to Bishop Healy whenever Joe had made some less-than-supportive comment about the conservative retrenchment going on in the church. Joe wondered if Father Fitzgerald was already composing his next letter. Father Fitzgerald was definitely opposed to any support for illegal immigrants. Maybe he'd found out about Casa Magdalena and was wondering if Joe had been helping produce counterfeit green cards instead of talking theology with Protestants.

"I find the game relaxing," Father Fitzgerald finally answered. "You look better tonight, Father Tierney. Your meeting must have pleased you."

Joe blanched. Father Fitzgerald's comment was too knowing. Joe pulled his hands out of his pockets and began to stretch his back and arms, trying to look cool. "It was okay," he said. Joe decided to bolt. "But I'm really tired now. I'll see you guys later."

Joe nodded to the two men and then left the room, walking slowly to cover his flight response. In the hallway, everything seemed darker and narrower. He held out his hand to balance himself against the wall.

Back in his room, he could feel his heart race. It was this diagnosis that made the difference. The comment from that little prick in a collar wouldn't have bothered him if he weren't HIV positive. Joe could deal with conflict. That was why Bishop Healy had sent Father Fitzgerald to Mater Dei. Bishop Healy had told Joe to wean Father Fitzgerald off EWTN, the rigidly orthodox Catholic news channel that Bishop McGee appeared on, and to loosen him up.

Maybe Joe really was losing it. He'd felt good about getting back on track with Casa Magdalena. But now ... with what was probably an innocent question ...

The phone rang. Joe had just closed the door to his suite. He hurried over to get the call. Surely it was Pascal. Joe had promised to tell Pascal about the first meeting. Pascal probably couldn't wait any longer.

It was Pascal, and he sounded excited.

"I can't talk specifics about the group," Joe said, reiterating the new prime directive as his first words after "Hello."

"I know, I know," Pascal said. "But tell me something. Tell me how *you* feel."

Joe walked over to the exterior wall and leaned against it. The room was still dark. How did he feel? He thought back to earlier in the evening. "When I left the meeting, I felt as if a burden had been lifted away." That was accurate. Joe had even felt the looseness in his muscles as he'd walked back to his car. He'd almost jogged.

"So you'll go back?"

Pascal had interrupted Joe before he could explain his latest panic attack in the rectory living room.

"In two weeks. It's a good place for me now." Joe would have to learn to deal with the fear of being found out without Pascal's help. Pascal probably couldn't understand that kind of fear anymore. Pascal's life was an open book.

"And did you talk about doctors?" Pascal asked.

Joe winced, remembering that Pascal had prodded him to see someone, explaining that Joe needed a baseline count of viral load and CD4 cells, that he might need to take drugs, that maybe they would need to find out what type of virus he had, that it was irresponsible not to know.

"We didn't get to that," Joe answered tersely. "None of the others seems to be in my same position."

"Same position. That means no other Catholic priests?"

"I didn't say that!"

"No, you didn't. Sorry for being snoopy. I'll try to be better. I won't bother you anymore. Sleep well—and think about seeing a doctor," Pascal said. "You're a dear friend."

After Pascal had hung up, Joe's good mood returned. He knew he had experienced that shimmer of hope everyone talked about. It had appeared for him, maybe just now in the parking lot. Hope ... like a small yellow balloon that floated up into the air, aimless and unhurried.

He went over to the loveseat to sit down. He left the lights off. It was easier to reflect in the dark. He was enjoying the sense of uplift again, thinking of the guys in the meeting. Joe stretched out his legs and put his hands behind his head. He liked Edward. And Jim was hot. But Edward was vulnerable, bright, and mature, older than the rest. And Rocco ... Rocco gave off a scent of danger. There was a vortex spinning in him, wild as a prairie tornado that might Hoover you up into its maw. He was young like Kenny, too. He was redheaded with ghost-white skin.

Joe took a deep breath. He pulled up his legs. He hadn't thought about Kenny all day. He had planned to call him, to talk about this new circumstance.

Joe stood up again. He walked to the middle of the room and stared at the phone. Should he call tonight? Should he get it over with? Didn't he have a duty?

But if he talked to Kenny, he'd definitely be toying with a tornado's pull. What if Kenny couldn't handle the news, broke down, got angry? Or what if Kenny insisted on coming to visit? That would complicate everything. Joe wasn't sure how he'd react in Kenny's presence. Part of him—the part that scared him almost as much as this disease—wanted to reach out and hold onto his young blond buddy. Joe's life was crumbling. Kenny could provide a new strength, a supporting wall—that is, if Kenny still cared about him.

But what about his priesthood?

Joe's head started to pound. He rubbed his forehead. He decided tonight was not the night for Kenny.

Chapter 12

R on was dialed up and working from home in the morning. After a quick review of the latest computer virus threat reports, he planned to follow up on Angela Roth's suggestion. He'd make a phone call, pursue another angle.

Ron was nestled in his warehouse condo's back bedroom, his home office. The simple square room had no windows or natural light, just two desks, three monitors, a server, two laptops, a couple of modems, and lots of wires. He could work on security issues uninterrupted in the utilitarian space. And when he wanted to, he could roll over to his second desk and work on a story. That's what he'd do today.

Angela was right. There had to be similar stories in other denominations. And Ron had a good source. A *"Deep Throat,"* he thought and smiled.

After closing out of the listserv, Ron rolled his chair over to the writing desk, picked up his phone, and then dialed the old number. Riverside UCC. He asked to speak with the Reverend Jim Nilsson. "Tell him it's Ron Saville-Jones from the *GLRegister*." Ron was pretty sure that Jim would take his call. When Jim had first moved to town, they'd had a pleasant six months together. Both had known their relationship wouldn't be anything serious. The only things they had in common were an interest in legislative gay issues and sex seasoned with light bondage.

"Hello, Ron, long time no talk," Jim said. "What's up? You said you were calling for the *GLRegister*."

"I'm working on a story, and I'd like your assistance," Ron said. He wanted to get the "yes" before he explained much more. His experience with Angela had burned him. Church people really shied away from the scandal topics, bona fide as they might be.

"What's the story about?" Jim asked.

Ron had expected a "Sure, I can help." He grimaced. Now he'd have to pitch the idea again. It had to be easier with Jim, another gay man.

"Have you followed the story about AIDS in the Catholic priesthood that just broke?"

"Well ... not closely," Jim said.

Ron jerked his head back. That was a strange answer. Ron knew Jim was deeply involved with AIDS issues in his congregation. And, after all, Jim was a gay minister.

"Oh, I thought it would have interested you."

"Because these guys were gay clergy?"

Jim's tone was challenging, and it annoyed Ron. He picked up a red ballpoint pen from the cup on his desk, one with his company name and logo on it, and started clicking.

"Yeah, because they were gay clergy who got the current-day leper's bell hung around their necks." Ron could feel the anger reach into his voice. "Guys who suffered a lot. Guys who should be more than statistics."

Ron paused. He had to get control of himself.

"It seems more like a Catholic story," Jim said.

What? He was getting stonewalled again—and by Jim Nilsson, one of the poster boys for the local gay clergy.

Ron took a deep breath. He put the pen down. He had to sound calm. "It's not just a Catholic story, though, is it, Jim? Aren't there UCC guys with HIV?"

There was a longer silence. Ron could hear his server drives whirr.

Finally, Jim answered, "No one that I know."

"Really?"

What kind of a question was that? Ron shook his head. No wonder he was getting nowhere with this story.

"Really. Listen, I've got to go. There's a meeting about to start. It's good to hear your voice, Ron. I hope I see you around."

The conversation was obviously over.

"Okay," Ron answered and then hung up. Ron turned around in his swivel chair. He couldn't believe it. Jim's reaction didn't make sense. Ron knew Jim well enough. His old friend was hedging. There had to be a reason Jim had brushed him off. Suddenly, one of Ron's terminals started to blink, and the server started to chime. One of his clients had detected an intruder. Ron quickly rolled back to the other desk. He started to flip through online logs.

*   *   *

Angela stood on the landing of the chancery's ornately carved majestic stairs. She often snuck up there for a few seconds to breathe in the composure of the heavily polished wood and to cleanse her mind before a stressful meeting. And this meeting would be stressful. Bishop Healy wanted an update on how the sex-abuse issue was playing out in the media. And he wanted Angela's update on local fallout from the AIDS story.

Angela heard the cathedral bell chime the hour. She was on. She walked down the steps and moved across the marbled entry hall to Bishop Healy's office. The routine was always the same. The supplicant would knock, and Bishop Healy would press a button under his desk to unlock the door, which would then open slightly. Bishop Healy loved gadgetry—gadgetry and cars. They were his substitutes for drink.

Bishop Healy was seated behind his desk. He waved her in. She went over to his desk and remained standing. Maybe she could make this meeting quick.

"It seems we've had a couple of quiet weeks on the abuse front," Bishop Healy said as he adjusted the tab of his Roman collar. "As for the AIDS story itself, evidently Bishop McGee is making an Augean stable–sized stink about it. He's called in the local provincial of the Salutarians and told him he might ban Catholics from attending their high school if the provincial didn't get control over his men. McGee's chancery issued a press release stating that the faithful needed to pray for vocations from those who would 'bravely follow their commitments.' I think they're ramping up their message."

Bishop Healy sat up in his chair. He drew in a deep breath, one moist with frustration. "I hear McGee's on the warpath against gay seminarians. He's contacted the nuncio with a proposal to force American seminaries to declare a moratorium on accepting gay candidates."

Bishop Healy leaned back, folding his hands in front of him. "In light of all of this, what do you have for me?"

Angela had listened attentively to Bishop Healy, already guessing what he'd say. She knew he was as frustrated by the sex scandals as she. Angela took up her notepad and stared a second at the writing. She wanted Bishop Healy to know she had been pondering this matter.

"About local interest in the AIDS-priesthood issue, there doesn't seem to be much at the moment, except from a small gay news magazine, the *GLRegister*." Angela stopped to look up from her notes into Bishop Healy's eyes. She couldn't tell if the contact worried him.

"I've told the reporter that we have no comment at this time and, off the record, that raising the issue now would link homosexuality and sexual deviancy in the minds of any conservative readers who got a copy of the article."

Bishop Healy leaned forward only slightly, a sly smile on his face. "Good point. But I hope that network sweeps month doesn't come around to bite us in the rear. Some station could be out there whisking up dirt that our brooms don't know exists."

Angela knew Bishop Healy had experienced several ratings sweeps exposés, one about his own alcohol problems and another about a principal with a gambling problem and a less-than-rigorous accounting discipline.

Angela smiled back. This was her moment to ask one of the questions that had been exasperating her.

"Bishop, wouldn't you know of any local clergy who are HIV positive? You have to pay their bills, I'm imagining."

Bishop Healy shook his head, as if he wanted to remonstrate with her. "HIPAA, et cetera, et cetera, keeps everything private, Angela. But we get some ballpark information about diocesan employees, which includes the priests, who are all men, unlike most of the other employees. Health trends. And some men, the wealthy guys, have their own health plans."

Angela waited a second.

"Would it be all right if I checked the diocesan records?" Angela asked, acting as geisha as she could, with a demure nod and a sweet tone. "Just so we'd know."

Angela knew the secrecy of medical privacy was a field of hallowed ground and that she had already trampled over it, calling around in the gay community to ask where the skeletons might be hidden. It was her job to know things, after all.

Bishop Healy hesitated. He was a bishop who trusted his clergy. Angela assumed most men told him about their sicknesses, their frustrations, their fears. It was the culture of his diocese. She knew that priests under psychiatric care informed Bishop Healy, but Bishop Healy didn't insist on knowing details or diagnoses. He had even instructed his administrator, Sister Cecilia, to keep all such treatment data private to her alone, even if the priest was open about the disease. No gossipy tidbits would emanate from his chancery. He had told Sister Cecilia that the information in health documents was nearly as sacred as confessional truths. And he let his priests know this policy.

So Angela expected no help in this arena, but she had to try. She only hoped that any employee of the diocese caught up in this scandal would come forward before the news broke.

Bishop Healy was still thinking. Angela leaned forward, putting her hands on the desk. Maybe ...

"Ask Sister Cecilia—no, I'll write a note for you to give her," Bishop Healy said after several moments of silence.

He picked up a sheet of five-by-three white paper topped with his Episcopal crest and wrote:

Sister Cecilia, please inform Angela Roth of the number of employees who are being treated for chronic STDs, including HIV.

"That should get you some of want you need," he said, handing the note over to Angela across the desk. "I'm not ready to play the name game, which I suppose I could figure out how to play, somehow. Let's just gather statistics. Let's not be surprised."

Chapter 13

J oe had just parked his car when the day's drizzle turned into a downpour. It was 6:55 p.m. Time to gather for the evening's "Round Table," the nickname Dan Beecher had given to their gatherings.

Joe looked out the car window and saw Jim, the UCC minister, and Edward, the Episcopal priest, run from cars parked further up the street. Joe got out of his Honda, checked the traffic, and then ran across the street, suppressing a desire to wave his hands or yell a greeting. Joe knew that a great sad fact drew together the men in that evening's group, but right then, he was feeling a sense of giddiness.

Joe joined up with the other two at the reception desk, greeting them with their first names. His companions responded at the same time, "Hi, Joe," which made him realize that they didn't know his last name—that he didn't know theirs. The thought distracted him, and he clammed up. Luckily, Edward was talking about his drive in from the suburbs, describing an accident that had slowed traffic. Joe half listened, thinking how normal the story sounded. Any three men could be talking like this—except the three of them were clergy with a sexually transmitted disease made famous for its ability to kill with a gruesome persistence.

The threesome walked quietly down the hallway. They entered the library in single file. Joe was the last to go in, and he only heard the tag end of Dan's comment that the newly arrived looked as soggy as newly baptized believers struggling out of a river's current. Laughter followed. Joe only smiled. He noticed, as he passed Paul, that the man seemed annoyed. Maybe it was the joke. Joe had assumed Paul was a fundamentalist of some variety, perhaps with one of those upbringings that didn't include anyone other than poor, red-white-and-blue evangelicals who lived in double-wides and shopped QVC—not that different from his own family.

"Let's get started," Dan said as soon as the three of them had sat down. Just like at the first meeting, Joe sat and looked around at each member, taking in the faces and postures. Everyone was back in the same seat.

"Does anybody have something to start with?" Dan asked.

Joe wanted to talk about doctors. Pascal had called him again in the morning. This was his chance.

"I haven't seen a doctor yet," Joe said, blurting out the words. "What do you guys do?"

Everyone got quiet.

Jim, the UCC minister, signaled that he'd answer first. He placed his ankle across his knee and then flashed Joe his killer smile. "I see Dr. Trongard. He's got years of experience with this disease. You want to make sure your doctor understands HIV. A lot of general practitioners don't know how to mix the drugs. The wrong mix could prove ... unfortunate." Jim uncrossed his legs. His pants fit tightly, and Joe briefly looked away from Jim's face to study the place where Jim's legs joined his torso. "You could develop resistance to some part of a life-saving cocktail if you don't have the right combination—and follow the dosing to the letter."

Joe's eyes were back on Jim's face. Jim didn't seem to have caught Joe ogling his flat stomach and promising crotch, or if he did, he didn't mind. Now that Jim had finished, Joe looked around at the other men. They were all nodding, except Paul, who was shaking his head at Jim.

Paul shifted in his chair, turning to look at Joe. Paul's cheap orange knit shirt wrapped oddly over the rolls around his waist, and Joe reminded himself to keep eye contact. "I have a different perspective. I visit a hospital across the state border." Paul stopped to cough, a dry cough, as if this different perspective made him nervous. "I go to their ER around 3:00 a.m. I only go once a year, for a general physical, to make sure nothing awful has happened." Paul was obviously sweating; he had beads on his forehead. His breathing was shallow. "The ER staff is used to me now. They take my counts and keep them on record under an alias I've managed to create. I don't take any drugs. Last visit, they told me my CD4 count was five hundred and my viral load twenty thousand. I attribute those results to prayer and the Lord's loving mercy!" Paul finished with his hands raised, palms up, and his eyes closed.

Joe's stomach grumbled. The sweaty man's plan sounded like a ruse Joe would have concocted. Joe looked around at the group. He saw signs of discomfort. Edward sneezed twice and reached for a Kleenex. Søren leaned forward and put his head in his hands. Dan, his jaw grinding, was looking down at his outsized hands, which he held together tightly in his lap. Rocco's mouth had opened wide, in what looked like amazement. This must've been the first time he'd heard Paul's story, too.

Jim moved forward in his chair and started to speak. He clasped his hands together, entwining the fingers. "We all believe in prayer." His tone was part kindness, part exasperation. Joe had heard the mixture in his own voice many times when he had to deal with the pigheaded or insanely zealous. "But I think your stats, Paul, are the result of the viral strain you have and the quirks of your immune system. Bottom line, you're lucky."

Paul's eyes narrowed, and he seemed about to answer when Edward cleared his throat, as if he were a father interrupting a sibling dispute, and began to speak. He looked directly at Joe. "I go to the county clinic on the south side. They have a practice that deals with many low-income individuals who are positive. They have the expertise. They're professional. And I'm not going to meet any of *my* parishioners in that waiting room," Edward finished, laughing.

"I go to this clinic, also," Søren added, his head nodding briskly. "It has a reputation, even in Europe."

"I go to the university," Rocco said, jumping in. "I'm on the student health plan. That's one of the reasons that I'm struggling to stay in the doctoral program. I like my doctor. And I like my therapist. I'm also seeing a psychologist and taking Prozac."

After Rocco, the group's silence returned, a condition that Joe was starting to wonder about. Did they not really trust each other?

"Did this help?" Edward asked, turning to Joe.

Joe smiled back. "Yes, it did." He liked the sound of Edward's voice, especially when its words were delivered with a sparkle from those blue eyes. And Joe had been thinking he felt closer to Edward because he was an Episcopal priest with a parish. Their ritual lives were similar. Plus, Edward seemed the most pastoral, a man like himself.

"I'm betting you'll want to go to the county clinic," Edward said, smiling. "We're in similar straits."

"I think you're right," Joe answered. "Maybe you could give me a contact."

"After the group, let's talk," Edward said.

*   *   *

Before the two of them went back into the damp night, Edward suggested they go to Antoine's for a late-night cup of coffee. "It's a couple of blocks away. We can park in the neighborhood."

Joe looked at this watch. He knew Father Velker and Father Fitzgerald would be occupied with their own entertainments. Pascal would call for his "Round Table" follow-up, but he could leave a message. Bishop Healy would be at Mass that weekend, so Joe didn't have to prepare a Sunday homily. Inside, he laughed at himself. He was always concerned about his schedule. He should make a rule that this evening was his night off—like the ones he had with Kenny—truly a night for his needs.

"Sure, let's go," Joe said, zipping his still-wet Windbreaker. "I hope Antoine's doesn't turn away squishy customers!"

There weren't many people at Antoine's, maybe because the rain was pounding down again. Joe and Edward settled into a corner occupied by a long coffee table, a sagging yellow settee, and a pair of ball-and-claw club chairs placed next to each other. They both sat in a chair.

Edward studied his Peruvian dark roast a second and then looked over at Joe. "I think you'd feel comfortable at the clinic. The feel is definitely institutional, but the people are considerate."

Joe smiled. "I'm pretty used to the institutional feel—and I know the clinic, from my immigrant work." He felt peaceful. Maybe it was the low-key atmosphere, the promise of friendly conversation, or Edward's attentive presence. Whatever it was, it was a nice change. He took a sip of his coffee. "I like the poor. I'm one of them. Always have been." Joe looked at Edward over the rim of his mug. Edward was built like his father, angular and lanky. Given even that small similarity, Joe was surprised that he found comfort in being around Edward.

Edward took out a small notebook from the pocket of his sports coat. He ripped off a page and then wrote down a number and a name. "Here's the number to call," he said, handing it to Joe. "Dr. Treloar is an Episcopalian and a man of many refinements. He comes from a long line of Episcopal priests and definitely understands a priest's need for privacy."

Joe reached over and took the note, stuffing it in his pants pocket. "That's my chief concern," Joe said as he returned to warming his hand over his cup. "I stay awake at night wondering how long I can keep the secret." After a deep sigh, he continued, "Then I wonder how long I have to live."

Joe saw Edward's strong blue eyes lock onto him. "With the drugs, we can live much longer than the ones before us, poor guys," he said. "That's what I believe. Maybe even a full lifetime, if we're lucky—and can afford the pharmacy bills."

Edward looked down at his long hands, which he began to clench. "But keeping the secret has become harder for me the longer I'm positive. It's such an important part of my life, yet the only one in the family who knows is my brother, an attorney, who helped me with my will. My children, whom I love immensely, don't know. Other members of the parish staff don't know. I've grown fond of several families from the community." He paused. "But they don't know or suspect. The secret starts to weigh on you." Edward settled back into his chair.

"It's the fear that weighs on me," Joe said, leaning forward and speaking quietly. "The fear of being found out. I feel so ashamed— like I'm a criminal, a sex pervert, someone even the other inmates would slaughter." Joe stopped to remember the recent death of an incarcerated child molester. "Like the other day when I was hearing confession. In comes a married man who talks about this dalliance. A couple of kisses and hand gropes. Nothing, really, by today's standards." Joe stopped and closed his eyes a second. "I was at a loss for words. I could hear the man shuffle on his knees. He needed my engagement, and I wasn't fully there. It's the sort of situation I was always good at. I could have helped that man, helped him clarify, helped him get his self-control and self-worth back. But all I could think of was my own failing. What I had become. I kept wondering how I was worthy to comment on his sin. I finally told him his sins were forgiven and then ended it. We were both relieved."

Chapter 14

Joe called the county clinic the next morning. Edward had insisted he see a doctor, stat. To Joe's dismay, Dr. Treloar had an opening that afternoon. Joe decided, after a quick inner struggle, that he could rearrange his afternoon meeting with the diocesan treasurer and told the clinic's appointment secretary that 3:00 p.m. would be fine.

Joe changed out of clerics for the visit. He often dressed in civvies. No one at the parish would wonder at his clothing. He almost considered acquiring another fake moustache but discarded the idea. He had to buck up.

Joe parked in the clinic's back lot, behind the glass and brick building, a new addition to the sagging neighborhood. Soon, he was at the building's front where two large glass panes let him peer inside. Joe had been to the county clinic several times, mainly to visit clinicians he knew through his immigrant ministry, people he talked with about vaccinations and maternity assistance for illegals. He scoped the large hall for anyone who might recognize him. He wasn't 100 percent ready for this first medical visit. He hadn't expected to take this step so soon, but Joe had awakened remembering Edward's words: "It's a disease, Joe. You need to see a doctor."

Suddenly, the clinic's sliding doors shifted open; a man and a woman speaking an African language walked past him, uninterested in his presence. Joe stepped back, waited a couple of seconds, and then forced himself to step inside.

The receptionist, Aisha, a woman with Lucy's poise and long corn-rolled hair, didn't bat an eyelash when he said he was there to see Dr. Treloar. Still, Joe wondered if she had classified him as another gay man with a terrible medical secret. It was hard to tell. She seemed indifferent. But perhaps she had perfected the facial disguise. She must be wondering.

Joe shuffled his feet as Aisha clicked in some queries at her PC. "You're new to the clinic?" she asked, looking up from the screen.

Joe nodded his head. He was starting to sweat. He wanted this to be over.

"Okay, I'll need to have you fill out these forms. You can sit over there." Aisha pointed to a row of orange plastic chairs. "Here's a pen. Bring them back when you've completed them. And I'll need to see your insurance card at that time."

Joe surmised she had said these words many times, but Aisha's eyes seemed to be studying him. *Maybe new patients intrigue her,* he thought. Joe took the pen and clipboard and smiled at her. She smiled back and pointed again to the row of chairs.

There were five people already seated: two African-American women, a couple who looked *indígena*, maybe Maya—they were shorter and darker like his *mamá*—and a young white man. Joe avoided all their eyes as he walked over to the seat next to the young man. He so wanted to be invisible.

Joe started to fill out the forms, holding the clipboard just so, hoping the young man couldn't see his name and details. When he got to the section about medical conditions and saw the checkbox for HIV, his underarms started to steam up. His hand had quickly checked "No" for everything else. This answer would be so obviously different.

The young man might have detected his hesitation. Joe looked over to see if he was studying his answers. Luckily, Joe's eyebrow-pierced neighbor appeared to be caught up in the events calendar of the *GLRegister*. Joe quickly checked the HIV box and then turned over the form. He got up to return to the receptionist's desk.

"Here they are," Joe said. He felt queasy.

Aisha took the forms with a thank-you and then started to review them.

She was checking that everything was filled out. She'd see that "X." Could he count on her to keep it private? Joe clamped his hands under his armpits. This was awful.

"Fine," Aisha said. "Can I have your card? I'll make a copy to put in your file."

Joe still couldn't read her. She must know by now. She must know this poor sap in front of her had it. And he was going to die a wretched death.

Joe reached back for his wallet. It took him a minute to find the health insurance card. He fumbled through all the junk he had there. When he got the right card, he handed it to Aisha and asked, "Should I sit down?" He felt like a child. This young woman was controlling him now. Soon, the whole medical establishment could be controlling him.

"Just a sec while I make the copy," she said.

Now she'd see that Joe's insurance was from the diocese. Her information was expanding. At least the card didn't say, "Father." He'd had it since the seminary when he was just Joe Tierney.

* * *

Another ten minutes and Janelle, a matronly brunette with a haggard face, brought Joe back through the warren of rooms behind the reception area and into an examination room. She weighed him, took his pulse, blood pressure, and temperature. Once she had noted down his vitals, she flipped through his information. Joe was in a daze through it all. He couldn't even make small talk. She'd said his blood pressure was high. He'd managed to say, "I'm nervous." All his words had abandoned him.

Finally, Janelle put her clipboard down on the small desk. She looked Joe in the eye. "And why are you here to see Dr. Treloar?"

Joe's eyes opened wide. He hadn't expected the question from her. Didn't she know? Couldn't she see it on the form?

His face must have flashed his anxiety. Janelle smiled and said, "Dr. Treloar likes to know before he comes in here. That's all."

Joe looked down at the floor. "Oh." He was on the verge of crying. Where did that come from?

"That's okay," Janelle said as she rose from the chair. Obviously, she wasn't ready for his emotions, either. "I'll just tell him you're ready," she said and then exited.

Joe let go. He began to sob as soon as Janelle shut the door. He was alone … in this disinfected clinic. How did he get here? How did this happen? Why him? He sobbed for several minutes and then tried to pull himself together.

Another five minutes and someone knocked. Before Joe could answer, the door opened. A short man, fiftyish and gaunt with floppy gray hair, wearing a tweed coat with a stethoscope around his neck, walked in. There was a name tag on his coat pocket. "Dr. Treloar, MD," it read.

Joe watched Dr. Treloar quietly close the door. Joe didn't move. The new man walked across the small room and held out his hand. "I'm Jack Treloar."

Joe didn't get up. He shook the doctor's hand. "Joe Tierney."

Dr. Treloar settled into the desk chair. He flipped through Joe's stats and the forms he'd filled out in the reception area. Dr. Treloar studied them a few seconds.

"You've never been here before," Dr. Treloar said without actually asking a question.

Dr. Treloar had that professional, well-aged maturity about him. Joe was relaxing. He'd often dealt with this type of man.

"A friend recommended I see you." Joe had asked Edward if he could mention his name. "Father Edward Brockton."

Dr. Treloar shifted when he heard the name Brockton. Joe noticed a small amount of stress creep into the doctor's face, around the eyes and lips. The doctor had put it all together. "I know Father Brockton well."

Dr. Treloar sat back in his chair. He placed his hands in his lap. It was clearly Joe's turn.

Joe felt as if his body had turned into a swamp. Every crevice was hot, sticky, and wet. And he was exhausted. The crying had wrung out the anxiety. He was just tired now. It was time to get this over with.

Joe leaned forward. "I came to see you because Father Brockton said you would understand the situation I'm in."

Dr. Treloar nodded.

Joe took a deep breath and then sat back. He wanted to get on the floor and curl into a ball. But he had to do this.

"I'm a Catholic priest. And I'm HIV positive."

* * *

An hour after leaving the clinic, Joe was back at his office desk. He sat for a moment and studied the phone. A sense of happiness filled him. Just taking that first step into the world of HIV medicine had made a big difference. Joe picked up the phone to call Pascal. His friend would want to know.

"I'm relieved you finally did it," Pascal said. "So how was your first examination?"

"I was a basket case to start with. I'm so paranoid! You know how I can get." Joe swiveled his chair to look out the office window. "But I didn't know anyone there. This time. And Dr. Treloar assured me that confidentiality was a key to the clinic's success."

Joe stopped a second to reflect. "I guess I'd say no one looked at me like I was dying. No one treated me like a pariah. I was just another patient."

"So what did they do?"

"They took a lot of blood, that's for sure. Dr. Treloar gave me a thorough physical, poking everywhere, even an X-ray. Then he sat me down for a talk."

"Is he gay?"

"Not that I know. I don't think so. Anyway, he told me to come back in a week and he'd discuss my results. He explained what viral load was and CD4 cells. He talked about safe sex and reinfection. He said the best things I could do were exercise, eat well, and sleep well."

"Not pray?" Pascal asked with a joking lilt.

"He knows I'm a priest, but we didn't discuss it. I'm a patient to him, not a sinner. The Episcopalian, whose denomination I never mentioned to you, was right. I feel safe with Dr. Treloar."

Chapter 15

R on went out to Chester's that night. The day had presented one
security meltdown after another. This new breed of foreign
hackers seemed government-supported, with uncanny insights into
the most complex security schemes he had devised. Fighting them
drained him.

And Ron was horny. Fretful days revved him up that way.
Chester's was the perfect spot to find someone to scratch his lust itch.
Chester's was the hot new place where the boys Ron liked, with their
chokers and tattoos, came to watch videos on the new flat-screen
TVs or circle the oval bar with beer in hand and roving eyes.

Ron found a seat at the crowded bar. He ordered a Sam Adams,
his regular, a beer he thought implied he was manly yet had good taste.
He spent a couple of minutes gazing at the videos, sipping the beer,
letting his body sync up with the pulse of the DJ's sound track.

When Ron finally relaxed, he began to focus more carefully on
faces. He settled on the face of a man who looked deep in thought
when he wasn't studying the low-slung jeans of the tall barback. This
man had a military-style haircut, but Ron could tell the hair was red,
almost carroty. The man finally looked over at him. Ron smiled. The
man smiled back. Good. It felt good to connect with someone solidly

sexual, not like those conflicted priests he'd been reading about in the background books Pascal had suggested.

Ron slipped off the stool and then walked around the bar. His eyes and the other man's kept their lock. Ron was already feeling the pull. The beat of the music was in him. This would be a good night—not a lot of chatter, just sex, relieving sex.

Ron sidled up to the new man's side and held out his hand. "I'm Ron."

"Rocco, here."

*　*　*

Ron was the first to stir in the morning. He pulled part of the top sheet over his torso and looked at Rocco's still-naked form. Ron smiled, remembering Rocco's initial comments about the lovely iron-frame, king-sized bed with wrist and ankle restraints barely hidden under its four posts. It had been a good night, though he had hesitated after Rocco had whispered he was HIV positive. Ron had stopped unbuttoning Rocco's jeans for a second, considering his options. But he was horny. And safe sex was good sex. Nevertheless, as he reflected this morning, he might not want to bed Rocco again. There was something about being only one thin latex layer away from the disease that didn't sit well.

"Would you like some breakfast?" Ron asked, patting Rocco's flat stomach. He had enjoyed Rocco's tight body.

Rocco began to stretch his limbs. "Breakfast?" Rocco sounded groggy. They hadn't had that much sleep.

Rocco stretched his arms and then stifled a yawn. "You don't have to dash off to work?"

"I work my own hours." Ron was in no rush this morning. He had hoped to do some more research into the Catholic priesthood— if a customer didn't contact him about a freshly coded worm.

"Then breakfast would be great," Rocco said, sitting up and supporting himself on his elbows. "I can help. I make great omelets—or were you thinking of going out?"

Ron scratched his head. He didn't want to waste too much time. "I cook. I am gay, you know," Ron said, tweaking Rocco's left nipple. "I got the decorator gene, the cooking gene, and the dance-till-you-drop gene. Those should qualify me."

"You got another gene, too, honey—a big long strand of gene," Rocco said as he touched the sheet over Ron's crotch. Ron began to think, maybe he would do this one again. He got up, stretched, and then put on a set of old workout clothes. Rocco got up, too, and dressed himself, but while he was dressing, he kept glancing at the clear outline of Ron's morning desire. Maybe Ron was rushing breakfast, but Rocco made no move.

Out in the kitchen, Ron stood back and watched Rocco, in tight T-shirt and blue jeans, get to work on the breakfast. His overnight guest explained, as he rummaged through drawers and cupboards picking out plates and utensils, that it was his duty to offer something in return for a night of pleasure. Rocco finally turned to the refrigerator and the countertop baskets finding eggs, cheese, onion, garlic, and maple bacon. Then he began to chop the onion, crack eggs, press the garlic, and fry the bacon. Ron was enjoying the sight. He walked over to the coffeemaker to begin a pot.

After the coffee had started to brew, Ron moved over to Rocco and nuzzled the nape of his neck, saying, "Smells great." The man might be HIV positive, but he was hot.

Rocco turned around to kiss Ron on the lips. That was nice. And saliva was safe.

Soon the breakfast was ready, and Ron shooed his Abyssinian, Imhotep, off the kitchen table. They sat down to eat. Both dug in. They had been very busy during the night.

"You mentioned you do some writing," Rocco said as he buttered a second piece of toast. "What are you working on now?"

Ron hesitated. He didn't want to say too much about the article. Confidentiality seemed to hover everywhere around this topic. And he wanted to be the first local writer to cover it. But Rocco didn't seem like a rival, or someone who would even care.

"It's an article about clergy with HIV," Ron said, sitting back to let his stomach expand.

Ron bolted upright when Rocco's knife hit the china plate.

"I'm sorry!" Rocco exclaimed, his eyebrows raised in disbelief. "You're writing about what?"

Ron shook his head, startled. What had just happened?

"An article on local clergy with HIV." Ron raised his shoulders into a question. "Like that newspaper article on Catholic priests with AIDS. Did you read it?"

Rocco was nodding his head. There seemed to be a ghost of fear racing inside his eyes. He started to hyperventilate.

"Did you know?" Rocco finally asked. His marble-white face was reddening. He appeared to be getting angry. "Is that why I'm here?"

Ron smiled back, blinking. He didn't know how to answer. Should he be afraid? He looked over at the rack of knives on the counter.

"Know what?"

"That I'm a priest."

Ron almost dropped his coffee mug. He steadied his hands and then set the mug down. He was actually shaking. Was this one of those unexpected coincidences, or what?

"I didn't know. Really. I did not know," Ron said. He leaned forward. He immediately saw what their meeting meant. Ron needed to get beyond Rocco's anger. "This is pretty unusual, huh? You've got to admit it. I'm looking to write an article on clergy with HIV, and I just slept with one? That's a … a weird piece of fate."

Rocco sat silent across from him, not at all fascinated by the quirkiness of fate. Instead, his face had begun to close down. The blood had drained out. Ron could almost detect Rocco's heartbeat dropping near zero.

Ron needed to salvage this contact.

"You don't look much like a priest," Ron said, trying to start up the conversation again. He grimaced. Maybe that sounded really stupid, like saying, "You don't look gay."

Rocco stirred. He didn't seem to take offense. "I'm a grad student, like I told you last night." His tone was flat. He clearly wasn't going to storm off. The slouch of his body said, "I give up."

They sat a moment eyeing each other. Ron was clicking through interview questions he could finally ask, sorting them in order: important ones, leading ones, minor detail ones.

Rocco started up again. Now he was looking into Ron's eyes as if he were imploring him for mercy. He opened his hands in supplication. "I was just ordained last summer. I do mainly campus ministry in my spare time."

"Okay," Ron said, wondering if he dared to ask any of the questions that were sporting through his brain. He'd try one. He didn't want to sound like an interviewer, but more like a concerned acquaintance. "Have you been HIV long?"

A pause. Ron surmised Rocco was considering whether he should say anything more.

"Less than a year. At least that's when I found out."

Rocco's voice had the sound of someone still in disbelief.

Ron wanted to reach out to touch him but didn't. He was feeling really awkward—awkward yet jazzed. "It must be tough. I'm sorry. You just get ordained and then the … the infection." Ron wanted Rocco to open up, to spill the story without being prompted.

Rocco took a sip of coffee. He placed his elbows on the table, clasped his hands together, and rested his square jaw on them.

Then Ron noticed the change. *He's starting to unwind. Maybe he'll talk.* Still, he had the look of a scared young man—an exhausted, scared young man.

Rocco sat back in his chair, placing his hands in his lap. "I've never experienced anything worse. It's so hard to study. I'm behind on everything. I think they'll expel me." Rocco gulped. "My order has been supportive—so far. They've offered to let me take a sabbatical."

Ron was getting a part of the story, but Rocco's voice sounded hollow, as if he were reciting facts in a trance. Ron wondered if he could cheer him up, get him to become even more chatty.

"The sabbatical sounds like a good option," Ron said. In reality, Ron didn't have a clue about how to deal with an HIV diagnosis. Maybe he should have researched that experience. He said a quick prayer that he'd never get news like that.

Rocco shook his head, rejecting Ron's sabbatical opinion. "I don't want to take a sabbatical. Doing the campus ministry stuff is the only thing that keeps me going. That and the support group."

Chapter 16

Dan Beecher had called a special meeting of the Round Table for that evening. His phone message was sketchy. "Something's come up. You all need to be there." Joe didn't like this emergency summons. Now he had to ask Father Fitzgerald to meet with the social ministry team, which he knew would be a disaster. If only that guy would dial into Jesus on the Mount rather than Mother Angelica on the airwaves. But Dan Beecher's tone was clear. Everyone on deck!

Joe was late. He had had an overly long conversation with the social ministry team leader, who questioned the need for Father Fitzgerald's presence. Maybe she was right. Joe merely thought a cleric should meet with such an important ministry. It showed the group's significance. His brain was on that argument when he stepped into the Round Table's library gathering.

All eyes turned to him. However, no one spoke to him, not immediately. Something had happened in that room. Joe smelled the stench of horror, as if the group had just witnessed a pig's slaughter and the men had been washed in the creature's wild-eyed anguish.

Dan Beecher beckoned him in with a wave of the hand and then looked at his watch. "You're a little late, Joe. Things got going without you." Dan sounded annoyed. He was usually so calm.

Joe sat down. He nodded at everyone in the room, except Rocco, who was bent over in his chair with his head in his hands. "Sorry, guys," Joe said.

"I'll summarize where we are so far," Dan said. He was brusque—and pissed. Joe was all ears.

"Here's the headline: Rocco told a reporter about our group. This reporter, who works for the *GLRegister*, wants to do a story about us."

The news flashed over Joe with the force of a brushfire hooking onto a house. The flame-catch was immediate and hot. Joe exploded, moving forward in his chair, fighting the urge to stand. He turned to Rocco. "You told a reporter! You ratted us out!" Joe bounced the palm of his right hand off his forehead. "What were you thinking?"

"Calm down, Joe!" Dan Beecher yelled. His voice echoed down the library aisles. "Calm down. We've all said what you just said. What were you thinking? But the fact remains—"

"That we've been betrayed," Joe said, interrupting.

"Like I had just explained before you arrived, Joe, we'll handle this! As a group." Dan's anger seemed to equal Joe's. "And I'll start—"

"Our anonymity is compromised! We're compromised." Joe was shouting again. He couldn't stop. "Don't you understand that?" Joe had wanted to talk about his visit to the clinic. Instead, he was boiling in a spitting vat of fury. He could feel his skin sizzle.

Dan inched forward in his chair. It appeared as if Joe's grizzled, short-fused wrestling coach had taken up residence inside the bulky Episcopal priest. "We'll handle it," Dan said, curtly, flexing his biceps as if he were readying them to wrestle Joe into submission.

"And *how* will we do *that*?" Joe couldn't turn down the heat. His heart was hammering the beat of a war drum.

Edward reached over to touch Joe's arm, and Joe jerked his arm away. Joe glared back at Edward, who now retreated, eyes wide, mouth agape.

Edward's reaction chilled Joe. He saw the scene. On a peaceful evening, in a church library, he had transformed into an unstoppable ranter, in the manner of his father. Was this his inheritance? Joe shut up. He slouched back in his chair. But he had reason for his anger. He waved his hands in the air, the gesture of a sensible man who'd lost an argument to idiots.

Joe felt a sudden chill fill the room—after all that heat and sweat. He stopped to look around. Rocco was sitting up now, but his eyes hadn't discarded the horror-scene gaze. His cheeks were wet with tears. Joe's eyes swung around the group. Now Paul was bent over, holding his head in his hands. Jim's and Søren's faces had frozen into a granite-hard, Nordic grimness. Edward was slumped in his chair and studying his hands. Dan was shifting, uncomfortably. His was the look of an accident survivor—all sore muscles, confusion, and fright.

Rocco reached for a Kleenex and then blew his nose. He looked at no one in particular as he started to talk. "I just told him about me. I didn't give him permission to write anything," he said and sat back in his chair where he balled his hands into fists.

Joe started to rev back up. "But you mentioned the group!"

"Yes, he mentioned the group!" Dan said, leaning further forward and bellowing anew. Dan raised his broad mitt of a right hand and aimed its palm at Joe, telling him in totally clear language: "*Stop.*" "Rocco mentioned the group—so the group will address the issue."

Startled at the rebuke in Dan's gesture, Joe sat back and folded his arms, setting his stubbly chin on his chest. Scenarios played through his mind. He envisioned Ron stalking him, waiting to get a picture of the AIDS priest saying Mass or baptizing a baby. He would be a prize catch for a tabloid.

Dan coughed. The group members turned to look at him. "I suggest we consider meeting with this reporter—"

"And say what?" Joe said, interrupting again, his voice still dripping bitterness, but quieter.

Dan inhaled deeply. "That's what we need to decide. We are public figures. And we should all understand the public's interest in our lives." It seemed Joe's old wrestling coach had decamped from Dan as quickly as he had arrived. Dan Beecher now sounded resigned to a bitter fate.

Paul raised himself up from his bent-over pose. "But they're our lives!" he bleated, shrilly. He held out his hands. "I don't want my transgressions to tarnish my reputation!"

The group now turned its worried gaze at Paul. Joe had categorized him as a tolerated, out-of-sync observer in the group. But now Paul was saying something Joe could agree with.

Edward, next to Joe, as usual, shifted in his chair, pulling his legs under it. "You speak of transgressions. But I think our transgressions can also be a way to salvation," he said. Joe was studying Edward's face. His friend's eyes darted around the group with an anxious hurry. "I know that sounds trite. And I hesitate to say it to this group. But many of us preach that very thing regularly. Some with conviction." Edward smiled a moment, as if he'd made a joke. "Without sin, there is no salvation. Do we believe that?"

Jim bolted upright, the night's earlier granite freeze cracking. "So being HIV is a sin?" Jim challenged. "I don't think I've sinned by contracting a disease. Not by getting HIV."

Edward exhaled a deep sigh. "You're right, of course." He reached his arms up so he could pull at his earlobes for a few seconds, nervously, and then quickly let his hands drop into his lap. He stared down at his resting hands a moment, as if an answer might be written on their skin, and then winched his gaze back up at Jim, locking on. "But I don't always feel that I'm blameless. I had sex outside of marriage. HIV is a result. So far, to be honest, I've gotten little good out of it. It's no gift to me. It feels like the reward of sin."

Joe had listened carefully. Edward's words resonated inside him, although the resonance hurt.

Jim's head was shaking his dissent. "Sex outside of marriage is one thing. Contracting a disease is another," Jim said. With that, he folded his arms and sat back in the chair.

Joe wanted Jim to continue. He wanted Jim to say something that would make him feel better about having contracted HIV. Instead, Jim lowered his head and started to cry softly. "This is all such a mess," he blubbered. "All such a fucked-up mess!"

Søren stirred. "I cannot be outed by some reporter. My situation would become unbearable." Joe saw that even stoic Søren's lips had started to tremble. "I am just surviving as it is. My wife ... my wife is not sure she wants to stay with me. She could not stand the publicity. It would end our relationship."

The group inhaled together. This was the most personal item Joe had ever heard from Søren. But it arrived laden with a long sorrow.

Then Paul moved again. "I don't know what I'd do if this came out." Paul's voice was muted this time, and his words were spoken in a hushed, secretive monotone.

Dan spoke, sounding worried. "I don't know what you mean, Paul, but if you feel desperate, be sure to give me a call."

Paul didn't answer. Now his head hung limp.

Joe looked away from the group, over at an old banner. He knew a reporter's outing would change everyone's lives. He had lived with the fear for weeks.

Dan spoke again, and Joe turned his head back in. "I know this is hard for everyone, but what about my suggestion? The press can be persistent when they smell a story."

Edward scrunched forward, which surprised Joe. His friend had seemed to clock out after his sin reflection.

"Perhaps it wouldn't hurt to talk to an outsider," Edward said. "It might help us all, in some way, if more people understood our situation. Maybe we can arrange something safe."

Joe's reaction was immediate, but he stifled the urge to start ranting again. How could Edward, his new pal, suggest that? Anonymity was the key to this group. It's why Joe was here.

Joe sat back a second. No one spoke. Joe looked around the circle. This group was good for him. He didn't want to lose that.

And he didn't want to explode again. He hated the pit bull inside him. He had to get back to reason. "Tell us more what you're thinking," Joe said, breaking the edgy silence.

Edward turned to look at Joe. Joe saw a spark of dread flicker in Edward's eyes, the sight of which made Joe afraid he'd been an unforgivable ass. "I was thinking about how I raised my children," Edward said. "I told them they needed to confront their fears. Talking to this reporter would be like that. Maybe a start."

Joe waited a second before answering. He couldn't offend Edward any more. "Aren't we responsible for the health of our congregations? Wouldn't our HIV status diminish that health, weaken their faith, alienate many?"

"Perhaps," Edward said, nodding his head a couple of times. "But I've wondered what would happen if my congregation found out. I'm sure we've all wondered that." Edward stretched his long legs into the center of the circle. "Some of us believe miracles happen." He looked around the group, deploying his handsome pastor smile again. He folded his hands in his lap. "Still, I'm not suggesting we all come out. I'm just saying we create a safe environment for the discussion. Maybe it will give us more control over the reporter. It would be better than having him stalk Rocco until he discovered the group."

Everyone turned to look at Rocco. Joe hadn't thought of that. Rocco was now a significant danger to them all. Rocco seemed to shrink into himself.

"Edward is right," Dan said, his voice calm, once again rowing through still waters. "I've dealt with the press. It's best to establish ground rules."

Now Joe was intrigued. This tack had promise. "What kind of ground rules?"

"Something a lawyer would set up," Edward said. "I'm thinking of my brother. He's dealt with media law."

Jim stirred again. "We'd write a contract? To ensure our anonymity?"

Joe was glad the cute man was back, participating, talking as if there were hope for a good outcome. Jim and he were gripped by the same terror. He had known it from the first night at the group. They were both golden boys, with glittering reputations to lose.

"Yes," Edward said. "A contract can be written to assure anonymity."

Joe looked around at the group. They were considering the possibility—everyone but Paul. Joe could see the struggle in Paul's face, in his tight jaw and nervous blinking. He was rubbing his legs with his hands. Paul could be a problem.

"Paul, what do you think?" Joe asked.

"I'll do whatever the group decides," Paul said. But Joe knew they were robotic words, spoken without emotion. Joe wondered what was going on inside Paul, but he didn't want to press the point. That wasn't how this group worked. This group let things flow out at their own pace.

"Are we agreed to contact a lawyer, to explore an interview with the reporter?" Dan asked.

Every head nodded, even Paul's.

This could work out. But Joe knew his was a special case. Ron had to be the "the reporter." Joe knew Ron. Protecting Joe's anonymity would be a challenge. Still, he was too exhausted to worry about that now. He just wanted to get home and take a pair of the sleeping pills Dr. Treloar had prescribed.

"I'll contact Edward's brother. He'll contact the reporter," Dan said. He started to rise from his moderator's chair. "I'll try to arrange the interview for our next meeting." After that announcement, Dan forced himself out of the soft chair, stood up straight, and lifted his muscled arms above his head in a yoga move Joe knew was intended to relax a tight frame. But he felt too stressed to try yoga himself. He just wanted to pop a couple of pills and dive into sleep.

Chapter 17

Angela's message light was blinking when she got back from noon Mass. The message was a brief statement from Sister Cecilia stating that the statistics had changed. But an unusual tremor had crept into Sister Cecilia Montpelier's typically staid delivery, causing Angela to step out down the hall and up the back stairs to visit the old nun.

The first lot of statistics Angela had received from Sister Cecilia had contained no surprises. Diocesan insurance records showed one single male living with HIV. Angela assumed it was Father Peterson. Sister Cecilia's records did not contain the names of individuals, only the number of people in a given disease group and their age cohort. After Angela's Healy-blessed request, Sister Cecilia had asked for a new report that showed disease categories by gender and marital status. The insurance company had balked at first but then relented once privacy concerns were clarified and spit out a new series of reports.

Besides the HIV man, Angela had learned there were two single males in a category titled: "Other STD." Sister Cecilia had been more than thorough in her disclosures. She had gone beyond Bishop Healy's request and informed Angela that thirty-eight single males were on heart medication, another twenty-six were on antidepressants, and five were diabetics. What statistic could have changed to make Sister Cecilia sound ever-so-slightly off balance?

Angela stood a moment before knocking on Sister Cecilia's door. She was certain the nun had heard her ascend the creaky stairs. Sister Cecilia would be ready. Angela tightened the green sash on her white summer dress and then knocked. The "Come in" was instantaneous.

Sister Cecilia sat at her desk, not rising to greet her guest. Her eyes remained on the papers before her. The old nun's face was flushed. Angela's concern flared, and she quickly crossed the long, narrow room to stand at Sister Cecilia's right shoulder. Finally, Sister Cecilia looked up at Angela and then back down at the papers carefully set before her.

"This one column has ticked up," Sister Cecilia said, tapping on the report that lay on the smudgeless glass of her desktop. Her tap was sharp, full of annoyance. "The statistic you are interested in."

Angela bent over Sister Cecilia's shoulder. She squinted. It was hard to read the small print. "Which column?"

"This one. The HIV column, single male. It's gone up by one."

Angela shuffled back toward the old room's window to support herself on its sill. The news shocked her. She raised a hand to cover her mouth. She hadn't expected this. She had been asking around quietly, the type of confidential calling she could do from a bishop's office. No one had heard of an HIV priest except Father Peterson. The gay priests who were still active lived cautious and conservative lives. Maybe it wasn't a priest. Maybe it was another single male employee. The Cathedral's choir director? But Sister Cecilia was concerned.

In the guise of that simple number, Angela felt the sudden entrance of a bigger, more brutish threat. A "loose thread" dangled from the diocesan fabric. Someone could pull it and *poof!* Reams of fabric would rip apart.

Angela removed her hand from her mouth. Her breathing was shallow. Sister Cecilia had swiveled around to look at her. The nun's face told it all. They had stumbled on the unwanted skeleton in the closet. What now?

Angela couldn't ask Sister Cecilia to ferret out the name. Bishop Healy had stated as much. He had called it "Healy's Health Policy Law," his own version of HIPAA. The skeleton would remain nameless.

Until it rattled out to haunt them.

Angela righted herself and then pressed down her dress. "Well, that's that," she said. "Thank you, Sister. Of course, you'll keep this between the two of us."

"Of course." Sister Cecilia's face was unchanged.

Angela started to walk to the door. Midway, she turned to say, "I'll inform Bishop Healy."

*　*　*

After seeing Sister Cecilia, Angela needed a breather. She decided to go for a walk through the chancery's high summer garden with its aroma of blooming roses and beds of colored daisies.

However, the news of this "uptick" bored into her gut with the bite of a vicious parasite, and the garden sights and smells did nothing to calm her. She felt an immediate, gnawing fear. She knew it couldn't be Joe, but she had the fear anyway. All she could think of, out in the garden, was how strange he'd been lately, as if something had happened in his life. Angela couldn't put the thought away. She cared about him, even though she knew it was a caring that would never wend down a garlanded bower to bliss.

Angela shook her head. She had to think about the big picture. That was her job. She had to come up with a plan, a strategy. Deep inside her, where her greatest angst kept a low fire burning, she knew that the next steps in this drama would be unpleasant. Bishop Healy might want a name—on the sly. He was cunning. Angela might have to use her less enticing skills—the skills that dug up dirt.

Angela stopped to smell one of the yellow English roses. She desperately wanted to breathe something other than her fear. A tap on the shoulder startled her. It was her secretary.

"Bishop Healy wants to see you *immediately*," Doris said with her youthful sweetness as ever intact. "It's something about the bishops' conference."

Angela thanked Doris and then walked around to the front of the chancery. It was the least efficient route to Bishop Healy's office. She needed more time. She wasn't ready to speak with Bishop Healy—not about this new development and certainly not about her suspicion.

Angela entered Bishop Healy's office and found him pacing. She'd never seen this behavior before. He rarely used movement to relax himself—teasing her about her yoga practices. His reliefs were humor, sarcasm, and motionless prayer. Now he was pacing with the fury of a caged lion in heat.

"He went and did it," Bishop Healy said, shaking a letter at Angela. "McGee submitted a proposal to the bishops' conference. He wants us to discuss it at the USCCB meeting in Philadelphia. Damn him!"

"What's the proposal?" Angela asked, trying to set aside the new worry. She forced herself to concentrate.

"I'll read the pertinent part. *No man professing to be a homosexual or with any past homosexual experience shall be admitted to any seminary in the United States or American territories.*"

Bishop Healy nearly spat out his anger. "McGee doesn't go after the current gay priests—or bishops—that would be too difficult. He'll start by barring the seminary doors."

Angela didn't move. "Does he give a reason?" Angela tried to sound calm and distant, although her mood was all storm clouds. At least Bishop Healy had stopped pacing in response to her question. They stood facing each other.

There was a moment of quiet in the office. Angela knew Bishop Healy was editing out a lifetime's worth of sharp critiques of McGee and trying to come up with a simple, on-point answer to her question. This animus with McGee was one of her bishop's greatest burdens. But the McGee proposal hadn't shocked her with the brutal force of Sister Cecilia's revelation. Every chancery in the nation had heard the scuttlebutt about a prohibition like this. It wasn't unexpected. But still it stung.

As she waited, Angela's shoulders slumped. Her arms hung lifelessly at her sides. She was suddenly very tired. The vocational concern came back. Why do these old men get to ruin the church? For a fleeting moment, she wanted to cry.

Angela looked away from Bishop Healy's gaze for a second and closed her eyes. She was a professional. She had to steel herself. So she stood upright, reminding herself again not to turn angry and shrill, that her job was to bring peace and clarity. She opened her eyes and waited for Bishop Healy's response.

Bishop Healy seemed to have calmed down. His eyes had softened. "He references Cozzens, citing a page about the disruption gay seminarians cause to straight men, and concludes that the current sexual abuse crisis and the latest news on priests with AIDS '*is clearly the result of homosexual deviancy that would never have occurred if the priesthood were kept clean from that stain.*'"

"May I sit?" Angela asked after drawing a loud, deep breath.

"Oh, sorry. Please." Bishop Healy pointed to the two scarlet-and-gold-striped high backs in the corner of his room. She sat in one; he sat in the other.

A few seconds passed.

Angela had decided not to tell Bishop Healy her other news. It would just complicate this issue. She turned toward him. "Are you thinking we need to respond?"

"I'm afraid we have to." Bishop Healy sounded defeated, even before he'd faced his foe. "McGee and I are on the same committee. The one dealing with seminaries. I have to formulate a response."

He smiled. "Or *you* have to formulate a response."

Angela nodded. She knew Bishop Healy had hired her because he wanted the face of the church to be womanly and beautiful. Bishop Healy thought of the church as a woman, as a nurturer, a teacher, and especially a mother.

Angela held out her hand. "May I see the document?" She needed time to connect with that nurturing drive, if it hadn't just been blown away in this day's squalls. Even with a moment to relax and take in the news, she didn't feel a peacekeeping urge. She felt a rage start to spread out from her gut. Angela wanted to suggest warfare. But it couldn't be brutal and blunt. She had to play smart, like a chess master, measuring the impact of each move. She had to make the bishops see the sacrifices they would make with such a law, make them see how their game pieces would dwindle further. She had to make them quake.

Angela finally spoke. "We may need our own campaign. A defense of the good gay priests who serve us now."

Bishop Healy's eyes widened. Angela knew he wasn't much for political crusades. He was more of a debate-it-and-vote man.

Bishop Healy's head nodded just as Angela saw his shoulders slump. "See what you come up with. At the minimum, we need to put out something countering this proposal—and then send that to the other bishops and the press."

Chapter 18

The evening after Rocco's revelation, Joe went over to the Catholic Workers' house, Casa Romero, for communal confession and Eucharist. While still in his office, he had thought of canceling but decided he had no good excuse. He turned off his computer and then stood up and tried to stretch out the knots in his back. How do you tell a community its chaplain is about to be caught up in a sex scandal? That's how he thought of Ron's reporting: a sex scandal in the making—with Father Joe Tierney in the paparazzo's viewfinder. And with communal confession at Casa Romero, he'd have to tell a lie: "Sorry, folks, no major transgressions to report." This sex sin wasn't something he could bring up with the community. It was way too personal. He'd invent a less explosive transgression, again. The thought of his many bad confessions made his mood sour more. Maybe he should call Father Boyer and get it over with, tell him the truth. The whole truth was going to come gushing out soon, anyway—spurting like blood from a punctured artery.

Joe's trip into the old neighborhood had helped settle his heart into a calmer rhythm, helped him slow down the fear grinding from last night's meeting. The Catholic Workers' community, made up of two couples, two kids, and Pascal, occupied a three-story wood-frame Victorian in the Walker neighborhood, his old neighborhood, a lightly gentrified plot of land whose street corners transformed at night with the hum of a sex and drug emporium. The area had its problems, Joe thought, as he stopped at the busy Water and Harrison intersection, but they were problems he knew how to confront.

Besides, here he could get a whiff of *México* and *el Caribe* in this cold city. He looked over at the bodega and *carnicería* that had opened a year ago. Ever since he was a kid, the Walker neighborhood had been a magnet for Hispanic migration. Joe chuckled. If it hadn't been for a bus driver's suggestion, his mother never would have wandered into the once-bustling Tierney's Market, a two-kilometer walk from downtown.

Soon Joe parked the car on a quieter side street. He looked at his watch. He was right on time.

Pascal met Joe at the door carrying the community's stole, a patchwork of Central American weaves.

"Evening, Father," Pascal said, playfulness in his voice. "Everything's ready. I'm here to vest you."

"Hi, Pascal." Joe reached out to hug his friend. This was the other precious element in the Walker neighborhood that calmed him—the warm presence of his good friend. Tonight, he'd hug him more tightly.

Pascal hugged back, pulling Joe tighter into his flat chest and then whispering into Joe's ear, "We all love you."

Joe fought back tears. "Thanks," he said as he released his hug to take the stole. He wiped his eyes with the back of his hand and then looked around to see if anyone had noticed his emotion. Pascal gave him one of his recently developed looks of concern, paused for a moment, and led him into the living room where the community had gathered around the wood trunk-turned-coffee-table that they used as an altar. Joe managed a smile for everyone. The two kids, Mary and Matt, ran up to hug his legs. He took a deep breath and felt the muscles in his chest relax. This was a comfortable space. The rituals would be hassle-free like the rites of his youth when Father Bob, an old high school classmate of his uncle, would come to their house and celebrate a family liturgy. Even his dad had enjoyed those evenings. Father Bob had a way with words. People loved him. Joe gulped, suddenly wondering how this group would react if they found out about his HIV. Or was that *when* they found out? Would they keep their children away?

After Mass, Pascal took Joe up to his room. "The Darlings are coming over for dinner and called to say they would be ten minutes late. Come upstairs."

While Joe sat down on the bed and leaned back on his two elbows, Pascal shut the door. Joe raised an eyebrow. He was worried Pascal would try to pull out the whole story of last night's meeting, stormy bit by stormy bit. But Joe couldn't say much. They had all vowed secrecy. Too much was on the line. He waited nervously for Pascal to start. Pascal always did.

"That was a beautiful liturgy," Pascal said as he walked over to turn his desk chair around so he could face Joe. "You seemed very peaceful," he said as he sat down.

"I don't know why." Joe rose up from his elbows, sitting on the edge of the bed and folding his hands in his lap. "I don't know if it's peace or resignation or depression. Probably depression. But I do feel relaxed in this space. It reminds me of my youth."

"Father Joe Tierney, the one-time radical." Pascal smiled and made a protest fist. "You were arrested once, at a hotel-workers' strike, weren't you? Soon after I'd left the seminary? It was quite the scandal, I recall."

Joe shrugged his shoulders. "I was angry then, because you didn't leave on your own. I hated that they kicked you out. It was a safe way to protest the clerical bastards and the hotel bastards at the same time."

Joe was glad they were talking about the past. He didn't want to talk about today's woes. They sat quietly for a moment. He could hear Mary and Matt running and yelling outside. The air was warm and lush. It was a good evening to be a child.

Joe remembered how things were once different. He scooted himself back on the bed and supported himself on Pascal's wall. Maybe he'd say something about what he was feeling. "I once prided myself on being a righteous man. And now, it's like a switch was flipped, and I'm not a righteous man anymore."

"Because you had unsafe sex?"

Joe nodded. He could feel the blood drain from his face. Pascal had summed it up. "Sex, first of all. Unsafe, secondly. And third—I can't even confess it. I'm too ashamed."

"You need to cleanse yourself." Pascal reached a hand over to touch Joe's knee. "Not that I think sex is wrong, but I understand your feelings. I used to have them myself. So you need to cleanse yourself."

Joe smiled. This was how Pascal talked. He should've been a priest. He believed in rituals, which reminded Joe to look at his watch. It was time. He stared at Pascal, who was waiting for a response. Joe reached into his pants pocket and pulled out a pillbox. He'd make a joke. "We're about to have dinner, so I better take these. I'm sure they'll cleanse me."

Pascal's eyes widened. "You're on the cocktail?"

"My viral load was high, 350,000. But my T cells are 600. Dr. Treloar says that's pretty good, but he wants to lower my viral load."

"How are you feeling?"

"A little draggy."

"A little?"

"So far, just a little." How could Joe tell Pascal that he was scared out of his mind and that the fear was pulling him under as surely as if he had a block of concrete cast around his feet and he was floundering in the fast-flowing river? How could Pascal understand? He wouldn't try to explain it now. "I'll let you know when it's more than a little draggy."

Joe knew he'd have a week until the meeting with Ron. He knew the fear inside him would continue to fester like a wound from a dirty blade. It couldn't be good for his health—or his spirit. Slowly, he rose from the bed. He felt the intense weight of that knowledge. "Let's go downstairs. I'm hungry."

*　*　*

Ron Saville-Jones would attend the next Round Table meeting. He'd agreed, in writing, to keep all information confidential unless he was otherwise explicitly permitted to use some facts or quotes. Edward's brother had drawn up the contract. Edward had assured them his brother was a specialist in intellectual property law and a fierce litigator, if need be.

Joe still felt sick. He'd been dreading the meeting all week. He lingered outside the building, thinking about the upcoming encounter. He'd met Ron when Pascal was dating the "dark-souled Internet consultant," as Pascal had described him. To Joe, Ron had seemed a self-satisfied circuit-boy at the time, not a dark soul. Back then, Joe couldn't understand why someone who appeared to be a clone from gay casting was dating someone as sincere and committed to an archaic form of existence as Pascal LaVigne, hair shirt and radical faerie. He had joked it was because Pascal could cook—or Ron had a taste for the waifish sort.

Joe looked at his watch. He was a minute late. Dan would be angry with him. Joe whispered a prayer for strength and then opened the church office door. He nodded politely at old Dennis behind the desk, who had gotten to know Joe's face, and hurried down the hall and up to the library.

"You made it," Dan said as Joe entered the library. "Ron should be here in five minutes."

"I'm sorry," Joe said, checking his watch again. He looked around at the men in the chairs. They were all there and looking stoic. No one was talking. Joe didn't feel like speaking either. He needed to conserve every bit of his psyche for what came next.

He didn't have to wait long.

The first knock sounded timid, the second louder. Dan shoved himself up out of his chair and hurried to get the door. He acted as anxious and jittery as Joe felt.

"Welcome, Mr. Saville-Jones," Dan said. Several heads swiveled to see Ron. Joe had sat with his back to the door. He closed his eyes a moment. He'd see Ron soon enough.

When Ron sat down, he began a scan of the men in the room, beginning with Rocco, smiling at each face, as if he were trying to say, "I'm not here to hurt you." But he stopped over long at Jim's face. Joe gave Jim a quick look. He looked pale.

When Ron's welcoming gaze got to Joe, he stalled again and his smile evaporated. Joe's heart nearly stopped. This was what he had dreaded: the sudden realization, the shock of recognition. For days, he had lived in fear of it. It was a sword in his heart. It was the beginning of the ostracizing, the setting apart, the cordoning off.

Edward, who regularly sat next to Joe, shuffled in his chair. Joe was sure Edward knew what he was feeling. He had told the group he knew Ron. Everyone must have seen the surprise in Ron's face.

Ron finally moved on to Edward's face, offered a brief nod, and then reached into his leather satchel and brought out a notepad and pen. Joe studied Ron's movement. He knew the contract permitted Ron to take notes on paper. And if nothing came of the notes in three months, if no article was published in a print medium, then he had to hand them over to Edward's brother who would destroy them. Online media publication was not permitted in the contract, except as the electronic publishing of a print page by an established media outlet. The group didn't want Ron to write his story and then concoct a website or compose a blog to disseminate his findings.

"I understand none of you want to become identifiable, to come out in this story," Ron said, his tone matter-of-fact. "My readership understands the closet, the pros and cons of it," Ron continued as his eyes roved around the group. "I don't think they're interested in a story about the pressures of being gay clerics or a story about why some of you remain in your churches, given the seemingly ubiquitous denunciation of gay sexuality within most religions." The group all shifted at that comment. Joe wondered if the comment was directed at him. Maybe Ron would single him out.

Joe's eyes couldn't stay away from Ron. Here was his executioner, sitting feet away. Joe felt helpless.

Ron was taking charge. He'd already made the group squirm once. Joe had expected an initial assault. Ron was a go-getter, with a taste for the dramatic. That's what Pascal had said.

"This is what I want to know," Ron said and then paused. "I want to know what it's like to be a religious leader who knows he's one small voice, one whispered comment away from being declared a leper."

Leper.

Dan began coughing loudly as if he'd sucked a horsefly down his windpipe. Joe turned to watch him, wondering if he was going to make some leader's comment, draw some boundaries, ban some words. Instead, Dan lowered his hand from his mouth and said, "Sorry." What was there to say? *Leper* was the word.

Edward leaned forward, causing Joe to turn again. "I think your question could be phrased less sharply," Edward said. Joe raised his eyebrows. He heard steeliness in Edward's voice. The hardness of it sounded unusual coming from his genteel friend. "Don't you really mean to ask us: are we out to our congregations? And what's been the response?"

"Fair enough," Ron answered. "I guess I was using a little purple prose," he said, chuckling. Ron stopped to wipe some sweat from his forehead. Maybe Ron was uncomfortable, too. Why was that?

Jim cleared his throat. Joe turned to look at him. Jim seemed anxious to speak, ready to get it out, as if he'd prepared well for an oral exam. "I keep my status private, from family, certainly. Only a few friends know. And I'm celibate now. It's been a couple of years, but I haven't figured out how to live my life again. I know how pathetic that sounds. And if a person like me were to walk into my office for counseling, I would encourage a large dose of self-acceptance and courage."

Joe noticed that Ron was scribbling as fast as he could, but the rest of the group was staring at Jim. Joe didn't know Jim was celibate. The cute man had never said anything. Was it because he was too afraid to tell another person he was HIV positive? Or was he just super cautious? Would he have sex with another HIV-positive man?

Joe's mind had wandered off the topic at hand, but then Søren began to speak.

"I think Jim's comment sums it up for me. It's a difficult problem, this sero-status. There is no clear way to address it as a pastor. So, I keep it inside the box. My wife, of course, knows. She has known for years that I have bisexual appetites. Only rarely do I act on them. And, as is obvious, that has proven nearly disastrous. For us." Søren ended with a gulp.

Søren's little summation had Joe spellbound. The wiry Dane had never shared much before. Why was he opening up now? Did he think it was his duty? That he had to comply with the reporter's authority? And Joe now had a desire to meet this mysterious wife. He didn't know if it was a morbid curiosity or a desire to reach out and hug her.

Then Joe wondered what he should say. Was it okay to talk about this stuff? Søren had been honest. The Dane's words had grabbed him.

Joe turned his attention back to Ron. It seemed obvious Ron expected everyone in the group to speak to the issue he had posed. Why were they meeting in secret? What brought them into this closed-off room?

Ron's eyes next fell on Dan.

"You know all about me," Dan said, opening his arms wide and smiling. "I'm an open book. My story is public. I'll let the others speak." Joe felt a surge of pride. In Dan. He had created a refuge of stability for himself in this hurricane of a disease.

Next was Edward. Then it would be his turn. Joe felt the sweat gather under his arms and shoved his hands in his armpits. What could he say that was innocuous? That didn't mention Kenny? Kenny's dream image was still showing up every night. And recently, Joe had told Edward about Kenny, a brief summary. He couldn't lie here, could he? He took a deep breath and turned toward Edward.

Edward sat up straight. "I helped start this group. I had come to Dan after my diagnosis. We had known each other as Episcopal priests, as friends, as cocktail party pals. But when the doctor told me I was HIV, I didn't know where to turn. I called up Dan because he was gay. And I knew he was positive, although we had never talked about it before."

"And what was Dan's advice?" Ron asked. It was his first follow-up question. Joe relaxed. Maybe he wouldn't have to talk after all. And maybe, for some reason, and this was only a hunch, Ron didn't want to talk to Joe—at least not here.

"He let me do most of the talking," Edward said and then stopped to stare at Ron's scribbling form. Ron looked up for a second, and Edward continued, "But toward the end, Dan said something I still remember, that my HIV status would float out over time, that there was no rush about telling everyone, that when I felt okay enough with my status, knowledge of it would flow out among my friends and acquaintances, the way driftwood follows a current."

Joe was nodding his head. Edward's description pretty much described his experience. Then of a sudden, like a gangbanger's shot from a passing car, Paul exploded.

"I couldn't disagree more!" Paul was yelling, his face full of frenzy and wide eyes. "There's no need for anyone outside this group to know, no one at all needs to know! I am a respected member of my community. Knowledge of this disease would hurt my ministry." Paul was starting to hyperventilate. "No, it would ruin my ministry. And loss of my ministry would ruin me! I have a right to my privacy!" Staring directly at Ron he screamed, "Don't you dare try to take it away from me!"

All eyes were on Ron. The night's focus had shifted. It was no longer a polite kaffeklatsch. Paul was angry. And Paul's anger resonated within Joe. He didn't want this interview, either. Everyone sat bolt upright. Then Ron started to speak, his voice quiet but nervous. He was repeating the confidentiality clause. Joe felt his body relax. He knew he had escaped the inquisitor. For one night, anyway. Tonight's interview had been driven off the cliff. Who knew where it would land? Probably not near Joe.

Chapter 19

Angela slid into the booth across from Bishop Healy for their weekly breakfast meeting. Today was her day. She had the strategy to head off Bishop McGee's assault. It was a strategy that would appeal to women. Because women understood the weight, worry, and glory of quiet service to others. Angela was sure she could convince Bishop Healy her approach would work. Telling good stories to women had brought acclaim and dollars to many a marketing campaign.

Angela felt a smile spread across her face. This morning, she didn't even mind eating at the Wide Pan with its menu of five greasy breakfast platters or a watery bowl of oatmeal.

Bishop Healy looked her over. His eyes sharpened at her smile. He always was a crafty negotiator. He waited for her start.

Angela unfolded her napkin to drop it in her lap. She couldn't wait any longer. "We have to strike at the weak point of McGee's thesis: the presence of thousands of faithful and productive gay priests, men who give selflessly."

"And what do you propose?" asked Bishop Healy, squinting at the aftertaste of his grapefruit juice.

"We need to confront this issue head-on and in the press. The press is hot about Catholic sex issues right now. We need to get coverage of a fantastic priest, a man loved and respected, a real contributor, and he has to be gay and willing to come out. He has to speak about coming out in light of the current accusations from the McGee faction. And he has to be a new face on the scandal front and gay-rights front, but someone already recognized for good deeds in the secular media. Someone women will admire and dream about."

Bishop Healy set his coffee cup down and ran his finger around the rim. Angela knew he had never been overly fond of the secular press. His taste for sporty convertibles had several times made him the butt of sidebar stories. He'd told Angela the reporters had made him seem like an old flake, even though they said their intent was to show his "human side."

"Wouldn't we be sacrificing this man?" Bishop Healy asked, focusing his eyes on hers. "Wouldn't we be putting his congregation and family through hell—press hell, interviews, cameras, innuendo, allegations—and attempts to dig up dirt?"

It was easy to read the old man's concern. He lived a public life and understood the pressing need to keep some aspects of anyone's existence private. And the fear of possible allegations rang a warning bell for Angela. Still, she'd press on.

"I can't see that there would be any allegations," Angela said, as she stirred some milk into her just-arrived coffee. "What's to allege?"

Bishop Healy leaned in. "If this guy has ever done anything—anything sexual—they'll find out. Then they'll clamp him in the pillory."

"So, when we vet the priest, we'll ask him the sex questions. It'll be part of our selection process."

"And how would this selection process work?" Bishop Healy asked. "The chancery doesn't keep lists of gay priests. Not that I know of." He leaned back and smiled. "I don't run that kind of diocese, which galls McGee."

"I can find a man." Angela fixed her eyes on Bishop Healy. Maybe Bishop Healy didn't know that crusading housing priest Father Joe Tierney was gay. The old man might be set for a surprise—just like the entire diocese.

Chapter 20

"I've got a marriage counseling session in an hour," Joe said as he undid the cincture after morning Mass. Pascal had followed him into the sacristy. Joe knew Pascal was anxious for an update on last night's Round Table meeting with Ron. Pascal had neatly mouthed the question during the short homily. But it was a fair question from a good friend. Joe hung up his alb and then turned to Pascal and said, "I need some breakfast. Can you join me?"

"I'll scramble the eggs and make the coffee," Pascal said. "You make the toast and set the table. No one's in the rectory kitchen now. We can talk."

Joe looked at himself in the tall sacristy mirror. He retucked his black shirt. "Yes, but people come and go," Joe said as he stared at himself. He grimaced at his own face. He hated the whininess that had recently entered his range of emotions.

For a second, Joe thought he heard Pascal stamp his feet, and a grin passed over his face. He turned around to look at Pascal just as his friend began to plead. "You need to talk about last night, Joe. You need to talk or your feelings will compost inside you."

Joe raised a hand to silence Pascal. Then he went over to make sure the old closet door was shut, gave it a push, and turned to face

Pascal. He shrugged his shoulders. "What's to say? It's in Ron's hands now." Joe leaned back against the closet door. He shoved his hands into his pockets. He had been feeling normal during Mass. The time leading others in prayer still pacified him. But now with Pascal there, talking about the "situation," Joe felt the stabbing return. And the blade edge was getting harder with well-pounded fear. How long could he go on like this?

"Ron doesn't own you," Pascal said, moving forward to touch Joe's shoulder. "And he doesn't own me. And he doesn't own the respect and love that everyone has for you."

Joe looked up to study Pascal's face for a minute. He saw concern around the eyes, but his friend was gulping air as if he were getting ready for a fight. Joe smiled a bright smile and reached out to touch Pascal's shoulder. "Thank you, Pascal."

Pascal beamed for a moment and then turned toward the door that led down the hallway to the kitchen and beckoned back saying, "Come on, Father. Breakfast awaits us. I'll even make the toast. You just sit. And talk."

Joe was silent on their short walk and remained so until he had settled in at the kitchen table with a view to the main door. He'd keep an eye on it. "First work on the coffee, *Pascualito*." Joe knew Pascal loved it when he used that diminutive.

Pascal came over to Joe, kissed him on the forehead, and rubbed Joe's thick mop of black hair. "You're a sweet man. I'm sure this will all work out."

Oddly enough, Joe didn't mind this display of affection in his rectory kitchen. Everyone, even his two uptight assistants, understood how Pascal was. Joe looked up at Pascal, and then he looked down to study the scratches on the table's surface. Despite the shine in his friend's face, Joe felt the fog of gloom settle back in. "Out is my big fear. I'm out of control, out of my comfort zone, and soon to be outed."

Pascal turned around and went back to the counter. "Is that what Ron is going to do?" Pascal asked as he rummaged for coffee filters in a deep drawer.

Joe sighed. "He said he wasn't going to name names, but I'm sure he recognized me. He almost froze up when he saw me."

"I know he remembers you," Pascal said, turning to look at Joe. "You are rather stunning."

The compliment meant nothing to Joe; it was only background noise. He looked down at his hands, and his eyes traced the veins.

Pascal kept on staring at him at him. "What did you tell Ron?"

Joe shrugged. "He asked a good question." Joe's voice was weak. "He wanted to know what it was like to live with this secret that could destroy our careers. But he didn't get a very good answer. Almost as soon as he asked the question, the whole evening swirled out of control. The Baptist—or whatever, he won't say—started yelling and screaming and eventually crying. Paul's so young and so scared." Joe shook his head. "I'd be sorry for him if I didn't feel the same way."

The coffeemaker started to hiss, and its dark gift began to drip into the pot. The aroma was strong. Joe liked his coffee *fuerte*, and he knew Pascal would have added extra grounds.

Joe was remembering how he almost didn't go to the support group. "Before I went to the meeting, I called up Dan Beecher to tell him I didn't want to attend. That suggestion didn't go over well. He convinced me I'd be letting the others down, especially Edward, who had so much respect for me."

"Tell me about Edward," Pascal said as he stirred the eggs into the scallions he'd chopped and heated. His back was still to Joe.

"I'm sorry, I'm not supposed to use names."

Pascal looked back a second. "But you've just mentioned Paul the Baptist-or-whatever boy. And I already know about Rocco's fateful encounter."

"And you haven't mentioned Rocco to anyone, have you?" Joe was suddenly irritated. He moved his chair back, surely leaving a scratch.

Pascal lifted the frying pan off the flame and turned to look at Joe, holding the spatula in one hand and the pan in the other. He seemed startled. Then his composure returned. "No, sweetie, I haven't mentioned anything to anyone. I'm good at confidentiality. Better than you, obviously."

Joe drew in a quick, deep gulp of air—as if he'd been holding his breath too long. "I'm sorry, Pascal. I know you won't betray me."

The two lapsed into silence. It wasn't until Pascal had sat down with the eggs and toast that Joe got back to talking.

"I was going to show up but say nothing. I knew Ron would recognize me, so I wasn't going to give him anything other than my presence," Joe said.

"Did anybody say anything?" Pascal asked, nonchalantly buttering his toast. "Other than Paul crying."

Joe took up a forkful of eggs and studied them. "You know, it was interesting. The guys were starting to talk. We were going around in a circle, the next man saying a few words ... about why he hadn't told his congregation, about how hard it was. It was very revealing. I was next in line when Paul started in. After crying, he became stern ... even mean, which caused the group to freeze up. Ron didn't know what to do. He's obviously not experienced in these things. He looked over to Rocco with puppy-dog eyes. Rocco finally got the conversation going again, but by then, it was halfhearted. The mood had changed. The evening ended soon after."

There was silence while both men ate.

"And what did Rocco say?" Pascal asked as he pushed his clean plate inward.

"It's confidential."

"I know."

"As confidential as it can be with a reporter there," Joe added, a wry grin decorating his face. "You won't be talking to Ron about it, will you?"

"How can I avoid that? We see each other ... now and again. And he started his research with me, you know, when he had the idea for the article. He even told me about the group he was going to interview—in confidence, of course."

"He'll ask you about me," Joe said. He could tell his voice betrayed the arctic coldness that always accompanied this fear.

Pascal reached over to touch Joe's arm. "I'll do everything I can to keep you safe."

Chapter 21

R on called up Pascal that afternoon and invited him over to his condo for an evening chat. He was having trouble sorting through all his thoughts. The interview had been going so well. The men were opening up. Then bang, the bomb went off. And for some reason, Paul's bomb blast still shook him. It was all he could think about.

Pascal arrived on time, and Ron buzzed him in after struggling off his couch from a late nap. He hugged Pascal at the door and got a return embrace. The warmth of Pascal's welcome relieved him. He didn't want to lose Pascal from his life. He had been thinking all afternoon about losing people. The interview had done that to him. He was focusing on the idea of loss.

Pascal reached down to pet Imhotep and then suggested they go out to the balcony to watch the warehouse district traffic.

The evening was warm, so there would be lots of movement. Ron really just wanted to talk and was about to suggest ordering some Thai appetizers when Pascal picked up Imhotep and headed to the balcony.

They settled into his metallic-bronze-colored mesh lounge chairs and stared out at the street. Ron didn't know how to start. He couldn't talk about specifics. But he needed to say something, talk about these grim feelings.

Pascal finally turned his head to stare at him and asked, "So, what's up?"

Ron scrunched up in his lounger. "I just wanted to talk. About the interview. I've got all these ideas swirling around inside me. I'm in an exciting place, but it's frightening, too. As if I were watching a kid break-dance on a sidewalk too close to traffic." He paused to study Pascal's face. Did Pascal know his friend Joe Tierney was HIV positive? Ron's body froze a moment. He needed to steer a wide course around names. It was in his contract. This evening could be tricky. He hadn't thought it through. "And you know I can't mention names."

Pascal's response was immediate. His voice was sharp, the way a man commands a surly kid. "I don't want you to mention names."

Ron knew at that moment that Pascal was in on Joe's status. *He'll be angry if Joe's life gets ripped apart.*

They both were quiet. Maybe Ron should just shut up and wait for Pascal to go back to his sanctuary. Then Pascal spoke again. "I'm only here to talk emotions." Pascal flashed him a smile. Emotion was what Ron had, in spades.

Ron cocked his head to see Pascal better. He wanted to talk to a person, face-to-face—to Pascal who would surely understand. "They're a sad group in one way. They're all afraid to be found out. HIV is the scarlet letter. Their letters are hidden, still, but even wearing the cloaked red 'A' makes them sick with foreboding. Discovery means banishment into the perilous forest," Ron said, shifting sidewise in the mesh. He was getting it out.

"On the other hand, I think there's a feeling of solidarity, of dangerous solidarity, certainly a bleak solidarity. Like those Poles who helped bring down the Communist regime a decade ago. Except these guys aren't bringing down anything. Well, not in a big way. But in little ways."

"How's that?" Pascal asked as he rubbed Imhotep's ears.

"Okay, maybe not all of them. But two of them are out to their superiors. I'd tell you their denominations or orders, but I'm not permitted—which is going to make it hard to give this article life. I can say Protestant or Catholic. It took half an hour to wrangle that concession from their lawyer."

"And being out to their superiors is bringing something down?" Pascal asked, going back to the solidarity reference.

"Yes. It brought down a personal barrier between themselves and their superiors. One of them, an older man, toward the end of the evening, talked about rummaging through scripture and religious books before he went to see his bishop. He felt the need to protect himself with some 'doctrinal armor.' That's what he called it. Instead, he settled into a leather chair in the bishop's study and just blurted it out: *'I'm HIV positive.'* The bishop got up and hugged him. Simple as that. Asked how he could help. Told the guy he would do anything."

"Even keep the secret?" Pascal asked.

"Even keep the secret. His bishop said that secrecy was sacred in the church—since the earliest days. In order to live, some early Christians had to keep their identities secret. Some were called to martyrdom, he said. Others were called to quiet perseverance."

"If secrecy's so sacred, maybe you shouldn't write this article," Pascal said; he and Imhotep looked over the railing as a terrier sniffed its way down the street, pulling its owner.

"Silence can be sacred," Ron said, nodding and following their gaze. He heard himself talking pious language the way Pascal did and shook his head in amazement. He waited for Pascal to look back at him. This next bit was the comment that had hooked him so deeply.

Pascal finally turned to look at him. Ron continued, "But that same guy said that one of the biggest things he'd learned from being HIV was that secrets can kill the spirit."

That short commentary of Edward's had changed everything. It managed to contain the blast damage from the bomb Paul had thrown with his ranting about privacy and personal rights. It had rescued the night for Ron. He decided the meaning of those words needed to get into the article. He focused on the quote. It had become the engine driving Ron to do everything possible to get this piece published.

Chapter 22

Joe and Edward took the scenic route south on their minivacation, spending several hours looking off over valleys and floodplains. They stopped once at a lookout over the river to eat the prosciutto and tomato sandwiches Joe had made. Joe was as relaxed as he'd been in weeks.

Joe looked over at Edward, who was driving the red Miata, and smiled. This trip had been Edward's idea; he had friends with a B&B in an old river town. Edward had insisted they needed to get away—to release the pressure of the last days. Joe had been skeptical. Road trips were not a part of his life. His family had never traveled anywhere for pure pleasure. Now sitting shotgun, he started to grin. He was enjoying the warm air pulsing past his face and through his hair. He hadn't even thought of HIV or Ron for several hours. This trip was a welcome relief.

On the bluff during lunch, they hadn't said much. But it was a silence without strain. Joe was greedily soaking up the beauty of the wide river as if he were a desert flower after a long-awaited rain, sending out every one of its roots in search of moisture.

At the B&B, Chanticleer's Nest, Edward did the talking. The couple knew him by first name.

"Welcome back, Edward," Marie said as she hugged him at the door. "It's always a delight to see you. It's been, what, over five years? And how's your wife?"

"She's fine." Joe noticed Edward's face tighten. He knew the couple had once been regular patrons. He knew the divorce was years ago, but Joe immediately imagined it had been one of those swift, surgical separations that left a lot of scar tissue and a pile of moldering bandages rotting in a landfill.

"I'm here on a working vacation," Edward said, managing a laugh and pointing to Joe. "This is Father Tierney, an RC. We're going to talk about a common initiative between our communities."

"Wonderful." Marie hesitated a moment. "But we only have the one room with the double bed. When you called, we had expected Joan to come with you. I guess we could get the air mattress."

"That'd be great," Joe said, jumping in. "I'm not used to sleeping with someone else, you know. Even if it is another priest." Joe winced at the absurdity of that last comment, as if the whole world didn't know by now that priests slept around.

"I'm sorry," Edward said once they were alone in their room, a long, second-story space with two dormers, a love seat, and floral wallpaper featuring pale yellow roses and blue hibiscus. "I assumed you would be comfortable in one bed. Not that I'm making an advance," he added, grinning. "I don't snore terribly. And the bed is wide. And it would be a solace to have you there."

"Maybe," Joe said, suddenly jolted by a new view of Edward, a view of him as a comely man, in fine shape, and forthright. Was Edward coming on to him? Was he so clueless about relationships? "Let's eat first," Joe said and then turned toward the door. He needed more time to process this idea.

Edward led him down Main Street to an old railroad hotel with a dining room of red flocked walls and white tablecloths. Joe grinned at Edward, saying, "This place is pretty fancy for a guy like me."

Edward seemed taken aback. "It's my treat, Joe. I used to love eating a slow, savory meal here. I hope you don't mind."

Joe shook his head. He felt as if he were on a first date, except he hadn't planned for a date. He had planned for something like a retreat. His nerves began to sputter with low-level anxiety. He smiled at Edward but knew it was forced.

The maître d' sat them next to one of the large side windows that overlooked the old rail bed, which had been paved over into a bike path. Edward ordered a bottle of wine, listing a name and year that had no meaning to Joe.

"This is a beautiful place." Joe was trying to ease into the evening. He turned to watch the waiter and maître d' as they seated a new couple, showing a courtesy that seemed to come from another century.

"They would do well in the sanctuary." Edward was obviously commenting on the staff.

"Movement is part gift and part art," Joe said. Maybe they could spend the evening discussing clerical issues.

"And always perfected under the eyes of another," Edward added, lifting his wineglass and tipping it forward.

Joe smiled back but not for long. He was getting tense. His hand clutched the wineglass too tightly. After the diagnosis, Joe had vowed never again to have sex with another man, to live the celibate life he had promised to his bishop, to try to redeem himself through abnegation and good works.

"Something's wrong," Edward said. "Am I too flirtatious?"

Joe looked away. He wondered if he had the strength for this moment. He liked Edward. Maybe under other circumstances something would happen, but not now.

Joe looked back at Edward. "No, it's not you." He felt an itch near his left eyelid and rubbed it. He massaged his temple briefly. "It's that since the diagnosis ... since then, I've prayed to be truer to my vocation."

"And I'm not helping." Edward set his hands on the table.

"It's not your fault." Joe didn't want to reject Edward. He relished having this kind man in his life. "Actually, I'd been wondering … if I'd met you before, maybe things would have been different. But now … now I feel so dirty, so untouchable."

Edward nodded his head. "I think any priest or minister, when he sins, when he or she sins big and publicly, feels it more intensely. Your life has become the stuff of tabloid headlines. It's an awful reality to confront."

"Yes, but there's more."

Edward didn't respond. Their dinner of pecan-encrusted perch, wild rice, and julienned carrots arrived. After the servers left, Edward took out his pillbox and popped a handful of large tablets. Joe looked around the room. No one seemed to notice, so he did the same. They ate in silence. Joe knew Edward was wondering what the "more" was he had mentioned. He'd have to explain it.

Once the plates were removed and coffee poured, Joe decided it was time. This was his confessional story. He couldn't escape telling it. The telling would be an absolution. "You see, it started over a year ago." Joe paused to make sure Edward knew this was the big reveal. "When I got a laptop. I'm not much for TV, and who has the time? When I relaxed, I'd be with friends or pray or play golf, tennis … run. I got the computer because people were telling me how easy it was to do research, to find that special fact or quote you needed for a homily."

Joe looked down briefly at the china coffee cup. "But I had heard of other uses for it, too. From the confessional. I'd heard of AOL chat rooms, of gay.com. I started to become a lurker at gay.com. I'd watch the conversations and look at the pictures. Some of them were pretty explicit," Joe said, still unable to smile but keeping his eyes steady on Edward's face.

"I know." Edward's face had an attentive look, empty of judgment, the perfect confessor's mien. Joe kept going.

"Then a year ago, the parish council gave me a digital camera at Easter. And I took all these photos, of myself. Like I had no respect for myself!"

"Like you were a sexual being," Edward said, leaning slightly forward.

Joe knew Edward was trying to be supportive, but he had to make his point. He was almost whispering.

"It's never been like that for me. I've never been so out of control, wobbling morally. I don't know what tipped me over."

The waiter came to ask if they had reconsidered dessert. Edward shook his head. Joe didn't move.

Joe hunched into the table. "So one night, this guy, HndsmYngJockForOlder—that was Kenny's handle as he entered the chat room ... He was perfect. Smooth, tight, taller than me, a great smile."

Joe stopped. His eyes were closed. He had told Edward about Kenny, but never how they had met. How would his friend react?

"And?" Edward prompted.

Joe looked into Edward's eyes. "And I sent him a private message with a photo. His response was immediate. In twenty minutes, I was at his place. An hour later, we'd done it twice." Joe's voice had emptied of feeling.

"And not safely," Edward said.

"Never safely, although I protested at first. Kenny said it was okay." Joe paused. "That was my first gay experience. I let him lead."

"Do you think Kenny knew he was positive?"

"I don't know. I haven't tried to contact him since ... since I found out." Joe slumped back into his chair.

Edward's head jerked. "Why not?" He seemed shocked.

"I figure I got what I deserved. Why dump on him? He'll get tested someday. All gay guys do."

"Joe, stop. That language sounds awful. You didn't deserve to get HIV. None of us did. Even if you did sin. Even if you let yourself down, your parish, your bishop. You don't *deserve* this disease. It's not a punishment."

Joe watched Edward start to reach his hand across the table and then quickly pull it back. Edward must have read something in his eyes. Joe knew he was closing the solid cloister door, sealing himself inside. But it wasn't an easy closure.

"You must've been very vulnerable, isolated, to get so hooked on this guy, to let him do that to you," Edward said.

"I thought I was in love." Joe chuckled at the idea. "He was a blue-collar guy, like me. We understood each other. And he was sweet. I'm sure he didn't know he was positive. He was always honest about himself. He would've said."

"So why don't you call him? Tell him what you know now?"

"He was moving on. He asked me to go to California with him. I'd said no. I made a vow to break it off completely. I told you all that part, remember?"

Edward sat back. "I remember. But you didn't say he was the only one. I think you have to tell Kenny," he said as he signaled for the check.

Joe didn't reply. He knew Edward was right about telling Kenny, but he had so wanted to get away from this HIV drama. Now he was back on stage reading his lines, waiting for the director's critique. He pursed his lips. All he wanted was time away from it all.

Chapter 23

After dragging himself through Monday morning Mass and slogging through the weekly staff meeting, Joe finally sat in his office chair to review the rest of his schedule. Could his day get worse? He was booked till 4:00 p.m. And the day was to end with another dinner at Angela's. He suspected she wanted him to do her a favor. That was the way it worked. Dinner followed by the big request. But seeing Angela wasn't the day's major poison. That hazardous toxin had arrived early, with inky clarity, in the morning newspaper.

Thinking about it made Joe feel nauseous again. He crossed his arms on the desk and leaned forward to rest his head on them. He glanced at his watch and then closed his eyes. The liturgy meeting was in ten minutes.

After only thirty seconds, a truck stopped outside his window; the driver banged open and shut the truck's doors. It must've been UPS. Joe raised his head. Slowly. Now he saw the headline again: "Youth Pastor Commits Suicide." The headline rested just below the fold of the front page. A man's photo accompanied the article. The name under the photo was Rodney Stanfield, but Joe knew him as Paul. By the third paragraph, the scenario had become clear: "Several boxes of S&M pornography were found in his apartment along with restraints, masks, ropes, and other paraphernalia."

* * *

The phone rang at Casa Romero, and Pascal rushed out of morning prayer to answer it. It was Ron.

"We're reciting lauds," Pascal said, annoyed at the early phone call. "You know that." He closed his eyes and took a deep breath. This reaction was a perfect example of why he didn't have a boyfriend— because of his hesitant relation to the modern, connected world.

"I've got to talk to you. Have you seen the headline?"

"I read scripture in the morning." Pascal looked over at the kitchen table to see if the paper was there.

"Pascal, he killed himself."

Pascal stopped breathing for a moment. The thought was impossible. "Joe?" Pascal asked, gasping, nearly dropping the phone. Had it gotten that bad?

"No, one of the others."

Pascal relaxed.

"Don't tell anyone," Ron said in a whisper. "I shouldn't tell you. I can't believe it. I didn't mean ... I didn't mean for this to happen."

Pascal thought he heard Ron stifle a moan. He shook his head. His heart was racing. He had to act. "I'll be over in a sec. Don't do anything. Just wait for me!"

* * *

Joe got the call from Dan Beecher just as he pulled up in front of Angela's condo. The Round Table was to meet for an emergency session. He had an hour.

Joe felt relieved. He needed to talk with the guys. The Paul-

Rodney news had been dragging him down all day. But first, he had to get through the Angela dinner. He decided to tell her about his new dinner deadline right away, as he walked in, still palming the phone.

"I just got a call. I can't stay long. A parishioner needs me. Sorry. Forty-five minutes, max."

Angela looked miffed. Her usual warm embrace turned into an Asian handshake, formal and flimsy.

He raised his shoulders as if to say, "What can I do?" He couldn't tell her what was going on. He needed to get to the group, to discuss what Paul's death meant, where it might lead, what the group should do, and if the group should contact Ron.

Angela moved to shut the door. "Okay, let's eat right away. You still need food." He could feel the energy in her body. It was red and barbed. She was fighting her emotions. Angela was angry, but he didn't have the energy to soothe her.

In silence, Joe followed her into the kitchen. She reached up into a cupboard and picked out two plates. "We can eat at the table here. I don't want to keep you long—*if* you have to go." Her anger had cooled only slightly.

They both plucked out a helping of pasta and ladled on some sauce. For a few seconds, they sat and ate. Joe discovered his hunger and forced himself to slow down. He hadn't had an appetite all day.

He knew Angela was watching him. She was pecking at her meal. "Joe, this is important. It's something Bishop Healy knows about."

He looked up. What had she said? What was this about?

Angela smiled at him. It was an all-business smile. He froze. He couldn't take much more pressure. He was thinking of asking for a sabbatical. After the weekend with Edward, he was feeling worse. His fear was that he'd distanced himself from a wonderful man, a man who had already become a key force in his battle for sanity. His actions over the weekend, his becoming sullen and quiet after their dinner conversation, his sleeping on the floor, had strained his relationship with Edward. And now what did Bishop Healy want? Was this really important?

Or the question that really froze his heart muscles: had Bishop Healy found out?

Joe saw a new emotion take over Angela's face. She had a look of concern, as if she'd read some of that dialogue going on inside his head.

Angela coughed—a conversation redirector, phlegmless. Or maybe there was some anxiety there. "You've heard about Bishop McGee's initiative?"

Joe relaxed. It was just McGee. No one had found out about him. "Isn't he always ranting about something?" Joe asked, letting some frustration show. "Deriding practicing homosexuals who receive Communion? Women who want to be priests? Politicians who don't vote the Vatican line? What is it this time?"

Angela looked serious. This wasn't play for her. "He wants to ban gay men from entering American seminaries. There's talk of 'suspending' the studies of current gay seminarians until 'church policy catches up with the roots of these scandals.' He's serious. And he's got serious friends."

On most any other night, this information would have steamed up Joe's shallow pool of calmness, sending vapor out through his nearly onyx eyes. Tonight was different. His heart only pumped an oily grief—and confusion.

He didn't respond.

"It could be the first step in a campaign to eradicate gay men from the priesthood," Angela said.

"Good luck with that, McGee!" There was the spike. His anger. Its sudden presence delighted him. "He'd have to shut down half of the parishes in every diocese and probably all monasteries and nunneries."

No quick retort. Angela shifted back in her chair and then undid the clip on her blond hair, shaking her hair and letting it curve down to her neck.

Joe was struck by the beauty of her movement, and the grimness of her new pose. *She's getting ready for battle,* he thought.

"He's going to do it," Angela said, almost without emotion. "There is no way to stop him. We can only respond. We can respond thoughtfully, in a manner that will tilt opinion away from him. Or we can be quiet. Or we can respond rashly and angrily."

Angela's words cleared his mind. She was right. They needed to respond.

"I think it's really up to you to decide how we respond." Angela crossed her arms. "It should be an issue you care about."

Joe leaned forward and rested his chin on his balled hands for a brief moment. If only she knew his real story. He opened his hands to plead his case. "Of course I care about this initiative. But I'm not a bishop. I'm not a theologian. I'm not a writer. I'm not a Dignity activist. Who am I?"

"You're a gay priest. And a good priest. But what's of special value right now is that you are a good, *gay* priest."

"Angela, *you* know I'm gay. A couple of my classmates know. Pascal, of course. But who else?" He froze for a moment. There was Kenny, and the group ... Dr. Treloar. The number of "knowers" was increasing. But Joe recognized he couldn't become Angela's poster boy. He lacked the energy—and the courage—for this fight. He tried to shrug off her request. He let his arms hang limp at his sides, his hands dangling loose. "I'm not very gay, if you know what I mean."

"That's why you're the perfect man for our campaign." Angela slapped the palms of her hands on the table. "You're *not* very gay. You're *not* the usual suspect."

"I'm *not* a lot of things. And one of them is a martyr. I just can't get involved with this, Angela," Joe said, rising from his seat. "Not now. And I've got a meeting to get to."

* * *

Joe and Rocco walked down the corridor together. Neither spoke. Rocco looked gray, his pale skin taking on a sickly hue. Joe didn't want to make chitchat. Angela's words still churned inside him. She wanted to use him. Like a political pawn. It made him angry. He thought she was a friend. Or maybe he wasn't thinking clearly. Maybe he needed to see things from her perspective. She was no fool, not one to unsheathe the atomic bombs after a minor border skirmish.

Joe and Rocco were the last to arrive. The others rose from their seats to hug them. Joe had only once shaken Søren's hands. Now Søren was hugging him to his chest and nearly stifling his greeting with tears. It was that kind of night. Søren was speaking through his light sobs, repeatedly muttering, "Did vee do this to him?"

Finally everyone was seated, and silence settled in. Joe stared at the empty chair. He looked around. Everyone else was staring at the chair, too.

"I think we should spend a moment in prayerful silence," Dan said, his eyes still on the wood slats of Paul's regular seat. "And pray for Rodney Stanfield's soul, the man we knew as Paul."

Their heads dropped lower in unison. But Joe couldn't pray. He looked up to see Jim and Rocco wiping new tears from their eyes. Soon, the whole room was crying, deep, throaty sobs, uncontrolled. Edward reached a hand over to pat Joe's back as Joe leaned forward and bawled.

After a few minutes, Joe had stopped crying, and he heard Søren ask his original question in a different way. He sounded like a man pleading. "Why did he do this? The reporter's article, it may not happen, may not be published. Was he getting sick? Does anyone know?"

Joe looked over at Søren. He had assumed Paul killed himself because of the article, because Paul was afraid his HIV status would be exposed. But there could be some other reason. And then the other thought. Would other reporters be sniffing around, finding a trail that lead to a bigger story? Joe started to grind his jaw.

Edward began to speak. "I don't think any of us really knew Paul. The rest of us are theologically and culturally so different from Paul … *were* so different." He was wiping his eyes as he spoke, and his voice was cracking. Joe wondered why Edward continued on with the false name. Wasn't Rodney the truer one? "We had this disease in common, and our profession—but so little else."

A pause, then Rocco spoke. "Think about the stuff they found in his basement." Everyone turned to look at him. His tone was that of a grad student with a theory, excited by an idea. It sounded out of place to Joe. "He probably had that stuff for a reason. Maybe something had happened. Maybe somebody in the leather community was going to betray him."

"Not the leather community," Jim said, immediately taking up the thread. "That's a pretty tight group. It's not easy to get involved with them." Jim sounded like an authority. Joe couldn't believe where this conversation was going or that Jim knew anything about some leather community. "They have apprenticeships and initiations. I bet Paul was a solo actor. He seemed like an isolated man to me, the type that is often drawn to religious work, sadly—the lonely prophet."

"What about Ron?" Rocco asked, hesitating on the name.

The silence was deafening. What was Rocco getting at?

"I mean, he's probably feeling awful—like he caused this," Rocco said.

"He did!" Joe shouted. His eyes had narrowed, and he looked at

Rocco as if the redheaded priest were prey. His anger came suddenly. Angela's request still ground about in his mind. McGee's threat of witch hunts rang in his ears. "Why did he have to pry? Why did he have to write about us? We're people who need our privacy! Will the world be better off if this article comes out?"

The group was all staring at him, the way they had stared at Paul a few weeks before when he had erupted. Was he the only other one who didn't want this article to happen?

"Are you suggesting we contact Ron?" Edward asked, looking confused. "Tell him we think any article now would be inappropriate?"

Dan spoke up, answering Edward's question. "I think that's too late. We signed a contract."

"I'll have my brother call Ron anyway," Edward said, looking at Dan and then at Joe with an expression that was half tender, half worried. "To reinforce the contract guidelines. He can't connect Paul to our group."

CHAPTER 24

After Paul-Rodney's death, Joe and Edward decided to have Wednesday night dinners together at Edward's ivy-clad bungalow, far from snooping eyes, sheltered on a tree-lined suburban curve. Joe told his staff he was pursuing deeper ecumenical studies with an Episcopal historian. Joe was glad Edward hadn't cut him off after his ill-tempered displays in the recent meetings. He had decided he needed Edward in his life—as much as he needed Pascal.

The first dinner was after the burial. No one from the Round Table attended the funeral for fear someone might make a connection between Paul's death and Ron's article, which was still in the works. Paul was only a youth pastor. The presence of well-known local clergy from other denominations would be suspicious, could lead to further inquiries, could bring reporters knocking on their own front doors.

The one news channel that covered Paul-Rodney's funeral had lodged a dismal image in Joe's head. He managed to watch the coverage twice, once popping out of a council meeting to make an "emergency phone call." The service took place at a funeral home. The station's footage, which was shot outside the building, showed half a dozen people moving behind a gray casket as a pair of men walked it down a ramp. The station played a fifteen-second sound bite, a recitation of the bare facts. The funeral must have been bleak. Even the day was overcast. At the doors of the funeral home, no relative spoke up for Rodney or tried to explain him, tried to cast him in a positive light. One older man, his mouth tight with what seemed a barely suppressed rage, waved the TV reporter and his microphone away.

"I read in the paper that only two people from Rodney's church attended," Joe said as he shredded lettuce for the salad, positioning himself at the counter only a few feet from Edward. "A great show of Christian charity and forgiveness."

"I guess they think he's in hell," Edward said, concentrating on the pot in his hands. He was about to stir the beans into the chili. "No use praying over the corpse of one of the damned."

"But what about the family? His parents?" Joe had finished the lettuce and began to set the small kitchen table. He enjoyed discovering that Edward stored his utensils and plates exactly where he would have. "Those people need support."

Edward turned from the pot of chili to look at Joe. "You're a good man, Father Tierney." Then he winked and turned back to the chili. "But your priorities are not shared by everyone."

Joe shrugged his shoulders. He didn't respond. He was feeling that special contentment again. It was cool in Edward's little white square of a kitchen. The day had been a scorcher, and Edward had apologized that he was an addict to air-conditioning. Joe rubbed his arms. He looked out into the backyard at a cluster of slender mountain ash and a robust, well-tended vegetable garden whose tomatoes were already growing large. He was thinking a welcome idea: that he might be feeling more content than he had ever felt—well, at least a feeling to rival the bubble of happiness that filled him when he absolved a crying man or blessed a dying mother and a feeling akin to what he had felt with Kenny after they had spent several nights together, when the barriers of his clerical isolation just seemed to crumble away.

Joe sat down at the tiny kitchen table. He was still examining the aspects of this emotion. Was his contentment like those rare moments in contemplation when all traces of sadness disappeared, leaving joy? But instead of sitting in the presence of the Sacrament, he sat feet from Edward. He smiled. Once, as a confused and stressed-out teen, Joe had longed for the grace to become a contemplative, to fit into holy robes and pray with the absorption of a jungle predator, concentrated on subtle movements with complete expectation of the coming nourishment. Now he was happy just watching this gray-haired man stir chili, happy to consider the hair on Edward's arms, the black leather belt as it looped his thin waist, and the smile that would turn and greet Joe every few minutes.

Edward went out to change CDs. They were listening to jazz, which Joe knew nothing about but was enjoying. When Edward came back, he went to the stove and his chili. With his back to Joe, he said, "It needs constant attention now. I'll just stir, adding a few more of my special ingredients. You relax."

After what seemed a very short while, Edward brought over two steaming bowls. Joe dug in.

"Good chili," Joe said, approvingly, making that short thanksgiving his meal blessing. He looked up at Edward. "Not bad for a *gringo*."

"You can thank my two years in a Tucson parish. Joan and I took to southwestern living." Edward spooned in some chili and savored it, closing his eyes. He opened them to look at Joe. "I'm afraid that's where I learned to love air-conditioning. I even like the hum."

Joe nodded and gulped. He had discovered that the subject of Joan, Edward's former wife, made his stomach churn. Her name, of course, implied the breaking of vows, a subject that still left him in evening turmoil.

"It's not too spicy?" Edward was probably responding to Joe's wince.

"No, no." Joe didn't want to ruin this moment. He didn't want to bring up his anxiety about a shattered marriage, about his act of omission—as someone who did nothing to repair the damage. He was supposed to heal rifts. But this rift had proved good for him.

Joe looked at the kitchen clock. "Oh, I need to take my pills." He reached into his pants pocket.

"Same here." Edward got up and went to the cupboard where he kept his five bottles. He took out seven pills and downed them with a glass of water from the sink.

Joe was shocked. "You keep your meds in a public place?"

"I just started leaving them here a couple of weeks ago. It's convenient for me. I take them at mealtimes." Edward sighed. "Maybe I need to live more openly with this disease, so it won't weigh on me so much."

"So you don't end up like Paul." Joe put down his spoon and looked up at Edward. "You don't feel suicidal, do you?"

Edward still stood with his back to the sink. "I'm not the suicidal sort, but I understand Paul's desperation, the feeling of the room getting smaller and the air getting thinner. I don't want to have this disease. And after five years, I still don't want my children and parishioners to find out, and especially my ex-wife."

Chapter 25

On Friday, Angela made a special trip to the GLBT center to get a copy of Ron's article. Her secretary, Doris, whose brother was gay, told her about a piece in the *GLRegister* detailing a group of local gay clergy with HIV. "I'll go get a copy," Angela told Doris. "And my schedule may need to change today."

"Do you think they're related?" Doris asked as Angela headed out the door.

"I'm sorry?" Angela answered, turning back. She hadn't a clue what Doris was asking. What were related?

"This article and his death."

"Whose death?"

"The youth pastor who killed himself."

"Oh." Angela paused. Her skin started to heat up. There could be a connection, though she doubted it. "I suppose there might be a connection."

Angela sat in the GLBT Center's small coffee shop with an espresso and a rapidly beating heart. She unfolded the paper. The article wasn't on the front page, but it was on the inside front page as a sidebar to a larger piece detailing the current state of the disease.

She sized up the space and batted her eyes. She knew Ron wouldn't be happy with this tiny bit of print. She quickly reviewed the main article. It was a compilation of statistics about HIV infection in the general population with a reference to the "AIDS in the Catholic Priesthood" article. She read no new information in the main article.

She took a sip of her sweetened espresso and turned to Ron's sidebar. Paragraph one had the lead. "HIV is often a diagnosis accompanied by shame. When you're a clergyperson, the shame is intensified. We have met with a secret support group for clergy who are infected."

Angela emptied her cup. The rest of the sidebar was mostly a series of quotes from an anonymous Catholic priest who was a member of the group. This was not what she wanted to read.

"I am the modern leper."

"I feel I've committed the sin that cannot be forgiven."

"Confession doesn't seem to purify me."

"Thank God for the group."

Angela put down the paper. She felt dissatisfied—all this emotion but so little real information. She was no closer to knowing who this guy was. And Angela was sure she needed to know. She was certain this little sidebar was just the beginning. Its modest tale of clandestine meetings and holy men on the down low had too much drama in it. It wouldn't go unnoticed. In a month, it would be a story line in all the soap operas.

She decided to have another espresso and read the piece one more time. Two thirtysomething men queued up behind her at the counter. The one with the shaved head said, "I bet that youth pastor was part of that group." Angela almost turned her head to ask him why he thought there was a connection. *How do people jump to these conclusions?*

* * *

By the evening news, Angela's suspicions about the viability of Ron's story were confirmed. His story had legs. Every local TV channel covered Ron's sidebar. Certainly, they were hoping for weekend eyes. Two of the stations had Ron on tape. He was attractive and more articulate than she expected. His answers almost sounded rehearsed. This coverage moved up the bar of her suspicion detector. She needed to get ahead of the story.

Ron's TV interviews didn't reveal anything she didn't know already, but one of the TV reporters asked if the youth pastor had been part of the group. Ron's answer was smooth, way too smooth. "I can't talk about membership to the group." Someone had definitely prepped him. "Membership to the group" sounded like lawyer talk.

* * *

On Saturday evening, Angela skipped her yoga class to watch the evening news. One of the more aggressive channels had been touting new information about the "positive pastors" all afternoon, on radio and TV. She sat in her living room with a glass of chardonnay in one hand and the clicker in the other. Her gut was wrenched. She feared this story would get out of control.

She didn't have to wait long for the big disclosure. The first thing out of the anchor's mouth was an announcement about an anonymous source from the county health department confirming that Rodney Stanfield had been HIV positive.

The news stunned her. She knew what it meant. Rodney was a part of that group. The terror of being found out—it probably drove Rodney to his death. As if HIV weren't terror enough. And that meant the priest in the group had to be suffering immensely.

Angela put her glass down and reached for the phone. She muted the TV. She needed to speak with Joe. She needed to find out if the priest grapevine knew who the man was. Maybe that was why Joe was so skittish around her. He knew the guy and was protecting him.

Angela pressed speed dial. She was using his sacred private number, but there was no answer. She checked to see if the speed-dial number was the correct one. It was. Joe usually answered when she called that number. Was he angry with her, still? Because of that request to be the gay poster boy? They hadn't talked since.

Angela stared at the phone. She wondered if she should call Bishop Healy, who had left for a national bishops' meeting. He hated to be disturbed during those "snake-den conferences," as he called them. He was getting old and had fewer and fewer friends in the hierarchy.

Angela just sat and stared at the phone. She would have to wait. But she knew her quiet summer days would soon be over.

* * *

Monday's newspaper headline, this one above the fold but in the right-hand column, an important but not the foremost position, detailed the arrest of the clerk in the county health department who had leaked Rodney's HIV status from a secure public health database. She was quoted as saying, "God instructed me to tell the world about the evil of the homosexual lifestyle and that his punishment can't be escaped."

By noon, Angela had snuck into Bishop Healy's office to watch a local news reporter interview the clerk, Ruthanne Phipps. She wasn't tearful. She was angry and righteous—the perfect zealot. Angela shook her head. She had seen plenty of zealots in her religious work.

By Wednesday, the national reporters started to call. At 10:00 a.m., Doris rang her. She told Angela that CNN was on the line. They had already played the interview with Ruthanne Phipps and were interested in background information about the clergy support group. Angela almost snapped, stifling the urge to say, "It's a secret group!" Instead, she told Doris to take a number, that she'd call the reporter back. Things were moving fast. She needed time to think.

Angela went out to the garden. It looked ragged. There hadn't been much rain, and Bishop Healy's gardener, Warren, a retired teacher, was getting less and less able to manage the flower beds. The thought of Warren made her grimace. Maybe she was becoming Warren. Maybe he had stopped caring about the garden. Maybe he stayed on to milk the system. Maybe she had stopped caring, too. Maybe she should lay low. This thing would eventually blow over. The church always survived.

That was the problem, Angela decided. The church would survive, but would it be a church that welcomed her?

Angela tromped back to her office. She picked up the phone to call the CNN reporter. She had decided to do the simple thing: tell the truth. She didn't have any information about the group.

The reporter, Maxine Smithfield, sounded tough, like a woman who was all about the facts. Just the facts, ma'am. Angela wondered if she were a stringer asked to call around and shake the trees for bits of information. And shake, she did. As soon as Angela told Maxine that she knew nothing of the group, the shaking began.

"But the article was written in your city and a Catholic priest was quoted," Maxine said. "Surely you're following up."

"I'm not a reporter," Angela answered. She tried to be calm. She didn't want CNN to characterize her as a stonewaller. She needed her career. But she was getting angry. "We are not in the business of spying on our priests." Maybe that was too strong. Angela decided she should cool down. She took a deep breath.

"Maybe a little spying might've helped with your Catholic sex scandals," Maxine countered. Now Maxine sounded like an attorney, a prosecutor.

"Spying?" Angela replied. Her jaw tightened. "Do you want someone to spy on you? To check everything you do or say, to make a list of the people you visit?"

That shut Maxine up for a moment. She huffed a little and then asked Angela to call her if she got any information.

* * *

On Thursday, Angela was in desperate need of Bishop Healy's advice. The phone kept ringing. She had written up a press release and sent it to all the news outlets and national services. It said what she had told everyone: "We don't know about the group."

But the questions were getting more unsettling. The set of questions that intensified her need for Healy's advice came from a conservative coastal Catholic newspaper that was planning a major series on the topic of gays in the Catholic clergy. The writer mentioned Bishop McGee in every other sentence. Angela even wondered if McGee were on the line listening as the reporter grilled her. The questions, however, were good.

How many priests in your diocese are infected?
Do these priests share the chalice with their parishioners?
How much does it cost the diocese to treat them?
Isn't this more evidence that homosexuals shouldn't be in the priesthood?

The last question made her put a stranglehold on her phone. That question was a shot across the bow, a warning shot: surrender or be sunk.

* * *

It was Sunday night at the chancery. Once again, Angela was standing outside Bishop Healy's office on a lonely, dark evening. A thin light shone underneath the door. Sunday night was usually the time when

Christian religious professionals kicked off their shoes and stirred their cocktails or cracked open their mysteries. But there would be no such rest for her or Bishop Healy, not tonight. Over the phone, Bishop Healy had sounded as concerned as Angela about devising a game plan to keep the brewing witch-hunt fever from ruining the lives of any of their diocesan priests.

She knocked twice, and Bishop Healy pressed the button to open the door. He was seated at his desk and stared at her. She hesitated. His look was anger and pain.

"How's that counteroffensive going?" Bishop Healy asked, chuckling ruefully. "It seems the media tide have taken us even deeper into this stinking ocean. And McGee is stylized as the brave crusader, the only one with a ship that isn't sinking."

Angela nodded. Her smile was thin. She understood well the conflict between the two men. Healy and McGee had studied together in Rome at the North American College, just as the bishops of the world were unpacking their robes for Vatican II. Healy had been for modernization of the church, McGee against. That disagreement still played out today. But these days, it wasn't just a matter of opinion between two spirited young men. These days, the men both had power and sway, had their own armies and partisans. And she, unknowingly at first, had signed up for the war. It was becoming the theme of her days.

"I hate seeing him get all the attention on this," Bishop Healy said. "We need another voice out there, Angela. Don't you think so?"

Angela winced. Joe had left her stranded.

"I agree, Bishop." Angela looked down to straighten her skirt, biding her time. She looked back up. "But so far, I haven't been able to get much going on that front."

She stopped a second, still standing at the bishop's desk. She hadn't told Bishop Healy the name of her poster boy. "You know I'm talking with Father Tierney, to see if he'll come out?" As the words evaporated, Angela's eyes widened. She felt like a Judas, like a betrayer. As if she had done something irrecoverably wrong.

Bishop Healy didn't move. In the passing of five seconds, Angela grasped that Bishop Healy hadn't known Joe Tierney was gay. His mouth didn't hang open, but his eyes said he was busy pulling together memories and sorting them into different columns.

Angela took a deep breath. "Father Tierney turned me down point-blank. He wants to keep himself far away from sexual scandal, which I guess I understand. And now, I'm overwhelmed by the national inquiries ... and—"

"You're handling it well," Bishop Healy said, interrupting, raising one hand palm outward. He sounded resigned, ready to count his losses. "You're doing very well. Just keep our message simple, kind, and upbeat."

"As you know from our last phone conversation," Angela said, "I've been asked to join a nationally televised panel this week. Do you think I should accept the invitation?"

Bishop Healy pushed his chair back and put his hands behind his head. She knew he was generally against unscripted media events.

"I have to give them an answer." Angela shifted her stance. "But I think the story has already gotten too much media attention to address it with only a press release and a couple of sound bites. Someone from the diocese has to speak at greater length."

"Fine," Bishop Healy finally said, unlocking his hands and leaning forward. "You'll be the face of the church, Angela." He paused. "And what do you think you'd say?"

"I'll repeat what I've been saying. That we do have several priests with HIV."

"But tell them we don't know their names, that we follow HIPAA guidelines." Bishop Healy pulled his earlobe, a sure sign he was nervous. "I don't want this to turn into an inquisition." Bishop Healy stood up and walked around the desk. He placed his hands on Angela's shoulders, paternally, more like a grandfather. His look was serious. "You know about Father Peterson?"

Angela nodded.

Bishop Healy stood back, let his arms rest at his sides. "I assumed so. You're good at your job."

Bishop Healy's grandfatherly look then turned tired and ready for bed. "I want the new man to come to me when he's ready. If you discover his name, let me know, but no goading." Bishop Healy then told her that Father Peterson had called him last week, in light of all the media commotion, depressed and afraid. "I've been praying the new man would come in soon. I hope he's in that group. I hope he's reaching out to someone."

"I do, too," Angela said. "But it's getting hard to avoid answering the subsequent questions. These newspeople want to know everything, which, to be honest, is their job."

Bishop Healy laughed. His mood was lightening. "Just don't make us sound stupid." He started to pace the room. "We respect the rights of these men to privacy." Bishop Healy repeated the phrase twice—the phrase Angela had given him.

"Privacy will be our message." Angela turned to watch Bishop Healy move. "It will play well with today's heightened concerns about identity theft and the fear of big brother."

Bishop Healy stopped a moment and looked directly at her. "Yes, privacy and compassion," Bishop Healy said. "That's our theme."

* * *

It looked like the panel discussion was going to start on time. The national network had decided to do a local shoot, and Angela only had to drive over to the affiliate station.

Angela peeked again at the other panelists: Dr. Hannah Jordan, a fifty-something epidemiologist flown in from the CDC in Atlanta, and Richard Newman, a notorious Boston-based gay commentator whose opinions, she was sure, would ricochet off the studio's right wing then off the left wing and finally out into thin air—all of which made him a prized TV commentator. It was his tall, muscular presence that made her most anxious. She could see his biceps through his tweed sports coat and noticed brown chest hair tufting over his unbuttoned white oxford shirt. She wondered which audience demographic he thought this look played to.

Richard Newman was a cradle Catholic, but Angela wasn't certain which perspective he'd bring, a neocon Catholic horror at yet another clerical lapse or a gay radical's defense of the innocent victim. So far, she hadn't read any Newman opinion on the subject of the "AIDS in the Catholic Priesthood" article. Perhaps he was saving an explosive volley for tonight's show. He'd detonate his opinions and then fly back to the East Coast.

Angela felt her mouth start to dry up. She reached for the glass of water next to her. After she set the glass down, she looked over at Dr. Jordan. Angela assumed the be-suited epidemiologist would pose no church policy problem. Her published vita described a studied woman whose life was involved with science and public policy, not religious doctrine.

Finally, she looked to her right where petite Mary Ann Smith, the show's host, pretty in her pink blouse, was reviewing her notes. Angela's research told her that Mary Ann was an anthropologist by training and liked to style herself as a social-connector. Angela wasn't sure what that phrase "social-connector" actually meant, but she had decided Mary Ann could be placed in the "friends" category.

The director called for quiet. Angela smiled and placed her hands in her lap. She knew she looked good on TV. She had worn her scarlet Donna Karan cowl-necked dress with no earrings or pins. She had fresh highlights in her hair. She was attractive, but not ostentatious.

Mary Ann was talking, introducing the three panelists. Angela hadn't been listening to the host. She was watching the cameras. She warned herself to pay attention to the words.

"Let's start with the representative of the Catholic Church," said Mary Ann, leaning over to Angela and smiling a little too brightly. "Ms. Roth, how does the Catholic Church see this scandal of priests with AIDS in light of the recent scandal of clergy sex abuse? Are the two intertwined?"

Angela smiled back. She had been expecting that Ms. Smith would lead off with a version of the "McGee" question. This was Mary Ann's way of asking, should gay men be priests? But her tone was unanticipated. Mary Ann's question sounded like an attack.

"I'm not a spokesperson for the universal church," Angela said, hoping to push the tip of her PR sword gently into Ms. Smith's slim bodice and tell her to back off, "but in our diocese, Bishop Healy is fond of stating that the men who are his priests are made of the richest muck." She smiled more broadly and paused a second before completing Bishop Healy's often-expressed thought. "Only in that muck can the word of God grow into a luxurious plant."

There, she thought, *an answer with substance but hard to parse.* She hoped it would work in this environment.

"I think that answer is as lamentable an evasion of the clerical-crisis question as any I've ever heard," Mr. Newman said, chiming in from his seat.

Angela's eyes shot wide open as she stared at the now angry man whose chest hairs seemed to flutter with irritation. "The issue is not the presence of sin as a necessary precursor to salvation ..." Newman said. Angela steeled her mind. *Pay attention.* "The issue is clergy discipline. Indeed, the discipline itself. And by discipline, I'm referring to the modern canonical rules and regulations that enforce a celibate clergy in the Latin rite. The issue is this antique requirement of celibacy in a modern age that is, itself, exploring the frontiers of sexual spirituality, discarding the discredited exercises of darker ages. The issue is the absurdity—"

"Please, Mr. Newman," said Mary Ann, breaking into his sudden rant, "we'll get to you in a—"

"No, Ms. Smith. I protest," Mr. Newman snapped, cutting off the panel host with equal quickness. Angela was distilling his ideas. He was talking about clerical celibacy. She'd bring up the old explanations. They'd been around for centuries. They had worked in the past.

Mr. Newman continued, "There have been too many seconds wasted on repeating the same old cant. What we need is a spiritual revolution. And it needs to begin in the bedroom of every deacon, priest, and bishop."

"Not in the pope's bedroom?" asked Mary Ann, in what appeared to be another attempt to slow down Mr. Newman's charge. Angela noted that Mary Ann was afraid of him too.

"He, Ms. Smith, *is* a bishop, the bishop of Rome," said Mr. Newman, his head aslant. "Thus he is part of my complaint."

Mary Ann turned to Angela. "Ms. Roth?" The squint of her eyes showed annoyance. The small-framed panel moderator was losing control. Angela forced a return smile. "What is the church's opinion about the need for a spiritual revolution beginning in the bedrooms of its male clerics?"

Angela kept a smile on her face, despite Mary Ann's continued insistence that anyone in Angela's position could speak with the authority of a pontiff. Angela could feel the muscles of her back tightening. She was astounded at the rapid development of this conversation into a heated discussion of Roman Catholic clerical policy, and she feared she was about to come off sounding like a prim librarian who was losing her poise as she desperately flipped through a pack of laminated answers. But that was her job. She didn't make up the answers under the lamination. At least she looked good. She took a deep breath.

"Again, I am not a spokesperson for the universal church, so I can't speak to Mr. Newman's thesis with an official theological voice. I think what needs to be said is that priests, like any other Catholic, get drawn into activities that are both sinful and dangerous. But a man who has sinned is still a man who can be a priest."

"Of course we are a church of sinners," Mr. Newman said, breaking in again. He seemed to sigh with the frustration of a brilliant man speaking to the mentally infirm. "But the issue in this democratic, media-connected, and scandal-obsessed world is: can the church be open about its sinfulness? Or will it support the shaming of individuals with HIV by continuing to hide the names of these very public men, thus perpetuating an environment of gossip, distrust, and hypocrisy?"

* * *

Angela was exhausted from the show's fifteen-minute shootout. She shook her head in disbelief and shock as a young woman assistant unplugged her microphone. Almost in a daze, Angela asked her, "Did Dr. Jordan get to say a word?" The woman responded with a sympathetic head shake and warm eyes. But Angela suspected from the glint in her eyes and barely disguised smile that the assistant had enjoyed the grilling Newman had given her. Angela said nothing more. She felt a sense of defeat. Of shame. But that was the cost of being a paid shill. In truth, she agreed with Newman. The problem was celibacy—and a culture of secrecy. But priests also had a right to privacy.

"You did what you could," Bishop Healy said in his promised follow-up phone call that evening. "Newman should've been an inquisitor. I bet he'd have enjoyed consigning a wayward soul to the iron lady."

"Much the image I was entertaining as he kept pressing his argument about the need for a new direction," Angela said. "Although you know I agree with much of what he says, I wanted to yell, 'Hey, let's put away the rhetorical ack-ack guns!' But I could never get such a sensible comment out." Angela sighed. She was steamed. She felt bested at her own trade. And she hated that feeling. "Let's hope this evening's audience was out walking the dog or jogging in the park listening to a medley of love songs." Angela attempted a laugh. "To tell you the truth, I'm not sure what impression I made. And that's a scary place for me."

"You were calm. Calm, but defensive."

"So the church came off as defensive?"

"That's what McGee said. He's called already. Of course, the uber-Christian McGee had wanted you to slash Newman's throat with the sword of dogma and let his pestilential blood flow out. I think McGee had blown, as they say, a gasket."

"Slashing Newman's gullet might have done no good. I'm not sure blood flows through his body. He's cold. Calculating. A real pugilist. A rhetorical bully—and well-trained. Better trained than me."

"He was obnoxious, but he had passion. And he planted his blows at our weakest point."

"Which is?"

"The secrecy of it all. The damned, putrid secrecy of the clerical culture. And the shame attached to this disease. Together, they're poison. God help those men."

Chapter 26

Angela called Ron the next day. She had convinced herself to follow up on Bishop Healy's lead—they needed to get beyond the secrecy, because there was a man in need, a priest with a new HIV diagnosis, and they had to help him.

Angela wouldn't ask Sister Cecilia, the close-lipped vicar for administration, to dig up the name of the new HIV-positive priest, so she hoped to get it from Ron. He had been at a meeting with positive clergy. Surely the priest had been there. Ron would have written down the man's name. Maybe he had known him. He had written about one priest. Maybe there were more, but not locals.

The task she set herself wasn't easy. Ron owed Angela nothing. A couple of days before her panel disaster, he had called for a follow-up quote to his article. She'd congratulated him on his piece but rolled out her standard line about privacy needs. It wasn't going to be easy to make this request. She was opening herself up for mockery. But now she was on a mission.

Angela combed her hair and fixed her lipstick before making the call. *How silly,* she thought. Ron couldn't see her and wouldn't care anyway. But it was what Angela had. And prepping herself made her feel in control.

She called, and he picked up the phone immediately, as if he'd been waiting for a call. "Mr. Saville-Jones, I imagine this is an unexpected call," Angela said, aiming for jauntiness.

"Please, call me Ron." He sounded tentative, wary. Maybe the fallout of that article was wearing him down. "What can I do for you?"

"Did you see my television interview last night? The one where I crossed swords with Mr. Newman?"

Ron chuckled. "I did. He was a dog with a bone."

"And he didn't let go."

"No. He's like that," Ron said. "I had the 'pleasure' of his acquaintance at a GLBT journalist event. He was declaiming how those of us out here in the sticks are doing a disservice to the GLBT community by paying homage to every gay institution that dots our barren streets, as he called them, rather than digging up dirt and demanding the reformation of tired approaches to equality."

"Sounds like him." Angela grinned. "Newman puts the 'pont' in pontificate."

Angela sat back in her chair. She and Ron had something in common. Good. Ride into the warm feeling. "Ron, we've begun to wonder here at the chancery about Newman's direction—his questioning—about the secrecy we've pursued in light of your findings."

That should make Ron feel good: "your findings."

"You mean keeping the identities of any priests private?"

"Yes."

Ron didn't reply for a couple of seconds. Angela waited. She began to twist a loose strand of hair.

Then Ron answered. "I was permitted to attend the group and write the article with the secrecy of their identities as a part of our agreement. I hope you're not asking me to reveal names." Ron's tone was sharper.

"Names *are* a starting point," Angela said, thinking fast. "We don't want to out anyone. We don't want to frighten anyone. But we certainly don't want another suicide." She was relying on the street gossip. No one had proved that Rodney was part of the group Ron interviewed. But she pushed it out there as if it were a fact. "We want the priest or priests to come to us. We want to discuss what's happening with them. We want to reach out. To help. Perhaps you could relay that message?"

Ron laughed. "I'm to be the covert agent of the Catholic Church?"

Angela smiled again. Now she was sure Rodney had been a member of the group. Ron didn't deny it.

"You'd be our agent, in a way. Our messenger. Our angel."

CHAPTER 27

The day after Angela's panel discussion, Joe had two funerals at Mater Dei. He wished he hadn't watched her appearance. Every word of the TV discussion was a knife blade peeling off his soft flesh. Now he found it hard to concentrate on the rituals of mourning. He could only think of Newman's words: *Gossip. Distrust. Hypocrisy.* These two families deserved more.

The morning funeral wasn't as bad. The deceased was a nonagenarian widow whose kids had the relaxed look of retirees. Despite their tears, Joe knew that they were relieved. Their mother had needed increasingly personal care in her final year. Joe had known Alice. She had been ready to die.

The second funeral almost crushed him. Joe had seen the young father often. He was handsome like Kenny. He always kept a bit of stubble at his chin, as if he wanted to say he was more than a father and a carpenter. A brain aneurism felled him. He had died at a work site downtown, and Joe had rushed over. He had knelt over the man's unmoving body to anoint him. The sense of death on that rough concrete floor had been brutally fresh, pitiless in its emptiness, in the void behind the young man's eyes.

Oddly, he reflected in the sanctuary after praying for the young father's trip to paradise, the second of the funerals was the kind that Joe was starting to prefer. Better that death come down hard and cruel, like a big, overbuilt bully that made you stop and stare, made you fight the quick-draw desire to punch it in the face, forced you to look elsewhere for solace—in a deeper, more obscure organ, the "seat of mercy" as he had called it in his sermon.

Joe returned to the rectory after the young father's postburial gathering, just as Lucy was about to head home. She handed him a message slip as she rose from her desk. "This one's from Pascal. He says he needs to talk to you. Tonight."

Joe crumpled up the pink slip of paper and stuffed it in his right pocket. "Thanks, Lucy. Have a good night."

"You look drained, Father T," she said, straightening her soft yellow skirt, the one Joe had said made her look professional and elegant, "like you been dealing too much with death. You have a stiff Scotch tonight and lay down for a long rest." As a final message, she gave him a broad, slow wink.

* * *

Joe called Pascal about 9:00 p.m. He picked up the phone in his sitting room and stayed standing, waiting for a response. Pascal answered. "I never know if you guys are saying compline or performing some other communal ritual at this hour," Joe said.

"Once again, you display a deep-green jealousy at the profound spiritual significance of my lifestyle," Pascal said.

Joe grinned. "Yeah, right. The sexually active gay man living the life of a member of a thirteenth-century pious lay society." Joe stopped to wipe his forehead. He was feeling a little fevered. Last night, he'd sweat out a pool into his bed. It couldn't be night sweats. It had to be nerves. Or was he eating the wrong food?

"Why'd you want me to call?" Joe asked, fighting off the urge to call his doctor. He rarely thought about illness, but since the diagnosis ... "Lucy made it sound urgent."

"You won't believe this." Joe noted the glee in Pascal's voice. "The chancery is reaching out to you. They want you to come in and talk about your HIV diagnosis."

"They want what?" Joe nearly choked on the question.

The sweat began to pour off him. This was the worst news, totally shocking. And Bishop Healy had always been a stickler for privacy. Bishop Healy was himself a recovering alcoholic; he had spent many years "anonymous" and had credited those years with his successful reform.

Joe didn't know what to say. His voice was small. "They mentioned me to you?"

"No, no. They don't know it's *you*," Pascal said. "And they didn't talk to *me*. Come on, be serious. Ron called. Angela called Ron. Can you believe it?"

"What? Who called who? What was said?" Joe couldn't make sense of it. His brain had nearly ground to a halt. His words were all reflex now.

"Angela called Ron," Pascal said, speaking slowly. "Ron called me. It's like the telephone game. The message is: Angela wants to discuss this 'situation' with any priests in the group. *Situation* is such a meaningless word, don't you think? Anyway, she really doesn't know it's you or that Salutarian whom Ron's been nailing. I think it has to do with the panel discussion with that Newman prick. You saw that, didn't you?"

"I did." Joe felt a wave of exhaustion move from his gut into his limbs. *This is how illness feels,* he thought. It begins to settle into the bones. He walked into his bedroom and lay down on his bed.

"This whole drama is coming to a head," Pascal said.

Joe didn't say anything.

"Joe? Are you still there?"

"I'm here."

"You understand, don't you?"

"They want to see me." Joe couldn't believe he was saying those words. The door to his soul was being torn off its hinges.

"Joe, they don't know it's you. They just want to see the priest or priests, to reach out to them. Healy's that way. Surely you know that."

Joe stared at the ceiling, following a crack that ended near his bed. "Yeah, I guess," Joe said. He decided to end the call. There was nothing left in him. He was completely empty. He had nothing more to say.

"Are you okay?" Pascal asked. "Should I come over?"

"I'll be okay. I just need to get my mind around this. Thanks for calling," Joe said and then hung up. He lay with his eyes closed. He was thinking of this new information, of the funerals, of dinners with Edward, and even of Kenny. He decided to go to bed early. He knew he needed to sleep, but could he turn off his brain? He got up and went to the medicine cabinet to grab a pair of sleeping pills.

Chapter 28

Sleep didn't happen. Joe got up and stood naked in his bedroom darkness. The last image in his brain-wave kaleidoscope had been Kenny's. Joe had thought he'd wait for the opportune time to call Kenny, but tonight, his body was restless. He wanted to act, to do something, to move some plan into action. And after all, Kenny was in California. He was young. He was probably still up.

Joe got out of bed and grabbed his cell phone. He made his most private calls with the cell so the parish name didn't show on caller ID. He was sitting on the edge of his bed scrolling through the numbers, when he wondered whether Kenny would be alone. Maybe night was a bad time to call. A third person would make things even more awkward.

He dialed anyway. Four rings and there was a groggy, "Hello?" as if Kenny hadn't checked the caller ID.

"It's Joe. Joe Tierney. Sorry to call so late."

"What's up, old man?" Kenny said. Joe heard him get out of bed, heard the muffled sound of sheets and the squeak of old mattress springs. He heard the near-groaning sound Kenny made when stretching, followed by a yawn. "I thought I'd never hear from you again," Kenny said.

Joe's mind went blank. The voice, the tone—he could already smell Kenny, salty, slightly acrid, inviting. He visualized his young naked body bending backward to elongate the spine and then raising his muscled arms high above his head. It was an image that drove Joe wild. He went out into his sitting room where he'd have more space for pacing.

"I'm sorry I've called so late. I couldn't sleep, and I needed to call you," Joe said. This was going better than he thought it would.

"You must be desperate horny," Kenny said.

Joe chuckled. Some of that was happening. "That's not why I'm calling."

Silence on both ends. Had he sounded sharp?

"It's really late for me, Joe. Can we talk another time?"

Joe stopped pacing and leaned against a wall. "I didn't mean to sound abrupt, Kenny. I like thinking about you."

"Cool. I wish we could do more than think. You know that, don't you?"

"I know. I know. But that's not why I'm calling."

"You sound worried," Kenny said. Joe thought he heard Kenny sit back on his bed.

Joe was starting to feel the anxiety push through his arteries. *Just get it out.* "The last few months have been bad. I've got something to tell you. I've been putting this off. Can we just talk a little? You don't have anyone there, do you?"

Kenny laughed. "No one here but me and Mr. Big Vein, whom I think you remember well. Go ahead, what do you want to say?"

This was Joe's chance. He was the advocate of clear, blunt communication, to his seminary professors' chagrin. They had tried to polish out all his roughness, but he kept some pits and ridges. And this was how he delivered bad news, except this message was so awful.

The words stuck in his mouth, and he almost hung up. He began pacing around in a tight circle. Then he stopped.

"Joe? Are you still there?"

Joe took a deep breath.

"I found out some news. A few weeks ago. Some bad news." Joe knew that stress made him use short bursts of words, a problem he had worked on in his counseling techniques class, attempting to change his breathing patterns. The problem was definitely back. He had to get this out. He sat on the loveseat. "I went to get tested. At an STD clinic. And I found out I'm positive. HIV positive."

Joe heard nothing but silence coming in from California. He waited for a response. Should he ask Kenny if he'd been tested? Was that his next move? Surely Kenny knew how HIV was transmitted. Did he think he was just too golden to get it?

Finally, "They're sure? No false positive?" Kenny sounded distant, distracted. Maybe the fear was starting to freeze him.

"There's no doubt," Joe said. "It's there. I'm taking meds now."

Another long silence. "Do you think you got it from me?" Kenny asked.

"It had to be." Joe was suddenly so tired he could barely think. He was on the verge of shutting down. His heart was raw. Part of him, he realized in a flash, was angry at Kenny. If Kenny hadn't been Kenny, the way Joe came to know him, none of this would've happened.

"I'm so sorry. I'm so, so sorry." Kenny's voice was as quiet as dusk. "I never meant for you to get hurt. Especially you. I really thought we'd have something long term. I really did."

CHAPTER 29

Joe called early the next day to ask Edward to meet him for a quick breakfast. He told Edward to dress down. Joe liked The Hefty Platter. It was full of students and people busy with their own lives. He could sit in jeans and a T-shirt and work undisturbed, just another regular guy stopping for breakfast. And it was a good look on him. Working-man.

Joe had brought his file on the shelter for undocumented women. The project work was intensifying. In their last meeting, the committee had finally decided to build a new structure rather than rehab an old space. They wanted a special place for these women and their children. Joe had pushed the idea. Now he had to make sure it happened right.

Joe had ordered coffee before Edward arrived. He was sipping from it and staring at the initial contract. The problem was, he wasn't reading any of the words. Thoughts of Kenny were popping into his brain. If it wasn't HIV, it was Kenny distracting him from his duties. Joe felt his frustration start to bubble. The wild thoughts were coming more and more frequently.

Then Edward touched his shoulder from behind, and Joe startled, nearly flinging his now-empty coffee mug onto the linoleum floor.

Joe glared up at his friend. "Oh, I'm sorry," Edward said. What had been a smile evaporated. "I didn't mean to sneak up on you."

Joe wanted to yell but stuffed the urge. He had to get control of himself. He set the mug down and flexed his arms. "I'm just wired, I guess." Joe pulled out the chair next to him and said, "Have a seat." He began to wonder if seeing Edward was a good idea. His friend brought with him a special set of distractions. But Joe felt the need to talk, especially after last night. And Edward was discreet.

"You look more than wired," Edward said. "It's like your complexion has faded—and somebody has hit you in both eyes. Didn't you sleep last night?"

"Thanks, I needed to hear that this morning." Joe had let the sarcasm escape and immediately felt bad. Edward looked at him askance.

"I'm sorry," Joe said. "I'm on edge."

"I can see."

The waitress came to take their orders and filled Edward's coffee mug. Joe placed the contract in its folder and shoved it aside. He had hoped to relax in Edward's presence, but that wasn't happening. It was like breakfast at the rectory, where he was always wary of combat.

"I apologize," Edward said, turning to look at Joe. "I was too blunt. Sometimes I—"

"Don't." Joe interrupted Edward with a swift hand movement. "I'm to blame. I'm in a really bad mood."

"What's happened?"

"A couple of things." Joe leaned toward Edward. "One, Pascal called last night. Bishop Healy wants me to come in and discuss my HIV status." Joe had whispered the last two words. He turned to look around at the other tables. His heart beat slowly.

When Joe's face came back from reconnoitering the room, Edward was staring directly at him. "They found out about you?" Edward asked.

"Not *me* precisely. They know there's a priest or priests in that group—from reading Ron's article."

The waitress came over to warm their coffee. They both thanked her and then leaned back in.

"Why are they asking around? What are they after?"

Joe checked on the pair of businessmen who were just taking the table next to them. He didn't recognize either of them, but he would speak softly. "Pascal says they want to make sure there isn't another suicide." Suddenly, Joe wished he hadn't met Edward in this public place. That was a mistake. These topics were too private.

Edward reached over to touch Joe's arm, as if he were a man wanting to ask something personal. For a moment, Joe stared down at the table and closed his eyes. He knew the next question.

"Is suicide a possibility?" Edward asked, his question hushed.

Joe looked up and stared wide-eyed at Edward. He felt Edward's concern. "My uncle Dave shot himself when I was just a kid," Joe said, letting out a little-known family secret. "Uncle Dave and my dad both owned the store."

He sat back in his chair, wondering if he was starting to look like Uncle Dave with wariness and a sweet man's pain glinting in his eyes.

The waitress arrived with their breakfast platters.

Joe rested his arms on the table and then looked up from his food at Edward. He had to make this clear. "Not much possibility of a self-induced ending here," Joe said, trying to sound nonchalant. "But I have imagined it," he said, replaying in his mind again the scene from his youth, the tragedy that had occurred in their family's attic, that had deepened the well of his father's anger and marked the beginning of the dark period when his father lashed out at wife and children, which resulted in the summoning of *la abuelita*. "My childhood sense of security was collateral damage from Uncle Dave's dramatic exit."

Edward let out a sigh of relief. He seemed to relax. "I'm sorry about your uncle but glad you're not likewise inclined," Edward said. He took up a slice of buttered toast and lathered on strawberry jam.

They both ate quietly. Joe was hungry. He noticed the restaurant had filled up even more and a line had formed at the door. It was noisy inside the large room.

Edward's next question was a little louder. "What are you going to do? About your bishop's inquiry?"

That was the rub. Since the diagnosis, Joe had simply wanted to hide. The group and Pascal and his healthcare contacts were the only ones who knew his own little secret. But, maybe things were bending this way for a reason …

He hadn't thought it out yet. "I haven't decided," Joe said. "What's your opinion? You met with your bishop."

"I did. At 11:00 a.m. one Monday. It was one of the worst mornings of my life. I couldn't stay still. My legs actually ached. But once I settled into the chair and got the thing out, everything changed. His response, as you know, was kind and generous. I just relaxed after that. At least for a week."

Joe nodded and smiled, dabbing some Tabasco sauce on his remaining huevos rancheros. "It would probably be the same with me. This secrecy is wearing on me. I'm not used to living like this. I mean, I've had my secrets but nothing I'm truly ashamed of. But I am ashamed of this disease. It might be best to get the diagnosis out there. At least with Bishop Healy."

Edward nodded. Joe could see the compassion in his friend's eyes. "You'll do the right thing," Edward said. "At the right time."

Joe smiled broadly. Edward's words were a salve. "You should go into counseling," Joe said, chortling. "You certainly make me feel better."

"I'm glad to be of service." Edward's eyes had warmed even more.

They sat and ate quietly for a few minutes. When he was finished,

Edward looked at his watch. Joe knew Edward had a busy day, as did he.

Edward moved his plate away from him. "There was something else? You said there were two things bothering you."

Joe cradled his mug in his hands. He wasn't sure anymore if he wanted to discuss the other thing. But it was the real reason he had called Edward. Why had he kept the most important news for last?

"Yes, there was something else. The main reason I called you and forced you to eat breakfast with me," Joe said, "aside from enjoying your company."

Edward seemed really pleased to hear Joe's words and smiled broadly. "And what is that something else?"

"You know I've been talking about it for a while … about making the phone call to …" Joe started and then stopped, choking up. How had that sadness sneaked up on him? Or was it sadness? Maybe he was too tired. Things were getting out of proportion.

Joe saw Edward tense up. "You mean the call to Kenny?"

Joe nodded quietly. He felt the sadness ache in his eyes. Edward was right. He must look awful.

But Joe was surprised that Edward knew instantly what the call was about. He notched his head to the right. The need to make the call had hung in Joe's consciousness for so many weeks—but he'd always shoved it away. "I didn't expect it to be so painful. I mean, the call wasn't painful. It's my reaction this morning. I guess *pain* isn't the word."

"What did Kenny say?" There was hesitance in Edward's voice.

"There was nothing special in the words," Joe said, opening his hands. "Nothing mean. He said he was sorry. He said he'd get tested. He thanked me. I woke him up, you see. It was late, and he was tired. I wonder if he even got back to sleep. I feel bad about that." Joe settled his arms atop the table. He had another thing to say. "I think it was just being able to talk to him again. I felt the old connection. I was shocked by the feeling. I'm still shocked. That connection is such a live thing for me. Still, I had dreaded making the call. Now ..." Joe shook his head. "Am I making any sense?"

* * *

Joe had a parish council meeting that evening. The agenda was light. It was time to send the six-month financial figures to the chancery. All the numbers had looked good to him when he picked up the report from the accountant that morning. He hoped the evening would end early. Maybe he'd get some sleep.

They met in the parish hall, three men and three women seated around a long folding table. It wasn't very elegant for a parish of Mater Dei's stature, but Joe liked to keep these meetings simple and unpretentious. It was one of the attributes he brought to Mater Dei's prestigious pulpit.

Everyone seemed in a good mood. It was still light outside, and Joe was sure the council members would want to get home in time for a stroll or a relaxing run in the warm evening air. He picked up the report and started to look at the numbers again. But tonight, his eyes blurred. It was the comment that Harry David, one of the old-time parish councilors had made, the comment about the funeral of the young father who'd died of an aneurism. Walking into the meeting, Harry had said, "You seemed to take that death pretty hard, Father."

Maybe he had. Maybe everything was getting hard. His eyes wouldn't focus on the figures before him. He was thinking of Kenny again. What would it be like to preside at his funeral? Joe startled. He couldn't believe the thought had entered his mind. He shook his head.

"Are you okay, Father?" Harry asked, slanting his head.

"Sure, sure," Joe said. "I've had a lot on my mind lately. Sometimes a stray thought zings me."

Chapter 30

Bishop McGee's campaign to oust all sexual perverts from the Catholic priesthood was gathering national momentum after a priest in a rural parish in his diocese was arrested with a stash of child pornography—one plastic storage bin stuffed with pictures of young boys and a hard-drive full of photos of young boys and girls in sexual poses. Angela thought she read glee in McGee's televised harangues, now that he had an offender of his own to disavow and defame.

"This perversion has seeped into the bedrock of our beloved Mother Church," McGee said on national news. "Those of us on the inside have smelled its stench for years. And now the rest of God's people smell it. It's time to clean house."

"Bedrock and housecleaning. He was never a man to keep to one metaphor," Angela said aloud with little joy as she reran the tape of McGee's interview in the chancery's small media center/library. The chancery had begun to receive hundreds of calls, letters, and e-mails from across the nation urging Bishop Healy to clean house along with Bishop McGee. The Catholic Purists League had set up a website where the faithful could "nominate" priests who should be examined for their sexual purity and orthodox beliefs. Ten of Bishop

Healy's priests were already on the list, including Joe Tierney. The comments attached to his name mentioned his "fostering" of a gay Catholic support group, which Angela knew was a group Joe kept at a distance, letting the parish administrator shepherd it. Joe was vigilant about not coming out.

As the tape ended again, Angela wondered why she ever took this job. She had thought service in the church would be noble and uplifting. Angela looked over at her picture of the Angel Gabriel in swirling garments, one of the images that had once expressed the meaning of her own work, a triumphant beauty bringing great news. God, had she been duped?

Chapter 31

J oe wasn't happy driving to the chancery that Sunday night. His jaw was tight, and his hands gripped the steering wheel as if he were driving on glare ice. His name was on the Catholic Purists League hit list! Damn them! You couldn't be a priest anymore! There was always someone spying, ready to report any quibble you had with policy or doctrine. His anger burned inside. Who had done this to him? His squeaky-clean assistant Father Fitzgerald? Someone from the parish council?

Bishop Healy's voice mail had been brief. He wanted the ten priests named on the Catholic Purists League online list to come over Sunday night for a get-together. *Yeah, more like a preinquisition party,* Joe thought. It would just be Bishop Healy, the priests on the list, and Angela who had to help Bishop Healy formulate a response.

Most of the men on the list were gay, like Father Peterson. But Joe was on the list because of his policies. He and Monsignor O'Malley had fostered anti-Catholic ideas. At least, that's what the website claimed.

*   *   *

Joe stood a moment in the doorway of Bishop Healy's large study. Four chairs were empty. Joe walked over to the one next to Father Keegan, a round old man with a voice and gestures as queenly as Liberace's. Normally, Joe avoided men like Keegan, but tonight, he felt a pull to put that thinking aside. Everything was changing. He tossed Father Keegan a smile and patted the man's big thigh.

Then Monsignor O'Malley entered. Joe smiled at him, and O'Malley waved him a greeting. Monsignor O'Malley headed in his direction after uttering a balmy "Good evening, all," to the group. Joe wondered if Monsignor O'Malley thought they were the only two straight men there. Why should he suspect otherwise?

Joe patted the seat of the chair next him. He watched the old priest move slowly across the room, noting that his hair was still long and slightly ratted at the ends, the perfect antiestablishment hairdo. You could make an anarchist recruitment poster out of that craggy face.

"Monsignor," Joe said, nodding at his old hero. "This will teach you to bless gay couples and preside at Mass for Dignity." Joe hoped he sounded jaunty, as if the two of them were alike, soldiers of reform, Don Quixotes of *aggiornamento*. But as the words echoed away, Joe's spirit started to cool—the cooling agent: the thought that this old man was more genuine than he had ever been.

"Well, Father Tierney, I see that the forces of darkness have reached out and grabbed onto the shoulder of our lone Hispanic priest," Monsignor O'Malley said as he happily patted Joe's shoulder.

"I don't think it's my mom's blood that got me here," Joe answered, hurriedly rubbing his eyes as if he were tired—wanting to hide his quickening sense of shame. "It's more likely that bile from the old sod that my father infused in me that dragged me here," Joe said, playing off O'Malley's notorious Irish pride.

Both men laughed. Joe had to admit he was glad the other men assumed he and O'Malley were on the website for the same reason: unorthodox activity—like remodeling the sanctuary at Mater Dei, which made him throngs of enemies. But that he was gay, a few might suspect, but none of these men knew.

Joe shifted in his chair. His sense of discomfort was growing. He had planned to sit out this war council of Bishop Healy's, keep his thoughts hidden. He knew he was safe at Mater Dei. It was a fortress for him. All of a sudden, he wasn't sure he wanted to hide there. Maybe it was O'Malley's presence.

Just then, Bishop Healy and Angela entered the room, and the jittery conversations ended abruptly. All the priests rose in unison from their chairs. Joe saw Bishop Healy startle at the sudden silence and the deferential movement. He seemed reluctant to enter.

He knows we're on edge, Joe thought. *Is he?*

"Please, men, this is not a Tudor monarch's star chamber," Bishop Healy said. He gestured for them to sit. He moved from the door and stopped in the middle of the group. There he waited for everyone to sit down. Joe took a second to look at Angela. She had stayed at the door, closing it silently. She seemed delicate, or uncertain. Joe felt a bloom of sadness open inside him. It was sadness for Angela. He had helped get her involved in this—this religious muck.

"Relax," Bishop Healy said as he made a tight circle in the middle of the room, looking at each of his priests in turn. "I'm not Bishop McGee, and I can't abide what he's doing to our church, the church you've all sacrificed for, some of you in situations McGee would recoil from." Bishop Healy stopped turning and fixed his gaze on Monsignor O'Malley. Everyone knew the old monsignor had spent two years in federal prison in the eighties for protesting government policy in Latin America by damaging army property with his own blood. Joe had heard O'Malley talk of the ill will McGee bore him for that act.

Bishop Healy spoke more softly. It seemed to Joe he was only addressing O'Malley. "But you were following your faith with the steam engine's throttle wide open. Sometimes that approach means you get seared."

Seared. Faith searing. Those were the words Joe liked to hear. He nodded his head. When Joe was in seminary, he'd heard cautious whispers that Bishop Healy had made a name for himself as a young prelate with bold acts and bold words. The Bishop Healy Joe knew had always seemed old and wise, calm and deliberative. But Joe knew Bishop Healy had the determination of a prizefighter. He had seen it on the social justice issues. Bishop Healy never wavered on offering refuge to illegals.

Bishop Healy finally took a seat next to Monsignor O'Malley and then gestured to Angela to sit on his left.

Joe watched her walk across the midnight-blue Persian carpet. She glanced at him and offered a small smile as she approached his side of the circle. Joe hoped her smile meant something like: *I'm here to sort this thing out. I'm not an enemy. I forgive your aloofness.*

Joe managed to smile back, but it was a polite grin, lazy and tepid. His mind was elsewhere. His fingernails dug into the arms of his chair. He felt the sudden eruption of another feeling, an unexpected surge of outrage. Its flow was circling within and steaming his guts. Just as Bishop Healy had warned, he was searing inside. He looked over at Monsignor O'Malley. The old cleric was rubbing his arthritic hands, the hands of a faithful servant. Joe's anger began to intensify. He looked at Father Peterson, who sat slouched in his chair, and his anger turned up a notch. It wasn't just anger. He was offended. He was offended that these good servants were being singled out for abuse and disdain by the wolves who ranged through the flock. That pack of absolutists howled with exactly the type of high-handed disdain that awoke the Mexican revolutionary in him, that made the eagle of Tenochtitlán ruffle its feathers as if it might rouse out of a centuries-old coma.

And feeling this burn was a relief. He hadn't felt anger like this for weeks. The thought made him happy. And the happiness surprised him. Some tension flowed out, sluicing past the debris of other emotions.

He'd been shell-shocked by all this AIDS stuff. All his other anger was a woe-is-me anger—even his anger about Ron's article. Tonight was different. He felt something in himself coming back to life. He leaned forward and looked over at Angela, offering her a broad smile. She saw him and batted her eyelashes, as if she were shocked. He decided then that he needed to let her in on the secrets.

"We've gathered here tonight"—Bishop Healy began, interrupted by a spattering of coughs—"like the apostles after Jesus' death, numbed by what's happened, concerned about the future." Bishop Healy sat forward to look around the room, resting his eyes for a moment on each man.

More like we're in the upper room, Joe thought during that interval, *and Judas just fled. And death arrives tomorrow.*

"Tonight, I'm looking for your advice," Bishop Healy continued. "This Catholic Purists League continues to grow in influence. I'm getting inundated with calls and letters and e-mails, all asking what I'm going to do about the mess in my diocese—and listing your names as if you were relocated sex criminals."

That final comment sent a chill down Joe's spine. He saw the faces of the other men contort in pain. Joe looked over at Angela. Her head hung down, as if she were studying the intricate patterns in the rug. He knew better. He knew this latest assault had overwhelmed her. And he knew he'd done nothing to help. Until now. He had to do something. His former priestly ardor had to rekindle.

The group was silent. Joe looked around and saw Father Peterson blink his eyes. "Do you want us to resign?" he asked. Only his lips moved as he remained slouched in the chair.

"No! Definitely not! I want no one to resign," Bishop Healy answered. The sharp ring of his voice shocked Joe. Bishop Healy was feeling the anger, too.

"Then we organize," Monsignor O'Malley said, rising slightly, closing one hand in a fist. "Like Saint Catherine of Siena against the schismatic popes. We prepare arguments. We become cunning. We cross mountains if we have to. We protest if we have to."

Everyone looked over at the old rebel. Joe saw smiles flower on all their faces. *Monsignor O'Malley's spunk makes us feel like children again,* he thought. The group was coming alive.

"It may come to protest," Bishop Healy said, raising his right hand in a calming gesture and nodding kindly at Monsignor O'Malley. "But first I want to try another approach." Bishop Healy looked over at Angela.

"Okay, then what does Ms. Roth suggest?" Monsignor O'Malley asked. "Something with corporate polish?"

Joe watched Angela's head jerk up, as if she had been caught not paying attention.

He studied her. Her eyes said she was considering her response. She let a few moments pass in silence. "Bishop Healy and I are working hard with members of the USCCB to counter McGee's offensive. That's going well. There are many who fear what McGee is doing."

Everyone was looking at her. You could hear the men breathe. *Will she be our savior?* Joe wondered.

"Regarding the media, however, the local and national media, we can't go much further," Angela said. She sounded exhausted. That panel interview had to have devastated her. She had always been the one in control. That was one of her attributes Joe found most appealing. He thought they were kindred souls.

"Why can't we go further?" Monsignor O'Malley asked. The rebel was still in his voice.

"We don't have enough facts."

"I thought this diocese had dealt with all the pedophiles, openly and in the press. Or is it about the HIV scandal? You want names?" O'Malley asked, his voice rising with each question. "Names of the infected? Like the Nazis gathering lists of Jews?"

All the priests stirred at that accusation and turned to focus on Angela.

"We want to reach out to these men, yes," Angela said with a calmness that briefly filled the room. "But we also need to tell other stories."

Joe nodded. Angela knew what she was doing. And she was right. Only facts can prove a lie.

"What other stories?" Monsignor O'Malley asked.

"Stories of faith and commitment to show the lie in Bishop McGee's and the Purists' complaints," Angela said. "We need faces, the faces of good gay priests, the faces of good dissenting priests. They need to be willing to put their stories out there for all to examine. Without those stories, our message is hollow."

"Our message isn't hollow, Angela," said Bishop Healy, standing up with a groan. Joe was surprised. Bishop Healy's anger was gone. He sounded resigned. "I've just realized what the problem is, what my problem is: I haven't fully believed in my own faith and commitment. I was hoping that this group could come up with a clever strategy to deal with the Purists' onslaught. But I look at your faces now and I think differently." Bishop Healy was standing in the middle of the room again. He was turning around, stopping to look at each set of eyes, just as he had done when he entered.

"I want to apologize to you all," Bishop Healy finally said, staring now at Monsignor O'Malley. "I panicked. I was like Peter after the Romans took Jesus, looking for an easy out, ready to deny anything if it helped me. But I don't want to be that Peter. I want to be the Peter who willingly dies for his beliefs. That's who I want to be."

A blanket of silence, thick and wide, covered the room. No one moved. Joe's eyes were tearing up. He saw Monsignor O'Malley's were as well.

"You are all good servants of the Lord. I bid you good night. And ask you to pray for me tonight. Pray to give me courage." Then Bishop Healy headed swiftly to the door and exited.

* * *

Joe was the next man out of the room. He nodded at Angela and left. He hurried to his car, moving fast so no one could catch up. In the car, he put in the Cuban CD and drummed his fingers as he drove. He had made a decision.

Joe parked in front of Casa Romero. One light was still on. He jogged up to the front door and knocked. He needed to talk to Pascal. There was so much to do. He knocked again. He could hardly keep still as he waited for someone to open the door. This was it. He finally felt free.

The door opened slowly. It was Pascal. Thank God. Pascal looked surprised. "Joe?" he asked.

Joe started to talk about the meeting, but Pascal raised a finger to his lips. Joe could barely wait. Pascal ushered him in and shut the door. Without a word, he led Joe up to his bedroom. Before the bedroom door had fully shut, Joe said the words, "I'm coming out."

They stood a foot from each other, alert. Joe smiled. "Next Sunday, when Bishop Healy is celebrant at Mater Dei. I'd like you to be there," he said and placed his hands on Pascal's shoulders.

Pascal looked stunned. He reached back to make sure the door was shut. Joe kept smiling. The room felt warm. It glowed with candlelight. Pure Pascal.

"Let's sit down," Pascal said. He made Joe sit in his desk chair, and he took the bed. Joe continued to smile. He saw this news churn through his friend's mind. But Pascal had yet to feel the liberation. He would.

"Is that wise?" Pascal finally asked. "In light of current inquiries? Few people know you're gay. Most people think you're on the hit list because you're not orthodox enough. You don't need to rush into anything." Pascal stopped. He reached over to put his hands on Joe's knees. "You're fragile right now. You know that, don't you? You need to take care of yourself."

Joe almost laughed. He hadn't expected this response from Pascal. Pascal, apostle of radical honesty, was worried about opening a closet door. Joe had to make it clear.

"I've had enough of this … this circus act. And I'm not going to be the caged lion any longer. I'm going to bite the hand with the whip!" Joe felt his grin grow. "And I'm going to clamp down tight."

"Whoa," Pascal said, bringing his hands back and raising both palms. "Big tent imagery. Are you on something?"

"I'm hyped, but it's the Spirit. We just finished meeting with Angela and Bishop Healy—those of us whose names are on the website." Joe heard the bother that resonated in his voice. This might not be the easy triumph he had hoped for. But he wasn't going to stop. He was going to batter down his closet door.

Joe tried to modulate his voice. He was half excited and half irked. "During the meeting, Angela made a good point, something gay folks have known for at least a couple of decades: that you have to come out. Prejudice only ends when it's answered by people with real names and real faces, people with real families, people you see daily, people you may like or who annoy you, but people you know, people you can understand. You know these things, Pascal."

Pascal kept on staring at him, as if he didn't recognize the words or was deciding whether to believe them. Pascal must be wondering if Joe Tierney, always cautious about his emotions, was starting to crack. Maybe Joe should prepare himself for this reaction. He might be getting it a lot.

"Pascal, speak to me," Joe finally said.

"I don't know what to say," Pascal answered. "Are you sure?"

*   *   *

Joe pulled up in front of Edward's house, selected his home number from his cell phone's contact list, and pressed call, even though it was now past midnight. Talking to Pascal hadn't calmed him down the way it usually did. He was full of energy, ready to burst. He had been a cowering victim so long. Now he would act.

"What's up? Joe, is that you?" Edward asked, clearly struggling to wake from a deep sleep.

"It's me. Sorry for waking you up. I have to talk with someone. Can I come in?"

"Come in?"

"I'm outside your house."

Edward met him at the door. He was wearing dark-blue silk pajamas and looked groggy but elegant.

They went into the living room, and Edward turned on a small table light, at first sheltering his eyes. He sat down on the leather couch. Joe remained standing. He was learning that Edward didn't rouse quickly from sleep.

Joe turned away and paced a couple of times up and down the living room, to the fireplace and back.

"It must be important," Edward finally managed to say. His eyes were now open and clear. He was looking up at Joe.

Joe stopped his pacing. He turned to Edward and placed his hands on his hips. "It is important. It's a decision. At least I think it's a decision. I'd like to talk to you about it."

"Right now?" Edward's voice was still wrapped in a sleepy haze.

Joe looked at his watch and clamped his eyes shut. "I'm really sorry. I know it's late." Then he heard Edward laughing.

"I just looked at the mantel clock," Edward said. "This didn't use to be late for me! I've become more of a monk these last years ... at least the early-to-bed part," Edward said, chuckling.

"I'm really sorry," Joe said, finally sitting down on the couch next to Edward. They both moved to face each other.

Then Edward shot up. "I think this situation demands a cup of hot chocolate. Come on, let's make some," Edward said as he headed to his kitchen.

"Yeah, that would be good." Joe stood up and placed his hands in his pockets. He was feeling a conflict. What was he doing at Edward's house at this hour? What was he saying?

At the kitchen doorway, Joe pulled his hands out of his pockets and gestured to Edward. "Come here," he said. "I need a hug."

Edward turned around and stared a moment. Then he put down the can of chocolate powder and moved toward Joe.

They embraced for several minutes, hugging tightly and letting go and then hugging tightly again.

Finally, Edward released his hold and stepped back. His eyes were dewy. "I can't remember the last time I hugged someone like that in this house."

"That was nice," Joe said. "Thank you." He felt a warm energy flow through his body. He was actually content. The nervousness had bled away.

Edward notched his head to the left and smiled an awkward smile. "You're so very welcome. Are you still up for chocolate?"

"Oh yes, I am. Warm up the milk! But I'm already relaxing. I may need to crash here," Joe said, turning to eye the living room furniture. "I should fit well on your sofa."

"I have a guest bedroom," Edward said, hesitating on the word *bedroom.*

"A sofa is good. This is a sofa visit. We need to get that chocolate and go sit on it." Too many thoughts were running through Joe's mind. He decided he had to concentrate on the big one: the decision.

Neither spoke again until they sat in the living room, the small lamp giving off a gentle light.

"This tastes good, Edward. Ghirardelli's dark chocolate?"

"Guilty."

Joe took another sip and then placed the cup on the coffee table. He pulled one knee up into his crotch and turned toward Edward. He felt ready to talk.

"You know we had a meeting tonight, with Bishop Healy?" Joe asked.

"Yes, you told me there was a gathering, you and the other guys on that hit list."

"Right—"

"I hope your bishop is standing his ground," Edward said, butting in.

"Oh, he is!" Joe was smiling broadly. "At first, however, it wasn't so clear. He came in, with Angela, nervous and fidgety. That's unlike him, you see."

"I met him once. He seemed solid. I liked him."

"He is solid—or as they say, salt of the earth." Joe stopped a second to consider what he really wanted to say. How do you explain an epiphany? He shoved his hands under his armpits and clamped down on them. He flexed his chest muscles. "It was such an eerie evening. I was so anxious going there. It's not like I haven't been in tense situations before, but I've never felt so personally assaulted. I've never questioned my value before. Believe me, I was questioning it tonight!"

Edward reached over to pat Joe's leg kindly, as if he were petting a sweet child.

Joe didn't move. He looked intensely into Edward's eyes. He studied their blue calm. He'd only known Edward a few months, but he felt a growing connection.

"I'm going to need your help in the next few days and weeks," Joe said. He sighed. His mood changed again. He slouched back and stuck his legs out. In the early morning hours, with the energy of his decision wearing off, he started to realize how much risk it posed.

"Of course I'm here for you. Is something going to happen? I thought you said the meeting went well." Joe could hear the anxiety pushing into Edward, ever so slowly and subtly.

Then he found the decision again. He sat back up.

"It was a good meeting. Because it made my path clear. And the path was a revelation to me. Totally unexpected," Joe said, a swell of happiness now billowing in his words.

Edward raised his eyebrows. "And what is that path?"

"I've decided I need to come out. It's step one in dealing with my new situation. I have to stop being so afraid, so cautious about who I am." That was the decision. He would tell the truth, come what may.

"You've never been known as a shy guy, Joe, not in this city. But caution isn't always bad." Edward sounded uncertain, as if he thought Joe didn't really understand what he was doing.

"You're right there," Joe said, chuckling, his happiness still intact. He was on a mission. "But I've always been fighting for something holy and sanctified, for righteous stuff, stuff that gave me courage and drive."

"You think coming out is righteous?"

Edward was probing, the way Pascal had.

Joe stopped a moment and closed his eyes. That was a good question. He had never heard it phrased that way before. Joe drew in a great, deep breath and then exhaled. "I think being on the journey to the center of one's soul is righteous." Joe was nodding his head. He opened his eyes and turned directly toward Edward. "And sometimes the journey is dangerous. But aren't all important journeys remembered for the barriers overcome?" He wondered if that sounded trite or like a con artist's come-on. Inside him, it sounded spot-on.

CHAPTER 32

Pascal was on dinner duty the next evening. His mood was bleak. He moved about the kitchen, boiling another three cups of beans, slicing more vegetables, baking corn bread. He tried to hum a Taizé refrain, but his heart wasn't in it. The problem was the phone. Every time he walked past the phone, he paused. Pascal wanted to talk to Joe. He wanted to talk to him badly. But he didn't want to turn into a nag. Joe's "coming out" pledge made him nervous, more nervous for his seminary pal than he'd been in years. Pascal had seen the scars left by a bad coming out. He'd seen kids become homeless. He'd seen families break up. He'd seen alcoholism, withdrawal, and suicide. He wanted to save Joe from that back-alley drama. *Although, when a man is a priest,* Pascal thought, *the likelihood of a smooth closet exit is unlikely.*

Pascal was walking past the phone, heading to his boiling pot of beans, when it rang. He lunged for the receiver. "Hello?"

It was Angela. He almost muttered, "Damn!"

"Pascal," Angela said, "do you have a second? Can we talk? It's about Joe." His first reaction: she sounded like a woman on a mission, a worried woman on a mission. Pascal was caught in the middle again, trying to keep Joe's secrets secret.

"I can't seem to get ahold of Joe," Angela continued. "I've left three messages. He sent me an e-mail inviting me to Bishop Healy's Mass this Sunday. Joe said it's important I attend. And to bring my wits with me. What's that supposed to mean?" Angela asked.

Pascal was draining the navy beans. "You put me in a bind," he answered. Some of the beans escaped the colander. "Fudge!" he cried.

"I'm sorry, Pascal, is this a bad time?"

"It's not the end time, but things have been better," Pascal said, hoping he sounded funny.

"I'm sorry?"

"With Joe, I mean. Things have been better with Joe." Pascal set the beans aside and leaned back on the counter. He'd have to concentrate on this call. Clearly, Joe planned for Angela to be part of his coming out theater. But Pascal didn't want to give Joe's secret away. It wasn't his to give.

"Pascal, it's okay if what's going to happen Sunday is explosive. Maybe Joe warned you so you could act."

Did Angela expect him to bite on that baited line? She was a PR pro, Pascal thought. But maybe she was right. He felt a ripple of panic expand in his chest. "Angela, I'm a little busy right now. Can we talk later?"

"No way," she said. "You're not getting rid of me. Talk to me now or I'm coming over for dinner."

"Okay. All right," Pascal said, exasperated. "If you don't do anything to stop him, I'll tell you. Maybe you'll be better prepared to help him."

"It depends on what he's doing."

Pascal paused a second. "He's coming out. That's what he said to me. He's coming out." There. Pascal had said it. He didn't hold the secret anymore. But the telling didn't feel bad. Joe was going to need all his friends available and ready to help him.

* * *

Angela set the phone down and sat back in her office chair, letting her head dangle back and her hair fall down as she looked up at the old plaster ceiling. She didn't know if she felt relief or fear. How could those emotions be confused? Maybe because she had to break a trust. She had to tell Bishop Healy that Joe was coming out at Sunday's liturgy. Bishop Healy was her boss. She had to keep him from being unprepared.

Angela called Bishop Healy's secretary. She told Angela that he had a full schedule, but she could have ten minutes late on Friday afternoon. Angela took the time slot. That would give her time to reflect. She was amazed at Joe's decision, even though she had argued strongly for it. She knew it would birth a storm front of damaging consequences. Joe was such a private man. But she could help. If only he'd reach out.

* * *

Angela went for a stroll in the garden before her Friday appointment. The day was overcast, windy and dry. Forest fires blazed in the West again. The air smelled of ash and burning embers.

She walked through the garden yet drew no comfort. She felt drained. Her reflections since the call to Pascal had provided no new insights, especially about her own role in this drama. She was close to resigning. This job wasn't what she had expected. She had thought she'd find a different kind of camaraderie working for the church, something beyond funny jokes and restaurant raves. She even thought she might find love somewhere among the laborers in the fields of the Lord.

Angela grimaced. That thought hadn't popped up in a while. Where did it come from?

She looked at her watch and saw the time. She was on in a minute. She wouldn't have time to check her looks.

When Angela entered Bishop Healy's office, she was shocked. He seemed smaller as he rose from behind his desk. Clearly she wasn't the only one who had been diminished by these last months. All these sex scandals and orthodoxy probes were taking their toll on her boss. Angela knew he wanted desperately to move on, for the church to make amends for sins, for the pontificators to chill, for everyone just to move on.

Bishop Healy signaled for her to join him at the two high backs. Angela watched him sit down carefully. He was starting to show his age. She studied his face. There were some stray whiskers unshaved under his chin. She decided she wouldn't say anything.

He tugged at his collar. She knew those things could itch. "I'm working on my USCCB liturgy subcommittee project, Angela," he said. "We're meeting in a week, so I don't have much time. What's up?"

Angela didn't even try to smile. Her spirit was as gray as the day. She'd be brief. And blunt. "I've received information that Father Tierney is going to come out—announce he's gay—at your Mass this Sunday at Mater Dei. I thought you should know."

Bishop Healy closed his eyes and sat back into the stripes of the chair. It was 3:00 p.m., and the cathedral bells began to toll. Bishop Healy remained silent, as if he were praying with the bells or waiting for one more distracting noise to end. Angela couldn't tell which.

When the bells stopped echoing, he opened his eyes and sighed. He arched an eyebrow, looking over at her. "Did you convince him to do it with me there? Is there a plan to deal with the blowback, to put his announcement in the best light?" She saw a film of fatigue cover his eyes.

Bishop Healy must think Joe's coming out was part of her McGee counteroffensive and therefore well orchestrated. If only. "I haven't actually talked to Father Tierney. My information about his coming out is secondhand." Angela hated that. But Joe seemed to have cut her off.

"Oh," Bishop Healy said, rubbing his chin. "Secondhand. Someone ratted on him?"

"No," Angela said, raising her voice. She didn't want Bishop Healy to think less of her. She wasn't a common spy. "I followed up on a hunch."

Bishop Healy nodded. "Is this the future of our church?" he asked.

"I'm sorry?" Now she was on the hot seat. This job was getting to be too much.

"Never mind," Bishop Healy said, sitting forward and waving his hand. "He's not the first gay priest to come out. He may indeed be the savior you've been hoping for. Let's pray he makes some good points."

Angela noted a tiny sparkle in Bishop Healy's eyes. *Yes,* she thought, *let's pray he makes some good points.*

Chapter 33

Friday's gray and ashy weather had stayed over into Sunday morning. All the church lights of Mater Dei's vaulted nave and sanctuary were lit and blazing. Joe peeked out from the sacristy to look at the congregation. Despite the extra excitement that should come from Bishop Healy's presence, the Sunday morning crowd seemed somber. And Joe expected that the pomp of High Mass would do little to lift the gloom. Since his name had appeared on the website, Joe had been receiving more letters and calls about resigning. He'd spoken of them at a special session of the parish council, receiving warm yet nervous support. This was new ground for everyone. Joe assumed the whole congregation was talking about the website's accusations, but he couldn't seriously assess the congregation's opinions without a poll. Not many parishioners spoke to him face-to-face about the accusations, but he was getting more stares than usual. *They're in a quandary,* he assumed. *They want this to be over. They don't want to hear about sex and priests and tightfisted orthodoxy anymore.*

The Eucharist was pure rote motion. Neither Bishop Healy nor Joe made a mistake. But for Joe, at least, there was no spiritual participation. His mind was on the final announcements. To make the liturgy worse, Bishop Healy's homily was flat, full of old pieties, and the regular choir director was out sick so the music lacked its normal precision and bright movement. Joe couldn't even remember Bishop Healy's message. *Probably about Jesus.* He chuckled inwardly, as he distributed Communion while the choir sang a sloppy version of "On Eagles' Wings." His mind kept wandering. He felt like a sleepwalker up in the sanctuary.

Then the time was near—time for the announcements, followed by the final blessing. Joe could feel the sweat bead up on his hands. He rose from his seat on a small chair next to Bishop Healy. He reached under his chasuble to tighten the cincture and then looked over and caught Bishop Healy's eyes. They were opaque. *He's waiting for something,* Joe thought. *He's figured it out or he knows what's going to happen. Well, he's still in for a surprise.*

Joe went over to stand in front of the cherrywood altar and the vase of potted white chrysanthemums that fronted it. This was normal procedure. Each Sunday liturgy ended with housekeeping notes, parish reminders, and requests for donations. He liked to make the announcements himself because he was the pastor.

"Today's announcement is a personal note," Joe began. He saw the bodies in the congregation shift, the hundreds of heads moving to focus on him. Down on the left side, he saw Angela, whose face was as unreadable as Bishop Healy's. He saw Pascal, who had dragged Ron along. Pascal blinked his eyes, an old form of greeting between the two of them. And there was Edward in the back. He was sitting tall, straining to catch everything. The scene was beginning just as Joe had imagined.

His congregation was seated, and he had their attention. He froze for a moment. He felt a cold chill go up into his heart. Should he do this? It would be his leap of faith—from a height few could understand. Then he started. He didn't know if he was smiling his normal hospitable pastor beam or gazing with the expressionless eyes of a Roman bust. His sensory input had shut down.

"Jesus said, 'If anyone wants to be a follower of mine, let him renounce himself and take up his cross and follow me.' Today, I renounce my public persona and take up my cross. I am a priest of this diocese, as you know, and I am gay, and I am also HIV positive."

*   *   *

Silence. Then movement. Joe was becoming aware again.

Bishop Healy jumped out of his chair. He jogged over to embrace Joe. Joe felt the tears flowing down Bishop Healy's apostolic cheeks, as if the entire weight of the last years' scandals were being purged through his two brown eyes. Joe's own eyes joined Bishop Healy's purging.

The congregation, on the other hand, mostly sat in stunned silence. Joe heard some gasps and cries of "Oh, no!" and "My God!" Joe looked out through blurred eyes. The liturgy was not yet over, so most people had stayed put. But several couples stood to leave, slamming down their choir books as they exited their pews. Cell phones came out of purses and coat pockets. People began to talk. A murmur filled the nave. Two young men with pierced eyebrows and spiked hair stood to applaud. An older lesbian ex-nun joined the clapping pair.

Another man, someone Joe didn't recognize, stood up with rage in his face. "You're an abomination! Spawn of the antichrist!" he yelled and then stomped out down the nave.

Now Joe and Bishop Healy were both standing openmouthed gazing at the congregation from in front of the altar. Joe was trying to take it all in. Ron was bent over and crying. Joe watched Pascal reach his arm around him.

Then another person rose up. Angela. She was headed for the sanctuary. Her eyes focused on Joe as she took the first step onto the chalky-white marble platform. She reached out and hugged Joe.

They both began to cry. How had it come to this? What had he done? Joe felt like a child, like a kid whose emotional walls had been stormed by monsters from without. But he had family to cry with.

Next, Joe felt a tap on his shoulder. It was Pascal. Joe released Angela and then hugged Pascal. He stretched out his right hand to touch Ron's shoulder; his face was pale. Joe was finding it hard to concentrate. He saw another dozen bodies surrounding him: two young men who were holding hands, the wealthy Darlings in their Levis and wrinkled cotton shirts, several old women with hats and white gloves, and a few other solitary men, one of them Edward Brockton, priest of the Episcopal Church.

Joe took another swift look out at the nave. The majority of the congregation stayed seated, waiting, it seemed, for the curtain call on this unannounced drama so they could quickly return to the sanity of their own lives. Joe knew he should do something. Then he felt another hand on his shoulder. It was Bishop Healy's. He whispered in Joe's ears, "I'm going to do the final blessing." Joe began to cry uncontrollably. He bent over and placed his hands on his knees.

Bishop Healy stood forward. He raised his right hand to make the grand episcopal blessing and prayed in his best oratorical voice, launching his words over the sound of Joe's weeping and the noise of a stunned congregation standing for the blessing: "The Lord of Heaven and Earth, of Angel and Animal, of Sick and Poor bless every single one of us in this life and beyond." A few of the congregation offered a quiet, "Amen," as most trooped out of their pews. A handful seemed to wait for the final procession.

Bishop Healy turned back to Joe, who had now straightened up, his weeping suddenly reduced to sniffles. "Let's process out," he said. Joe nodded his head. This might be his last time as pastor.

The organ didn't play. The choir members, those still remaining, stayed silent. The altar servers were statues. Only the sounds of breathing, of whispered conversations, and of clerical footsteps filled the nave. At the end of the nave, a small crowd waited. Bishop Healy muttered some words about thanks and prayer and then maneuvered Joe through the gathering back up the side aisle to the sacristy. The sacristy was empty. The altar servers were gone. Joe looked around. He barely made out the details of the closets and cupboards. He was in shock. A part of his brain knew that—the streetwise kid part. Shock. He was in shock.

* * *

Bishop Healy's last words to Joe in the sacristy on Sunday were: "See me Monday morning." So now Joe stood before Bishop Healy's door. He was dressed in clerics, even though Mondays, he usually wore Dockers and a nylon sports shirt as it was casual day at Mater Dei.

Joe didn't know what to expect from Bishop Healy, but he knew their conversation would be serious and would have consequences. Things would change. Every fiber of his aching body told him he'd made a huge mistake with that public declaration. He had ruined everything. His life really was ending. None of his friends understood why he did it. He wasn't sure himself. That evening, he'd rejected all the offers of solace and companionship, telling his friends he needed hermit time, to reflect and to plan. Instead, he had sat silent and numb in the dark until he went to bed at 2:00 a.m. Now he stood alone outside Bishop Healy's door. His heart started to beat faster. He had to figure out what the next steps were. The time of quiet, mind-numbing lamentation was over. He had choices to make. His altar profession would really change his life—for better or for worse.

Joe opened the door and saw Bishop Healy hurry from behind his desk. His smile was broad and welcoming, and his stride excited. Joe wondered what the reason for the good cheer was. Did Bishop Healy think a tide of positive endorphins and a pastoral welcome could sweep away the trash Joe had scattered in Mater Dei?

They hugged, but this time without tears. Bishop Healy gestured for Joe to take up one of the two high backs. Bishop Healy took the other.

Bishop Healy's first question took Joe by surprise. He had calmed his face. "You've told your parents?" It was a good pastor's question.

"Last night," Joe said. "We talked briefly."

"And?" Bishop Healy prodded, raising an eyebrow.

Joe shifted. This was uncomfortable ground. He wanted to discuss his job, not the damage he'd inflicted on his parents. "They'd heard the whole story before I called. Both were on the phone at the same time, crying. My mom sounded frantic. It was awful."

Bishop Healy nodded. His face was neutral, neutral and attentive. "It's hard news to hear—the illness of a child."

Joe smiled a little. "My mom was already planning how she'd take care of me. My dad was mumbling stuff I didn't understand. He'd probably been drinking all afternoon."

"We fall back on old patterns when tragedy hits." Bishop Healy grinned a wry grin.

Joe thought a moment. He wondered if that was what he had done last night when he had burrowed into his cocoon.

They were silent a while. On the drive over, Joe had toyed with the idea of asking to be sent as a missionary to Central America, to a mountain village where no one would know his story, but Joe couldn't figure out how he'd handle the medical stuff in a land without twenty-four-hour pharmacies and state-of-the-art labs.

Then Bishop Healy asked a surprise question. "Do you want to confess?"

Joe froze. How could he not have seen that coming? Bishop Healy's first concern was for Joe's soul, not his job status. Joe took a short breath, held it a second, and then blurted out his answer. It was an answer from his gut.

"Not at this point, Bishop," Joe said. His eyes were steady, wary, almost apologetic. Of all the hard things he'd done recently, giving that answer was one of the hardest. He didn't want to hurt the old man, but his gut told him: no more lies. He didn't want to speak untruths anymore. He knew he had transgressed, especially with Kenny, but was he sorry? He wasn't sure. Certainly not about Kenny, he wasn't sorry about him—not today anyway.

"That's okay," Bishop Healy said quietly. "Give yourself time."

The conversation paused again.

"You can say anything," Bishop Healy said, sitting back and resting his hands in his lap. "What do you want for yourself?"

Joe puckered his lips. He wasn't sure exactly what he wanted. That was his problem. He ran his right hand through his hair. His thoughts were a tangle of half-baked ideas. He was just bubbling emotion these days. But there was the one thing he really wanted.

"I suppose it's unrealistic to say that my biggest want is a cure." Joe's eyes brimmed with that confession. He shook his head, angry that he still couldn't control his emotions.

Bishop Healy stared at him a moment and then looked down. "From what I read, you're likely to live a long life now." Bishop Healy moved to adjust the fit of his collar. Then he looked back up at Joe and smiled, as if to say, "Take your time."

Joe blinked his wet eyes but said nothing.

Finally, Bishop Healy shifted his bulk and settled back into the high back, taking a deep breath. "You will be a priest for many years," Bishop Healy said, looking over at Joe. "That is my prayer."

Joe tried to answer but started to cough. The answer stuck in his throat. "Yes, I guess I will be."

"And you're going to have some rough times. Even in your parish, one of our most liberal and humane." Bishop Healy folded his arms. "What with the scandals in the church, the pressure to "clean house"—not that I think you need to be swept out, but I'm getting heat all the way from the papal nuncio that I need to make a point about priestly celibacy and that I can't shove this scandal under the rug."

Now Bishop Healy's eyes were filling up. Joe felt an urge to reach out, to hug the old man, to tell him not to worry.

Then Joe sat back and grabbed onto the high back's arms. His eyes widened. He suddenly saw where this conversation was leading. Joe knew the reckoning was coming. And now was the time. Bishop Healy was leading him carefully to the inevitable resolution: a public demotion.

Joe didn't want to make it worse for Bishop Healy. "I'll do whatever you want," Joe said, his voice firm for the first time that morning.

Bishop Healy rose, extending his hand. "I'm glad to hear that, Joe. You won't have to wait long. I'll get back to you soon. Within the week."

CHAPTER 34

Tuesday morning's Mass was more of the same newly choreographed and awkward ballet. Joe saw himself as the dancer and the congregation as the audience. During the performance, some of the congregants' eyes appeared to regard him with a soft kindness as their attentive irises watched him kneel and bow and pray the prescribed words. Other eyes squinted tightly, which Joe assumed reflected a reservoir of ire deep in the brain and soul. The owners of those eyes resented that he was still their priest. For them, he assumed, he was the pestilence. The sharp coldness in those eyes made him want to run away.

Whether the eyes were kind or spiteful, no one shared the cup with him. He stayed at the altar during the kiss of peace. The tension was wearing Joe down. It degraded his spirit the way winter road salt erodes the underbelly of a car; it was corrosive yet unavoidable if a person planned to move about in a Rust Belt city. Was this his future? Could he stay in this city?

At Casa Romero that Tuesday evening, the Catholic Workers' eyes overflowed with compassion and acceptance. Their special kindness made Joe feel worse.

"I feel like the Elephant Man," Joe said up in Pascal's bedroom after Mass and dinner, "like the freak that needs to be coddled. I get reassuring looks, but I remain a freak. A freak knows he's a freak." Joe sat in Pascal's single straight-back chair. He had turned the chair so its back was to the desk and he could look at Pascal, who sat on the edge of the single bed.

Pascal leaned forward. "Everyone's concerned. That's all it is. At least in this house—what's it like at the rectory?"

Joe tipped back in the chair, raising the front two legs an inch. He put his hands behind his head and pulled forward slightly. He was trying to stretch the tenseness out of his neck. "Frigid. Like we need to turn on the furnace. Father Fitzgerald is gleeful. Yesterday, he asked me if he could begin an EWTN-inspired book club so they could read the works of the great minds who teach on the channel."

"Ewwwww," Pascal cried out, poking his finger in his mouth. "Books by sour old men. That's not spiritual reading; that's gulping down a spiritual enema."

Joe lowered the chair back down, moved his hands to his lap, and raised a fractional smile. He was thinking of Father Velker's sudden discomfort. "Father Velker asked Bishop Healy if he could move to a rural parish ... for health reasons." Joe started to laugh. All of a sudden, the absurdities that had been piling up inside his gut were bursting out. "I think ... I think he's afraid ... afraid I might infect him!" His laughter deepened, and he held his stomach.

Pascal smiled back but didn't take up the laughter.

Joe finally quieted down and placed his hands on his knees. "You don't think that's funny?" Joe asked.

"I'm not surprised by the old man's reaction. Maybe you see it differently." Pascal sounded remote. Maybe he was tired of Joe's drama.

Or there was another possibility. Maybe it was because Joe was positive and Pascal wasn't. Joe did see things differently now. Joe knew he was doing okay, physically. The meds were working. He was no threat. He'd read up on it all. And at least he'd laughed. He'd actually laughed!

The two friends stared at each other in silence for a few more seconds.

"So what are Healy's plans?" Pascal finally asked. That question was on everyone's mind, but only the bravest had asked him. Joe didn't have Bishop Healy's answer yet. He was worried, though.

"He's praying about it." Joe's mood had reset back to glum. "I'll tell you as soon as I know. To be honest, I don't have a clue what he'll want to do. He's getting a lot of pressure." Joe shrugged his shoulders. Bishop Healy respected him, so his penalty shouldn't be too harsh. "He'll replace me, probably. I'm sure I won't be a pastor anymore."

"But what do you want to do?" Pascal was drilling back with the main question.

What did he want to do? It was also Bishop Healy's question. "Do you want to stay at Mater Dei?" Pascal asked. "Do you want to come live here? You could, you know!"

Joe grinned at the invitation. "I'm not quite ready for the full Catholic Worker lifestyle, but I appreciate the offer. I really do. You've been a great friend."

"Thanks." Pascal reached over to hold Joe's hand. "But tell me, if you can, what do you want to do with the rest of your life?"

Joe pulled his hand away. "I'm still processing that, Pascal. I'm not really sure." Joe folded his arms across his chest. "I'm empty of ideas. I'm just empty." Joe knew that assertion wasn't 100 percent accurate. He was hiding a thought. The emptiness he spoke of was a lack of concrete plans—a waiting—but there was the flickering idea of going to see Kenny. Still, Joe wasn't sure he was ready for that trip—or that Kenny would welcome him. And he didn't want to share that option with Pascal, not yet. It was too fresh—and frightening. Was it a fantasy, he wondered, or an actual possibility?

* * *

Wednesday morning, Joe got another call from the chancery. Angela invited him over. It wasn't exactly an invitation. "Bishop Healy wants me to talk to you today," she had said. Her tone was official.

Joe wondered if she had another publicity scheme. Or maybe she just needed to talk. But why the trip to the chancery?

Before Joe left to see Angela, he had to deal with Lucy. She was bearing the brunt of the phone calls that poured in, most using the same language, something about the wolf among the sheep and God's cleansing fire.

Joe invited Lucy into his office for a chat.

"Close the door," Joe said as Lucy entered. "I think we should talk about those phone calls you're getting." He gestured for her to take the chair next to his desk.

Joe had half-jokingly considered setting up a parish complaint line with a recording machine to sop up the ranting. Whatever he did, he needed to help Lucy. She didn't deserve to hear all that crap.

Joe could tell Lucy was nervous. She hadn't complained to him, but her emotions were obvious. She was so unlike him in that.

"Are you doing okay?" Joe asked.

Lucy nodded her head. She kept her hands in her lap. "I'm hanging in there, Father T. But it ain't pretty what I'm hearing."

"They're reading from some right-wing pamphlet, Lucy. They're like robots ... or angry street thugs."

At that, Lucy shot up from her chair and started to pace in front of the desk. *Here it comes,* Joe thought.

"But they're screaming at *me*. Like I've got it too! Like everyone here is filthy! And that ... that boy priest ... he's been eyeing me at lot lately. An evil eye. He thinks he's going to be in charge. I can see it in the way he walks around, checking everything over. I think he wants to do something to me." Lucy waved a hand over her head as if a crow had just swooped by and pecked at her.

Joe sat forward, putting his arms on the desk. "You mean Father Fitzgerald?"

"Yeah, him. You know he never liked me." Lucy stopped to stare at Joe. "'Cause I'm no Catholic."

Joe stared back, a stunned look on his face. He suddenly realized that if he were forced to leave Mater Dei, he'd have to find a place for Lucy, someplace away from people like Father Fitzgerald. She was strong, but that young priest could wear away anyone's composure.

"I see your point, Lucy." Joe leaned back. "I won't let anything bad happen to you. I'll talk to Bishop Healy himself."

Now Lucy looked pleased. "That's good, Father T. Bishop Healy is good folk."

*   *   *

"What's up?" Joe asked as he strode into Angela's office. After his talk with Lucy, he was beginning to feel indignant. There was an edge to his question.

His warpath mood changed the moment he saw her. Angela stood up to greet him but stayed behind her desk. She kept her hands tucked behind her back, as if she were a disgruntled principal receiving a wayward student. Her face was drawn. She hadn't applied any makeup. Her cheeks looked hollow.

This isn't going to be good, Joe surmised. Thoughts of Lucy's plight evaporated. He slouched into Angela's side chair and turned to face her.

Angela settled into her desk chair, placed her hands on the desk, and then began to talk. "This is a somewhat irregular meeting." She rubbed her hands nervously a couple of times. "Bishop Healy wants a friendly face on his ... his decision."

Joe felt the air vanish from the room, out under the door and through the windows, as if a tornado were birthing around them. A surge of fear trebled the beating of his heart and moistened the palms of his hands.

"His decision?" Joe whispered. He feared he might start to cry.

Angela coughed to clear her voice. "Bishop Healy, with much cajoling from the USCCB, the nuncio, and beyond ..." Angela paused. The "beyond" sounded especially ominous. "... has decided that you should take a leave of absence."

Joe's jaw dropped, and he tilted his head, blinking a message of confusion with his eyes, but not tears. Just like that? This was Bishop Healy's decision?

"I am a priest. Forever," Joe said, snapping out the "forever" and clenching his jaw. Of course, he'd thought of taking a leave of absence. Every priest his age did. It was so common now and especially after his diagnosis—and with his relationships all adrift. But this felt like being shoved off the boat by some evil force from "beyond." He'd thought Bishop Healy would send him to a hospital as a chaplain or off to a rural parish or to a priest recovery clinic. He was a good priest! But a leave of absence! A forced leave of absence!

He didn't want to go easily. His jaw remained tight. "A priest forever, right? Am I not correct? I am a priest forever!" He no longer whispered.

Angela's paling face showed no emotion, but her body was stiff. "You are correct, Joe. And it pains me to say this, but Bishop Healy wants you to take a leave of absence." Joe noticed the modulation in her voice. She pronounced each word with care and with control—total control, but forced, so clearly forced. "It's a leave from Mater Dei and from your diocesan committee work. And you won't be able to perform any sacraments. Your faculties will be revoked until some final decision is made, that is." She seemed to stumble at that last bit.

Angela paused again. She lowered her eyelids for a brief moment. "We have to follow canon law, hold hearings, and send all the documentation to Rome. Many eyes are watching us. The judicial vicar, Monsignor Gregorovich, is already working on the hearings. Canons 1395, 1740, and 1741 apply. They address dealing with priests whose actions have caused sexual harm or scandal. Monsignor Gregorovich, or someone from the tribunal, will be contacting you soon. The hearings are confidential, of course. But, given current publicity, Bishop Healy wants your case to be properly presented to the media."

"My case? Presented?" Joe's mind was exploding. This was all so threatening.

"He wants us to provide the facts and a rationale for our decisions, for the tribunal's decisions. We have to control the message. You have to understand this, Joe." For a moment, Angela had let down her official guard and seemed to be pleading. "It will be done with dignity."

Joe wasn't placated. "What is the rationale for this tribunal? To humiliate me?"

Angela closed her eyes a second. "Please, Joe. I don't want to do this either."

"Then don't do it." He was steaming.

"I won't be doing it for much longer, I assure you of that!" Angela's voice was now sharp, and her body started to loosen up. An angry redness recolored her cheeks. "But I will do this last thing for Bishop Healy. And I know you will, too, because you're as loyal to him as I am."

Joe ground his teeth. He hated what she had just said, but she was right—about his loyalty.

Chapter 35

J oe called Edward after he got back to the rectory from his meeting with Angela. Or was that back from his sentencing? "Can we get together tonight?" he asked. "I'll pick up some deli food." Joe knew he sounded depressed, that Edward would sense it and make time for him.

"Uh, sure, Joe, about seven? I have an earlier appointment."

Since Angela had delivered her message of canonical legalese, a message which abruptly changed his status within the church, Joe had been swimming in a muddy funk. This little conversation with Edward almost triggered another flow of tears. Nothing was going the way he had expected. He knew there'd be change, but so drastic and harsh a change?

After leaving the chancery, he'd taken a half-hour walk along the parkway and then returned to the rectory where he spent most of his time in his quarters, calling Edward, sitting on his love seat, sitting behind the writing desk, lying on his bed, even doing his yoga stretches. He couldn't get into the planning groove. He was a good planner, but he couldn't plan his way into a "leave of absence." The whole phrase bothered him. Not that he was totally against the concept. Maybe he didn't like the "absence" part. It sounded so negatively charged—with the pitch of something that might explode and rip the flesh off anyone nearby.

Joe finally looked at his watch and saw it was 7:00 p.m. He'd be late. Damn! He had to pick up food and hurry to Edward's. When he got to Bernie's Deli, he frowned at the long line. Joe told himself to calm down. He'd be having a lot of free time soon. He should reset his engine to near idle.

Thirty minutes later, he pulled up in front of Edward's house. Edward met him at the door and grabbed him into a hug, deli meats and all. Neither of them spoke a word. For once that day, Joe found himself beyond tears and stood contented in the russet-red-tiled entryway with the taller *Anglo* wrapping his arms around him. It felt almost as good as a Kenny hug, muscular and tight.

A minute later, Edward released Joe from the bear-like embrace and led him into the living room. "Give me those bags," Edward said, pointing at the deli bags. "You sit down. I'm getting you a Scotch."

"A beer would be better," Joe said, smiling, gladly letting Edward maneuver him around. He sat in the middle of Edward's worn brown leather sofa and folded his hands between his knees. He could hear Edward bringing out plates from a cupboard and opening a bottle of beer. There was some chopping and the crinkling of bags. Soon, Edward was back with a tray of snacks and drinks, which he set on the glass coffee table. Joe looked up at him and patted the cushion next to him. "Sit down, please," Joe said. "Sit right here."

Edward moved around the glass table and sat where Joe had pointed.

"May I hold your hand?" Joe asked before Edward could say a thing. Joe needed the touch of another person. He didn't want to deny himself that sensation any longer, even if it was just holding another's hand. Edward reached out his left hand, an uncertain look on his face, and Joe took it in his right hand. "I need some comfort tonight," Joe said as he moved his right knee up against Edward's thigh. "Just some comfort. From someone I can trust."

"Did something happen?" Edward asked quickly, a sharp-edged concern in his voice. "Are you okay?"

"Health-wise, yes." Joe closed his eyes and began to cry. This seemed to be his new routine. It was as if some emotionally fragile person had taken over his body. He struggled through his tears to get the awful thing out: "They want me to ... to step down from Mater Dei. Take a leave of absence, lose my faculties. Go through some inquiry. A canon law hearing."

Joe looked up at Edward, to read his reaction.

"Some inquiry?" Joe read an angry confusion in Edward's eyes. Surely Edward knew about canonical inquiries, but the words did sound threatening. "About what?"

Joe felt deflated. "In light of recent events, you know. There's the need to be public in this time of scandal and lawsuits. Priests with AIDS. There are questions. What did I do? Did I harm anyone? An inquiry about all that stuff, I suppose. Probably to make sure I'm just a regular homosexual down on his luck, not a predator."

Edward's response was fast and loud. "You can't go through with that! An inquiry? In today's age? It's humiliating! Degrading. You've got a disease. You had sex with another man." Edward stopped a moment, shivering a second. "Not very Christlike of Bishop Healy, in my opinion. And who will be your Pontius Pilate?"

Joe slumped back into the couch, dragged out his handkerchief, wiped his eyes, and blew his nose. The numbness was coming back into his bones. Then he remembered.

"Damn!" Joe yelled, shooting up from the couch. He searched through his pockets for his pillbox. "I've got to take my pills. I forgot them this morning. And now I didn't bring my evening pills."

"Okay, okay." Edward looked at Joe and reached up to touch his arm. "We'll go over to the rectory and get your pills. Then come back."

Joe pulled away. "We?" Joe was now gripped by a fear of making introductions at the rectory. How would he explain Edward to his associates? Even after Sunday's public admission, he still had a coward's urges when it came to his intimate secrets. "I can do it myself. I'll come right back."

"You can't do everything alone—not anymore." Edward rose from the couch and picked up the tray. "I'll put this stuff away, and then we're off. You can finally show me your room and the pictures of your family—and of that sister you never talk about." Edward was talking like a man in charge. Joe decided to obey.

"Yeah, pictures of my parents just before they move into exile. I'm sure the neighborhood shunning has already started."

* * *

Joe and Edward entered the rectory through the back hall that led into the kitchen. It was already 8:30 p.m. Joe assumed no one would be there. Dinner was over. Joe froze when he saw Father Velker and Father Fitzgerald sharing a microwave pizza at the small kitchen table. He shook his head. They both loved their snacks.

Father Velker and Father Fitzgerald looked up from their greasy indulgence and stared at Joe and Edward. Joe thought they looked as shocked as he felt—maybe guilty. Joe looked back at Edward. He steeled himself. He had to stop being a coward. He had already come out—as gay, as positive. Why did he need to hide a friendship? Even if it was with an Episcopal, HIV-positive, divorced, and gay priest? These two could make up all the stories they wanted to.

"Good evening, gentlemen," Joe said as he moved forward. Edward followed him. "This is my friend, Father Brockton. He's an Episcopal priest."

Joe watched his two assistants grab some paper towels and wipe their hands. They rose to greet the new arrivals but seemed reluctant.

Then Joe saw an impish sparkle in Father Fitzgerald's eyes. *He wants to make mischief,* Joe thought. Monday night, toward the end of their mostly silent dinner, Father Fitzgerald had announced at the rectory table that he was going to pray all twenty decades of the rosary every night for the healing of the Mater Dei community, "to bring our Mother's healing touch to this awful wound." Now Joe wondered what new pabulum would tumble out of his mouth.

"Are you from Father Tierney's ecumenical group?" Father Fitzgerald asked.

Joe looked at Edward. Edward's face was blank.

"He's a friend of mine," Joe said, answering for Edward.

"A special friend?" Father Fitzgerald asked.

Joe knew what that question meant. Father Fitzgerald was asking if he and Edward were lovers.

"He's a good friend," Joe said.

"Oh, I see … by the way, Monsignor Gregorovich called for you earlier this evening." Father Fitzgerald had tossed off that comment as if it were unimportant information. "He told me he left a voice message for you."

Joe squinted at his young nemesis. What was going on? "If he left me a message, why did Monsignor Gregorovich contact you?" Joe demanded, maybe a little too loudly.

Father Fitzgerald's look of merriment vanished. Joe tightened his hands into fists.

Father Fitzgerald blinked, as if he were a man unsure of his next steps. He gulped and then started to speak. "He said there would be a canonical hearing. He asked a few questions and then told me I'd be called as a witness."

Joe watched the smile creep back onto the young priest's face as he finished speaking. The smile curved and moved as if it were a snake clutching a tree limb. Joe wasn't going to let this pass. "A witness to what?" He took a step closer to Father Fitzgerald, who was about three inches taller than he was and weighted with a baby gut.

Father Fitzgerald stepped back.

"I think I don't have to answer that," Father Fitzgerald said. Then he pointed his right index finger at Joe. "You'd better watch yourself, Father Tierney."

Joe's reaction was immediate. He raised his right fist, swiftly, as if he were a streetfighter again. But Edward was behind him and equally fast. Edward swung both his arms around Joe, grabbing him tight. Joe tried to lurch forward. "Let me at him!" Joe yelled. He pushed at Edward's hold. "Let me at him!"

Edward hung on tight. He wasn't letting go. "I think you two should leave," Edward yelled over Joe's head, pointing his chin at the door. His voice was sharp. He kept a tight grip on Joe.

Edward's words echoed. No one moved. Joe thought Father Fitzgerald looked triumphant, as if he wanted to take the blow. Then Joe looked at Father Velker, who hovered behind the younger priest. Joe saw that the old man was shaking. Joe closed his eyes a second, telling himself to let the anger flow away, the way his sister had counseled him when he would become furious at his dad. He began to relax his tense body.

Joe shook his head in disbelief. He took a deep breath and turned back to look at Edward. "I'm sorry for that outburst," Joe said. "I'm okay now."

After a few more seconds, Edward released Joe. Everyone stood frozen in place. Joe's assistants made no move to leave, so he twisted a bit to take Edward's hand and began to lead him down the long kitchen to the main hallway door. They'd go to the rector's suite, leaving the other two priests to their emotions and the cooling pizza.

"What a day!" Joe said after he closed the suite's door. He flipped on the lights. He imagined Father Fitzgerald was already calling Monsignor Gregorovich. What had he just done? Was he losing it?

Edward moved into the center of the room. He was looking around, seemingly unfazed by the kitchen incident, more intent on checking out the room. Then Joe remembered the reason they had come. "The pills," he said. He went to the wall safe where he kept his drugs.

"You need to unlock a safe every time you get your drugs?" Edward sounded like a man watching the unbelievable.

Joe stared back, a little shocked. What a fool he must seem. "It was a precaution." Joe paused a second. "But I guess I don't need to hide them anymore." Joe started to laugh, loud and unrestrained.

Edward responded in kind. "Yeah, I think your secret's out," he managed to say through his laughter.

It took a minute for them to recover, both men trying to catch their breath.

Then Joe went into his bathroom to take the pills. When he came back, he saw Edward standing at the sitting room window. From there, Edward could see the small rector's garden with an illuminated statue of St. Francis and several hanging bird feeders.

"Those drugs are now working their wonder," Joe said, quietly announcing his presence. Edward turned. He smiled at Joe and then walked over to the pictures on the long interior wall. There hung the family photos—four of them arranged in a square.

"I'm sure you can tell which one is my dad. He's the white one." Joe tried to sound nonchalant. Edward nodded his head.

"You don't have a recent picture of your sister?" Edward turned to look at Joe. "She lives in Texas?"

"Yes, Elena." Joe stood back from Edward. "She escaped from my father's grasp as soon as she could. She was sixteen. Now she's married to a Pentecostal pastor who thinks we're the spawn of Satan. We never see her anymore, but Mom writes." He paused a second. "I wonder if my mom has told her the news." The sadness was coming back, but it was not as bad.

Edward turned from the photos and said, "You seem in a better mood."

Joe smiled in response. "Yeah, I do. What's with that?"

Joe had an idea, something he wanted to do. "Hold on a second." He went over to the door and switched off the lights. Then he walked back toward Edward in the pale darkness. Joe reached out to embrace Edward, placing his head on his chest. Edward nestled his chin atop Joe's soft, dark hair. They stayed quiet for a while. Joe thought of all the lonely nights he'd spent in that space. But the thought seemed weak and dated.

Then he had more to say.

Joe pushed back a little, not totally releasing Edward. He wanted to get some things off his chest. "I'm not a saint, as you saw out in the kitchen. And I'm not pure. But I told Bishop Healy that I'd probably be a priest for a long time." He thought of Angela's message. "Now it seems I have to be cleansed through some kind of inquisition before I can even celebrate the sacraments again. That's not something I bargained for." He stopped a second. "These admissions came easily with Edward. "This situation makes me ask, who am I?" He hoped Edward would understand this. Surely he would. He had his own vocation to puzzle out. "I'm not a contemplative. I'm not deeply prayerful. But I do believe in my vocation. At least for now, weird as that must sound ..."

Edward pulled Joe back in. "Everyone's vocation is a walkabout, if you ask me," Edward said into his ear. "It just means we're all in need of a good hiking staff and a pair of thick-soled boots."

Joe breathed in deeply. Edward didn't think he sounded stupid or shallow. That was good. He relaxed even more.

Then Joe focused more intently on Edward's words. He had been feeling a little drowsy, probably the letdown from his kitchen confrontation, but now he perked up. He let his mind study the words, test them for nuance. He moved so he could look up at

Edward, who moved in response. "Walkabout. Interesting idea. Maybe you've got something there. Maybe I need to take a hike, go on pilgrimage, put on a shell, and head to Compostela."

Neither spoke.

Then Edward bent over again to whisper into Joe's ear. "If you go on pilgrimage, don't forget those of us who love you."

Chapter 36

The next morning at dawn, Joe made the decision. Then the planning began in earnest. He checked out websites, made call after call. The call to the Darlings was the most crucial. Next in importance was the long conversation with Edward, who had reluctantly left the rector's suite last night after agreeing to let Joe remain alone. Once those two pieces of the puzzle had fallen into place, Joe smiled all day long. Everything was coming together. By 2:00 p.m., he decided it was time to tell Pascal.

Joe reached Pascal at St. Martha's kitchen just as the crew was cleaning up after lunch and setting up for the next day's breakfast. "Can you meet me at the Nightly Bean at 5:00? I'll buy you a latte. I've got news," Joe said.

"Okay, good," Pascal said. "You sound better."

"You're right. I'm feeling better."

Joe arrived early to lay dibs on the table in the corner near the window. He ordered an Americano and sat to watch the traffic. The Nightly Bean was getting busy. Students, professors, and even old neighborhood folk trudged in. Looking for that late-afternoon lift, he surmised, feeling none of the need himself.

Pascal knocked on the outside window slightly after 5:00. Joe waved at his friend's broad smile. He felt a little nervous, but not bad—not like the last time he'd tried to reveal a secret in that aroma-rich room.

Joe handed Pascal a ten-dollar bill as soon as he reached their table and told him to buy his latte and leave the change as a tip. Joe was feeling expansive. He had energy. Wind filled his sails. Now he only had to navigate through the next few days.

"So what's the news?" Pascal asked as soon as he had sat down. Joe didn't even care who was listening. He started with the Darlings and told Pascal of his request.

"You asked them for what?" Pascal's eyes were full of disbelief.

"I asked just this morning. They had already called to say they'd help any way they could, money included." Joe coddled his Americano between his hands and remained calm.

Pascal sat back in his chair. "I can't believe you asked the Darlings for money!"

Joe hadn't expected Pascal to be indignant, but he didn't care. The request was his to make and the Darlings' to grant.

"You don't need money," Pascal said. "You can live with us at Casa Romero. The diocese doesn't order the Catholic Workers around. You can work at St. Martha's."

"I need to go on pilgrimage." That was how Joe had styled his decision—not a flight or a retreat, but a pilgrimage.

"Then go poor. Beg. *That's* pilgrimage."

"I also need thousands of dollars worth of drugs and lab tests, remember. My options are limited." Joe was still smiling. Everything was clear to him. He didn't even care that a couple at the other window table had gone quiet, obviously listening.

Pascal leaned in. "Just how much did you ask for?"

"Fifty thousand." Joe knew that sounded like a lot—especially to someone as frugal as Pascal. It was a lot of money. The woman at the next table turned around for a quick glance. Joe smiled back at her. "Twenty-five for a year's worth of drugs and labs, another twenty-five to get me somewhere and settled."

"Settled? I thought you were going on pilgrimage."

"I'm going away, far away. Then I'm going to live a different life. I'm going away to sort things out—and maybe pray again. That's why I call it a pilgrimage."

Pascal took a sip of his latte and licked his lips. He seemed to settle down. Joe assumed the "pray" part had reassured him.

"We'll have a farewell at Casa Romero." Pascal moved a hand to shield his eyes from the quick-glare reflection of sun off a silver SUV that was parking outside their window. He pointed at the hulk of metal and said, "Before you go drive off in one of those."

Joe grinned. "I'm driving my little Honda. I'm sure it has a few more miles in it."

"Good, you're not going to spend your money unwisely" Pascal said, sounding relieved. "So we'll have a party before we launch you and your Honda, which I christen the *Santa María*, or should that be *La Niña*, off to find a new world. But only if you promise to come back."

Joe's grin vanished, but he knew his eyes still sparkled with the shine of a little boy confessing a prank to a pal. His impishness had returned. "I promise to keep in touch. But listen, Pascal, I may not come back. Certainly not right away. My life is going to change. I'm going to change it."

Pascal sighed. Joe knew this separation would be hard on Pascal. That was one of the jagged downsides to his decision.

"I can visit, can't I?" Pascal's eyes were pleading.

Joe waited a second. "Sure, but after a little while, okay?" Joe's plan included a break from his past—at least for a while. He didn't want to host a slew of friends.

Pascal gave him a pouty look. "And where do you plan to end up?"

"Somewhere in the desert. Palm Springs."

"Palm Springs!" Pascal's cry was loud enough to startle two old ladies who were settling in nearby with a pot of tea and two cups. "I thought this was a pilgrimage, not a cruise to Babylon."

Joe laughed. He always enjoyed Pascal's wild reactions. But he decided to plow on with the facts. "I'm not telling many people—my parents, of course. Actually, I'm leaving in two days. I've been packing for a couple of hours—"

"No! I don't get this scheme." Pascal was shaking his head, holding on to the sides of the table with his hands. "It's not making sense. It's not who we are, going to Palm Springs for pilgrimage!"

Joe stopped a moment, studied his friend's face, and raised a finger to his chin as he tried to understand Pascal's worry. Pascal thought he was traipsing off on a flight to hedonism. Joe had presented his plan wrong. He had to make his reasons clear.

Joe told himself to rid his voice of giddiness and concentrate on calmness. There was a meaning in his choice. "Pascal, you and I both know what Palm Springs is. Yes, it's a gay Mecca. Crazy things happen there. But on the other hand—and forgive me for saying the obvious—Mecca is a holy place, a place of pilgrimage. Edward tells me he finds Palm Springs a great place for contemplation. He talks about becoming peaceful just gazing at the mountain. There's a mountain, you know."

Pascal shoved his chair back an inch. "You're sounding a little nuts."

Pascal's tone had turned grouchy, but Joe knew he would come around soon. He always did. Joe had to explain it right.

"I'm just pulling it all together for you. I've gone to Rome. Now I'm going to Palm Springs. I know what it's like to be a priest. But I don't know what it's like to be a gay man. It's that simple."

Both sat quiet for a second. Joe knew he had to tell Pascal about Kenny. Kenny was in San Diego, only a few hours away from the desert. He was about to tell that part of his story, but then Pascal started up again.

"Joe, you've always been gay." Pascal's voice was now low and gravelly. He was staring intensely at Joe. "You and I knew that in seminary. There's really not much mystery to it."

Joe closed his eyes for a moment. He opened them to look over at his friend. He'd hold off talking about Kenny. His motivation for going to Palm Springs was more than being near Kenny. Joe balled up his hands and rested them on the table. He was feeling tense now. This topic always screwed him up inside. "We both knew we were gay in seminary, true, but you know how closeted I've been. Back then and ever since. And you know what else I think? I think staying in that closet did something to me. Misdirected something in me. Made something grow crooked. That's how I got into this fix—and in a second, I'll tell you more about that." Joe raised his right hand to make sure Pascal stayed quiet and listened. "But, Pascal, listen to me. I need to go someplace where no one knows me and a place where I'm sure to find other gay men ... to explore that part of me. A safe place for me."

Pascal was shaking his head again, but not as forcefully. His eyes were getting dark. That was the Pascal-in-argument look. "That's not how it is, Joe. Gay is inside you. You just need to accept being gay. It can happen anywhere—even in the seminary." Pascal started to sound annoyed. "And you already know plenty of gay men. Edward, for example, he's a gay man. I would think you'd want to explore your feelings for him." Pascal winked at Joe. Joe knew that the Pascal wink always meant he was being serious. "And, by the way, you don't have to tell me how you got infected. I know you're too private to dispense that information easily."

Joe didn't respond immediately. He took a deep breath. This meeting definitely wasn't going as smoothly as he had hoped. Pascal made good points. Maybe Joe's reasons were muddy, but that lack of purity didn't weaken his resolve. He looked at his watch. He had more loose ends to tie up, but he didn't want to leave without clarifying two things. First, about Edward.

"Yes, I do have feelings for Edward, and that's complicated. But he's agreed with me that this is the right thing to do. In fact, Edward's helping me. He has friends who run a guesthouse in Warm Sands."

"Warm Sands! That's Whorehouse Gulch!"

Joe was getting tired of this drill. "Please, Pascal. Please. You get a little Jansenistic at times."

"I am *not* a Puritan! Ask my confessor!"

Joe had known Pascal wouldn't like this part of the plan, but it was pivotal for its success. Joe didn't want to be totally alone in his new world. He needed at least one point of contact in Palm Springs, even if that contact was just a friend of a friend.

Joe reached over to touch Pascal's hands, which were now both flat on the table. "Okay, you're not a Puritan. But trust me on this. Edward says these are good men. I've already talked to them several times."

There was a long silence. Joe could see Pascal's mind process this announcement, a waterwheel churning. Joe worried it would take a dozen candlelit meditations before Pascal came to understand his plan. Then, subtly, there was a change in Pascal's features, and Joe saw what looked like acceptance.

Pascal grinned. "So you're going to be a cabana boy," he said. Joe relaxed, from his tight neck down to his calves. Pascal had resolved things in his mind, at least for now, and was ready for some playfulness. "Father Joseph Tierney, priest of God Almighty, becomes a cabana boy."

Joe chuckled. "Yes! I'm going to be a cabana boy … to begin with. I'm going to clean rooms, make beds, scrub toilets, and serve lunch to guests. I'm still going to be a servant."

Pascal folded his arms and broadened his grin. "Like a priest should be."

Joe winced at the word. He wouldn't be a priest anymore, not legally. His choice to go on pilgrimage posthaste had canonical consequences.

But Joe wasn't concentrating on those consequences. They were quickly becoming the proverbial water under the bridge. Joe was thinking of new flows, of new landscapes.

It was time to tell Pascal about Kenny. Joe would keep it simple. He leaned in. This announcement was personal, confessional-box personal. The other patrons of the Nightly Bean didn't need to hear this.

"I've only had sex with one man." There, it was out. Now Pascal wouldn't wonder if he had become a rutting pig, if that was how he'd contracted HIV. Pascal would know he was still God-serious Joe.

Pascal leaned forward in response. He seemed to be waiting for more, eyes open wide, as if he were a child anxious about the end of a story.

But Joe knew the story wasn't ending. "That man's name is Kenny. He's young, younger than us, and he lives in San Diego. I'm going to contact him, after I get settled into a new routine. Why? Because maybe we could have a life together, or maybe not. But I'm going to check it out."

Author's Note

This novel is a complete work of fiction. It is not based on any real lives. However, three historical facts inspired me in writing this novel.

First, in January 2000, the *Kansas City Star* published an article by Judy L. Thomas titled "AIDS in the Priesthood." It can be found at http://kcsweb.kcstar.com/projects/priests/ststans.htm. I am a former Jesuit and knew several of the priests mentioned in the article. The quote used in this work is a piece of fiction and not from that article. The article in this work is entirely fictionalized.

Second, in December 2002, Cardinal Bernard Francis Law resigned as archbishop of Boston because of the clergy sex abuse scandal raging in his diocese. Law's spokeswoman during much of the crisis was an elegant young woman. I often wondered about her experience at that harrowing time. The diocesan spokeswoman in this novel is a creation of fiction and is in no way meant to resemble that woman.

In this work, I have set my AIDS article after the Boston scandal peaked.

Third, there is a reference in this novel to the book of Donald B. Cozzens, *The Changing Face of the Priesthood: A Reflection on the Priest's Crisis of Soul.* Cozzens's work is not quoted directly in this piece of fiction. His book is a good starting place to read up on the hot-topic issue of gays in the Catholic priesthood. It was published the same year as the *Kansas City Star*'s article. Since those early years of the twenty-first century, new restrictive language has been formulated to deal with gay men who seek to follow a vocation within the Catholic Church.

As in all works of fiction, the author has taken certain license. Of special note, this work is not a treatise on privacy laws, the medical treatment of HIV, or Roman Catholic canonical practices.

And finally, I am not done with Father Tierney. His journey continues.